# SOLOMON'S
# EMISSARY

# SOLOMON'S EMISSARY

REMI ARTS

ARCHWAY
PUBLISHING

Archway Publishing books may be ordered
through booksellers or by contacting:

Archway Publishing
1663 Liberty Drive
Bloomington, IN 47403
www.archwaypublishing.com
1 (888) 242-5904

This is a work of fiction. All of the characters, names, incidents,
organizations, and dialogue in this novel are either the products
of the author's imagination or are used fictitiously.

ISBN: 978-1-4808-7664-4 (sc)
ISBN: 978-1-4808-7665-1 (e)

Library of Congress Control Number: 2019903961

Print information available on the last page.

Archway Publishing rev. date: 4/8/2019

# ACKNOWLEDGMENT

Without extraordinary
understanding,
encouragement and editing,
my story could never have
come this far.

Thank you, Beverly.
Ingenium secreto

# PROLOGUE

Sgt. Stan Hogan stood under a tree on the sidewalk just outside the gate. His combat uniform made him look taller than his actual 6 ft. He was lean and in good shape. He'd only been with this particular squad 8 months, but the respect of his men was already well established.

That afternoon his captain had called him in to brief and assign the takedown. Normally, it would have been handled by Sgt. Arnie McCall, the original team leader but he had been called away on a family emergency.

It was described as a routine case, and he was assured all the information on the suspect was current. In spite of this, he felt uneasy and ill-prepared. He would have preferred more time to familiarize himself with the case.

He checked to see if the men were in place. Jerry Lenz was to gain entrance. A strict silence code was in force. Stan watched him circle the house trying the windows looking for a way to get in without breaking down the door. When he returned to the front, he shook his head and pointed towards the door indicating forced entry.

Stan nodded, and Jerry inserted the pry bar between the door and its frame, it slowly gave way. He cringed as the wood cracked and splintered. One could only hope that whoever was in the house was a sound sleeper.

When the door finally gave, Jerry pushed it open and stood aside listening. When he was sure everything was quiet, he waved and with his gun drawn he moved into the opening where he stood momentarily, waiting for his eyes to become accustomed to the dark. Stan remained beside the open door and no sooner had Jerry set foot across the threshold when a shot rang out. It caught him in the middle of his chest. The surprise more than the impact caused him to fall backward. Stan yelled. "Man down!" and without his order, gunfire sprayed the house from front and back. Stan immediately ordered, ceasefire, but it was already too late.

Jerry got up and opened his jacket. The slug was clearly visible embedded in his Kevlar vest.

Stan entered the house and turned on some lights. His worst nightmare was a reality; a moment in time that would hound him for the rest of his life.

The man presumed to be the suspected drug dealer was still alive. He was trying to cover the lifeless body of a woman holding a baby at the bottom of the stairs. Dazed and barely able to speak, all he said was, "we shot a woman and a baby for Christ sake!"

Stan steadied himself against the bullet-riddled wall, and as he did, he watched the suspect go limp trying to reach for his gun a few feet away. It struck Stan that this man didn't look anything like the drug dealer. He pulled the picture of the suspect out of his pocket; it confirmed his suspicion. He'd given the final order. He was to blame for an innocent man being shot and the deaths of a woman and a baby. He stumbled out of the house holding his head.

He knew there would be hell to pay and readied himself dreading the consequences. He sat down on the bumper of one of the vehicles and watched the usual array of curiosity seekers milling around. He needed to organize the events in his mind before his captain arrived. He didn't have long to wait.

"What the hell happened here?" The tone of voice telegraphed his anger.

"I don't know captain. I reviewed the intelligence I was given this afternoon. This is definitely the address but whoever lives here doesn't appear to be the dealer. To complicate matters even further, he wasn't alone; there were a woman and a baby in the house; both dead."

His superior chose to deliberately overlook what had been said. "And the suspect?"

"Paramedics are stabilizing him for transport to the ER."

"Jesus Christ, the media will have a field day with this. Don't say a word to anyone and I mean *anyone* until we sort out this mess. Do you understand?"

# 1

The gold lettering on the white glass read: Anastasia Whitefeather, Attorney at Law. The terrazzo floor, light walls, and flickering fluorescent fixtures were reminiscent of an old PI movie.

He grumbled as he took a second look at the piece of paper in his hand. It read Stacey Bogs. "Damn! There is no one here by that name, and yet this is the address." After some hesitation, he grabbed the door handle. He needed a lawyer, and this was the only one in the building. It didn't matter to him what his name was.

The door was locked. Looking around he decided this was one depressing building and the obnoxious hum of the fluorescent lighting did nothing to enhance it. Judgmental by nature, a character flaw he had been working on for some time, he quickly concluded that any lawyer working in such a "joint" was probably an ambulance chaser. He stuffed the scrap of paper back in his pocket and turned to leave. Peripherally, he caught sight of a tall, slender woman coming towards him from the other end of the hall. He recognized her, but it took him a minute to figure out from where. Then it came to him; he had seen her on the street near his office. She had intrigued him then as she did now. She pulled a key ring from her briefcase and asked, "can I help you?"

"I … I don't know. I'm looking for Stacey Bogs, the lawyer. One of the guys in my office gave me this address, but there seems to be some mistake."

"Well, I work mostly by appointment but I'm here now, and I do have the keys," she smiled. "Come in, I'm Stacey, and yes, I am the only lawyer in the building."

He followed her inside and saw how small it was.

"Have a seat," she said as she hung up her coat.

Looking around the sparsely decorated office, he concluded his evaluation of her qualifications as a lawyer were right on the mark. It was decorated in a style best described as "early poverty."

"Well, what can I do for you Mr …?"

"Benning, Thomas Benning."

She had seen his quick assessment of the room but chose to ignore it. "It is obvious that you are new here Mr. Benning," she said in a reserved tone. "I'm Anastasia Whitefeather."

Her attitude made him feel a little uncomfortable. "Yeah … I am. I've only been here about six months."

"From?"

"Alabama."

"You're American?" she asked with a heightened level of curiosity

"No, Canadian. I just lived there for a while."

"And before that?"

"Toronto."

"How long were you in the States?"

"About five years."

"Working?"

"No, I stayed with a friend."

He didn't appreciate this unexpected, unwelcome inquisition and countered by asking a few questions of his own.

"Is Bogs your maiden name?"

Her expression changed immediately, and she wasted no time in setting the record straight. "Well, Mr. Benning, some attorneys and law clerks call me that because my clients are mostly from the Tsakahena reserve which is coincidental, where I grew up. Quite frankly, I resent the tag."

"I'm sorry, I didn't know. I honestly thought that Bogs was a name. God, some people are moronic."

"Well, contrary to what most people believe, it is still very much a man's world and to complicate matters even more, a white man's world. There is very little we can do about it; prejudice is everywhere. I'm even willing to bet that you assumed Stacey was a man."

"True … but I don't think that makes me prejudiced."

"I like your style, Mr. Benning."

"Call me Tom."

"Okay, Tom. You need to know that I specialize in aboriginal matters so you might want to retain another attorney." Not waiting for his answer, she opened the middle drawer of her desk and pulled out a wad of business cards held together with an elastic band. While she shuffled through looking for the right one, Tom noticed hers off to his right on her desk stuffed into a purple, tacky looking holder with gold lettering on it, obviously a <u>freebee</u> from some insurance company or other.

"Why would I go and look for someone else," he said reaching for one of her cards. "I'm here now, and I just need some information on real estate. I don't need any legal stuff done yet, simply a consultation."

"Well … Mr. Benning," she continued in an abrasive tone. "You're probably here because you are interested in the parcel of land near the reserve."

"Well yeah, I saw the sign, "Tsakahena land.""

"Yes, and your friends probably warned you about the proximity to Indians."

"First of all, they aren't my friends. They're co-workers and secondly, what the hell do Indians have to do with anything?"

His sudden outburst surprised her but not enough to distract her from continuing. "Point taken, co-workers it is. As to the second part of your question, there is a consensus that nobody wants to live next door to a native family; you must have seen the way they live. I'll bet there is one thing your co-workers didn't tell you and it's the most valid reason of all to rethink your options. This parcel of land is a floodplain. It is too wet to be used for anything other than gardening. It looks nice and dry in the summer, but the rest of the year, it is a swamp. This year is an exception due to very dry weather. It seems we are both on the receiving end of a bad joke."

Her candor was refreshing. "I see. Thanks for telling me.

I had hoped for a nice building lot, but I guess I'll have to look somewhere else."

"That's probably a good idea."

He couldn't put his finger on it, but she seemed to be looking for an argument. Her face was no longer soft, and she looked back at him when he didn't answer her. "Now you can go back to your coworkers and have a good laugh about your new lawyer, Stacey Bogs."

He stared at her in disbelief. What was wrong with her? "Look, lady," he answered icily making no effort to disguise his anger. "Why did you have to add that unsolicited piece of crap? I need a lawyer. I haven't given you any reason to assume otherwise. It looks to me like you're the one with the chip on your shoulder. I came because I needed legal advice nothing more, nothing less. I thought I made that abundantly clear. I'm new here, unfamiliar with the surroundings and how real estate transactions are conducted. Perhaps you have a right to be bitter, I don't know … but I do know that you must be one very unhappy lady to be so harsh. Here's my card, send me your bill."

He dropped it on her writing pad and got up to leave. When he reached the door, he turned to continue venting, but he changed his mind and left without acknowledging her apparent upset. Even as he walked away, he could still feel the tension. His encounter with Stacey Whitefeather had left him somewhat disoriented.

A few days later, he saw her again, and his eyes casually followed her crossing the street but this time was different. The attraction was gone. He couldn't help but wonder why she had been so unpleasant and more importantly, why he had taken it so personally.

Ultimately the envelope with her return address on it arrived in the mail. He opened it expecting an invoice. To his surprise, it was a letter of apology. He read it and then put it aside on his drafting table. Throughout the day, he glanced over at it. He was tempted to call her but didn't.

The following morning, the guy who had given him her address, stood leaning against his drafting table. He pointed to the envelope and sneered. "Well, what's this, a love-letter from the squaw lawyer?"

Tom took in the tall, muscular man. He was the boss' son, a known bully who never anticipated that a mere drafts-man would give him any flack. Tom was well aware of how he had been set up. Some of his co-workers had been only too happy to fill him in. He was seen as a quiet guy who pretty much kept to himself so what followed was totally out of character. He slowly put his pencil down, stepped into the aisle and slammed his fist into the bully's jaw. He grimaced grabbing his sore knuckles as the jerk lost his balance and fell backward to the floor.

"You fucking asshole, you'll pay for this big time." He cursed holding his jaw, he got up and went back to his desk and picked up the phone. Tom shrugged and went back to work, well aware that he had been too quick with his fists. He knew there would be a reprisal for showing the bully up for who he was. He just didn't know where or when.

David Burganoff went into the bathroom and emerged a little later holding a towel against his bloodied mouth.

He kept a safe distance as he generously offered to let Tom off the hook if he apologized publicly. The entire office was spellbound. No one ever dared oppose the son of the famous James Adrian Burganoff, founder of the firm.

His coworkers waited for his reaction. He'd done what many of them wanted to do. Tom added insult to injury by yelling back, "go to hell you stupid son-of-a-bitch, you're a first-class prick! I would no more apologize to you than to a garbage rat in an ally. Come to think of it; I have more respect for the rat; he knows what he is."

David Burganoff walked out of the drafting room only to come back a while later with the police. Everyone watched Tom arrested, handcuffed and taken away.

He was booked and advised he could make one phone call. His personal effects had already been collected and put into a bag, so he had to ask the clerk for his wallet, pulled out a card and dialed the number. As he waited for an answer, he watched as his wallet, keys, and some change were being sealed for safe keeping.

"Ms. Whitefeather?"

"Yes, this is she."

"Ah ... this is Tom Benning."

"Aha, you're going to forgive me. Either that or you changed your mind and decided to buy the swamp anyway."

"No ... wrong on both counts. I'm in jail. I slugged a paleface in my office?"

He heard her laughing out loud. She asked him where he was being held and said she was on her way.

He felt good about calling her. She had laughed, and

that was a good sign even if he had called on a professional matter. He was in handcuffs when they brought him to the front desk. She may have laughed on the phone, but now she was all business. Pointing at the handcuffs, she asked icily, "are those really necessary?"

"Yes ma'am, for our safety as well as his. It is procedure for someone who has committed a violent act. His victim needed medical attention after the assault, and he is pressing charges."

Stacey didn't answer but rolled her eyes and then stared at him without saying another thing. She just kept staring. Tom had seen that same look in her eyes the first time they met. She knew exactly how effective it could be and so did he when the cop became visibly uncomfortable.

"Well … since you are here to bail him out, I suppose I might as well take them off.

"That is an excellent idea officer; we are so grateful for your understanding."

Her face was so sincere that it was hard to tell whether the comment was a put-down or if she meant it. She turned to Tom ignoring the police officer.

"Well Mr. Benning, it looks like the money you saved on the swamp is going to pay your bail. For starters, you owe me fifteen hundred dollars."

"Yeah, that's no problem. What do you prefer cash or check?"

"Check will be fine. Why did you call me? After all, you didn't answer the note I sent you."

"I only got it yesterday. Can we please get out of here?

This embarrasses the hell out of me. We'll talk over lunch if you like?"

"Sure, I'll finish the paperwork. I paid the bail before they brought you out so we can leave shortly." He watched her sign the documents.

They went to a small restaurant and ordered coffee. He couldn't take his eyes off her fine features, long shiny hair, flawless skin and full red lips.

"So, you got yourself thrown in the pokey … aggravated assault, no less."

"Which means?"

"You wounded somebody."

"Wounded? I gave the guy a split lip, that's all."

"Yep, you drew blood and according to the law that is wounding."

"Okay … now what?"

"You could be convicted and sentenced anywhere from a suspended sentence up to 15 years."

"Jesus … just for decking a guy?"

"Most likely you will get a suspended sentence with an anger management course thrown in for good measure."

"Damn, that's all I need."

"What happened?"

"Well … like I told you, I slugged the guy. Anyway, I'm glad that you were in your office. I'll get you the bail money and start packing."

"You're leaving?"

He took a sip of his coffee and stared out the window, "yeah it's time to move on."

"Out of the city?"

"Yeah."

"But you're coming back for the hearing, right?"

"No, I'm leaving for good."

"You'll lose the bail money."

"Don't care."

"Let me get this straight. You called me, but you don't think that I'm a good enough to get you off, is that it?"

"No."

"Then why?"

"Because I can't afford your fees, now that I'm out of a job."

"Nonsense, you wouldn't get fired for decking a guy."

"If the guy is the boss' son you would."

"Oh ... I see your point. Why did you hit him?"

He deliberately ignored her question. He wasn't comfortable giving her the details.

"It isn't important, ma'am, I just lost my temper."

"Please call me Stacey."

"Okay."

"Look, you might as well tell me. As the attorney of record, I'll find out anyway. It had to be something more than a simple difference of opinion. You're not violent, I've seen you lose your temper, remember?"

"Yeah ... I guess, but I'm out of here anyway so there won't be a court case."

"Oh, c'mon ... it can't be that bad. Have some more coffee."

"Let's forget about it and order; I'm starving."

"Okay, but I won't let you off the hook. You've got me curious now."

He shrugged. "Well … the jerk saw your envelope on my desk and said something that piss … ticked me off, that's all."

"What did he say?"

"It was kind of personal."

"It can't be that personal and anyway you're not supposed to hide anything from your attorney."

"Well, it wasn't a big deal. He said what's this, a love-letter from the squaw lawyer? That's all. Don't ask me why but I just lost my cool and let him have it."

He spoke from behind the menu. He hoped that she couldn't see him blushing. She didn't answer so he peeked over to see if she was looking at him. She wasn't. She studied the menu and stirred her coffee. After a short pause, she commented softly, "who said chivalry is dead. I'm sorry; I had no idea it would be a problem. If I had, I would never have sent it."

"A problem? Christ, I can't believe what you're saying. You wrote a letter, why should that be a problem? I appreciated your apology and was going to call you, but quite honestly, it never occurred to me that it would be to bail me out of jail."

She seemed intent on ignoring his attempt to lighten the mood.

"I screwed up, but then if I hadn't, we wouldn't be sitting here. It's difficult to imagine you were ready to get beaten up for a remark made by that stupid jerk. And, as if that weren't bad enough, now you're going to have a lawsuit to deal with."

"Whoa! Who said anything about a lawsuit?"

"People like him sue every chance they get. He'll wait until you are convicted and then he'll proceed. Waiting will make it easier for him to win a civil suit. He is probably at his doctor's office as we speak, getting X-rays, photos and medical forms which his lawyer will produce as evidence. I recommend that you start putting a good defense together."

"Thanks, that's just the type of encouragement I need. My plan to skip town is beginning to look better and better."

"You don't mind losing your bail money, do you?"

"Sure I mind, but I don't have much choice. Burganoff has a lot of influence in this town so I won't get a job here. More importantly, I don't want to go to jail."

Stacey suggested fleeing was not in his best interest. She went on to say her approach would be to subpoena his co-workers and base his defense on fighting slur and prejudice. She was certain the jury would be sympathetic.

"No thanks. I'm no hero nor am I a flag waver for native rights."

"You are a strange and complicated man, Thomas Benning. You don't strike me as someone who runs from a problem and yet here you are about to do just that. Won't you let me help you?"

He stared at her for a moment; but even though her offer seemed sincere, he shook his head.

She wasn't easily dissuaded. "I have to confess you intrigue me. You're like a breath of fresh air. My work consists of alcoholics, family violence, and child welfare cases. If you stay, I will take your case. Now, I know what you are about to say so please don't worry about the money. Pay me when you can if you insist."

He attempted to refuse her offer, but she pre-empted him. "I know what you are thinking. I saw you looking around my office but don't let appearances deceive you. I keep the décor simple so my clientele will not be intimidated. I handle all the band cases for which I am well compensated.

Additionally, my dad has a junk-yard, and he is shall we say ... prosperous and he believes in sharing his good fortune. I have more than enough money, but I don't flaunt it."

They talked. Lunch spanned the afternoon but he didn't care, he knew he didn't have anyone or anything waiting for him.

Their eyes met often. Each time intensified their new-found interest in each other. It was obvious they enjoyed being together, and he asked her if she would have dinner with him. She accepted smiling and asked if he would prefer to go "dutch" given his current financial situation.

He was suddenly upbeat.

"Wait-a-minute ... I just remembered ... I left a few bucks in Alabama."

"You're almost broke, and suddenly you remember that you have money in Alabama, of all places. How did you get it? You've already told me that you didn't have a job."

"Relax. You aren't exactly trusting, are you? The friend I lived with had money, and he left it to me in his will ... about $8000.00."

"It isn't a fortune," she laughed, "but converted to Canadian currency it will be enough to get things settled."

His smile confirmed he would stay, at least for a while.

# 2

There was something familiar about the old man, but Tom couldn't quite place him. His hair was grey and thinning. It nearly reached his shoulders. His skin was tanned and wrinkled like so many in Mobile. Had it not been for his clear blue, inquisitive eyes, Tom wouldn't have paid him any mind but this man looked intrigued. He couldn't decide whether he was being studied or whether the old man was waiting for him to decide whether he was going to keep the item in his hand or put it back in the bin. He started toward Tom as he returned the item to the bin. He obviously felt prompted to ask, "you sure you don't want it?"

Surprised and somewhat annoyed by the redundancy of the question, Tom turned and answered almost abrasively: "I'm sure but don't worry, your shop is the first on my list if I change my mind."

"Oh, but this isn't my place, I'm a customer like you." He grinned, extended his hand and introduced himself. "I'm Chaim Solomon, and I'm always on the lookout for a bargain.

The pickings are good these days with technology advancing at such an astounding pace. The downside is that we have no choice but to upgrade."

There was still a hint of arrogance in Tom but shook the extended hand. "Tom Benning. Keeping up isn't a priority for me. I just want to access the internet."

"So, you don't have a computer."

Tom hesitated. He wasn't interested in getting into a conversation, but he had to admit he was intrigued by the twinkle in this old man's eyes. What was the harm in taking a couple of minutes to talk to him? "No, not yet; I'm putting one together bit by bit."

Chaim was curious. "What kind of card are you looking for?"

"I need a PCI."

"I have quite a few PCIs in my workshop at home."

"Interesting ... how much?"

"Ah ... I have so much junk, why don't you come by the house and see what I have? If you find what you are looking for, you're welcome to it."

"Are you sure?"

"Sure I'm sure, but you can buy me a coffee if it makes you feel any better."

The prospect of getting the part he needed was enticing, and the price was right, so Tom and the old man went across the street into a little coffee shop.

"You're not from around here."

It wasn't a question but rather a statement.

"No."

"A snowbird, perhaps?" he chuckled.

"Well, I guess I qualify, I'm Canadian."

"You also are not from around here either, Mr. Solomon."

"No, actually I'm Israeli. I retired here to get away from never-ending conflict and to pursue my hobbies. Call me Chaim, please."

"Okay, Chaim it is … A Jew in Mobile of all places?"

"Oh … Munchen, Jerusalem or Mobile, what's the difference A Jew is a Jew, isn't it?"

"Yeah, I guess … but your name must be a real tongue-twister for people down here?"

"As a matter fact it is. Some people call me Shame or Came some Gayem others don't use it at all, they just say, you or, sir. You are the first person to pronounce it correctly."

"Perhaps that's because I'm half Jewish."

"With a name like Benning?"

"My father was English; my mother Jewish."

"How did they meet?"

He wasn't sure he wanted to continue being probed by a total stranger, so his answer was deliberately curt. "In Holland, during the war."

Chaim seemed oblivious to Tom's reticence. How could he know that this man's innate curiosity had led to his reputation of being a bulldog when he wanted to know something? Clearly Tom's attempt to dissuade further questions had failed.

"And how did she escape the concentration camps?" he proceeded with his inquisition.

"My mother and her brother were both blond, blue-eyed

kids. They were fortunate enough to have neighbors who helped them."

Tom hoped that would shut Chaim down, but no …

"You speak Yiddish then?"

"A few words; I was raised Catholic like my father. The Jewish religion, Hebrew or Yiddish were outlawed in our house."

"Your poor mother, it must have been hard for her?"

"Yes, but she was liberated when my father died."

There was a long pause, and Tom felt some degree of pleasure. His tactic had been successful. Subject closed. His optimism was short lived when yet another question arose.

"What is your profession, young man?"

"Profession? Hell, I would hardly call my work a profession. I'm a handyman."

"Now maybe, but I'm sure that you were schooled for something else."

"What makes you think that?"

"Oh … your hands for one thing; a handyman does not have hands like yours. The little nicks and scrapes tell me that you recently became a handyman. Your fingers are lean, smooth and callus free. The way you move, your inquisitive eyes everything tells me that you have had a good education."

"I am an architect but as you can see, not a very successful one."

"What happened?"

The conversation had been easy, perhaps too easy.

"It's a long story. Maybe I'm looking for a new future

but who knows what that might be. I may live out my days as a bum."

"That is a defeatist attitude, don't you think?"

"If that's what you think, fine. I, personally, don't care what people think anymore."

"Even so, there is a future for everyone. Actually, the future is an arbitrary constant which measures the materialistic and social aspects of society. Our role in this process is to strive for the well being of mankind while experiencing personal growth."

Tom pondered the statement. He was unwilling to admit that there was more to this man than he had initially believed. Still, he was in no mood to be more than civil and couldn't resist a hint of ridicule, hoping to change the course of the conversation.

"So … a philosopher, I see. I have a feeling that you are the kind of philosopher who believes that we don't get out of life what we put into it."

"What do you mean?" asked Chaim.

"Well, you must have heard the saying, you only get out of life what you put into it?"

Chaim stared a spot on the floor as if looking for an appropriate response.

"You're right. I don't believe that. If true, society would stand still, and we would eventually lose ground."

"Well, Chaim, believe what you will. I'm not quite up to striving for those ideals. It would be a waste of time, as far as I'm concerned. Mankind is already doomed. We're destroying ourselves."

"Not quite. Even if we falter or something interferes with our ideals, someone somewhere is always willing to take up where we left off. And, my friend, it often happens under the most unexpected circumstances."

"I hope that you will find what you are looking for, old man. I'm less optimistic and will putter along until I get my head straight."

"You are further along than you realize, Thomas. Perhaps we were meant to come together, and we have come to a point where we can be of great benefit to each other."

Tom dismissed Chaim's theory. "I doubt it."

"Regardless of what you think, why not come with me and pick up that video-card. It may give you some insight into my past and possibly your future?"

He had to admit that he did want to get his hands on that card. He paid for the coffees, and they left. As they walked, Chaim took the opportunity to continue questioning Tom.

"You're not married, I gather."

"No, I'm a widower."

Tom was surprised by Chaim's pace. Unlike many older people, it was quick and his gait easy. They walked along in silence until they came to a section of the sidewalk paved with cobble stones. Chaim stopped at a pair of rusty, cast iron gates. This was one of the city's oldest residential areas but the local heritage society had overlooked the dismal state of the gates and accompanying fence.

Chaim pushed one of the squeaky gates open.

"Like me," smiled Chaim. "My bones also squeak when I get out of bed in the morning. The gates can be fixed with a few drops of oil, but that won't work for me," he laughed.

The Building behind it was a large red brick mansion which appeared to have been built before the civil war. The walls and most of the windows were covered with ivy. The lawn was freshly mowed, and the shrubs and flower beds were neatly trimmed. A wide driveway, paved with the same brick as the house, led from the front gates to a coach house at the back of the property. It was impressive. A large portico extended over the main entrance at the side of the house. It was a testament to the elegance of days gone by. The area was quiet except for the occasional car. There was little to disturb the pleasant moment of trespassing into the past.

"You live alone … Mr. Realist … Philosopher … Solomon?"

"Go ahead, be smug. I have a housekeeper who lives above the coach house. She does some housekeeping and cooks one meal a day. The rest of the time she works for other people. It's a good arrangement for us both."

"I'm not smug … It's just that you haven't told me anything about yourself while you have conspicuously interrogated me."

Chaim seemingly ignored the comment. "Come on in," he laughed, motioning gracefully after entering the access code on the alarm pad. "Welcome to my home."

Tom paused and took it all in. "It's beautiful. I had once hoped to build houses like this. Today's architecture is more based on structural engineering."

As he entered the house, Tom commented rather

offhandedly that the alarm system wouldn't do much good for someone determined enough to get in.

"I know but it is a deterrent, and there are a few more surprises for someone who is determined enough to succeed," Chaim assured him.

The ceilings were high, and the wide pine plank floors were stained dark walnut. This home seemed to have escaped the fate of so many of its contemporaries. As they walked on Chaim pointed out an elaborate staircase. "These are used sparingly. But no matter what, I have to go up and down each day because the house only has one shower and it's upstairs" he giggled.

He led the way down to the basement explaining that these stairs were used more often because this was where he spent most of his time.

Expecting a dingy cave, it was anything but. The musty smell usually associated with old basements was non-existent. It was brightly lit. Fluorescents compensated for the small windows. The floor was covered with light grey linoleum, and the walls painted off-white. The most surprising feature was the ceiling. It was over nine feet high.

Tom stopped on the bottom step. This was indeed a unique space.

Directly to his left, was a long workbench with large closets on either side. The shelves above the bench were stacked with all kinds of electronic gadgets. The closet doors were padlocked. The wall directly facing him was where a treadmill, weightlifting bench, and a punching bag.

To his right was a large chalkboard and above it, an

air conditioner with a few paper streamers gently wafting. Except for the stairs, the wall behind him was blank. The center of the room was open and cushioned with a couple of blue mats, much like those used in gyms.

"Shit, this is more like a gym than a workshop. Don't tell me that you need all this space just to exercise."

Chaim paced the floor slowly stroking his chin. When he stopped, He faced Tom, and in a calm yet authoritative tone began. "I have to be honest with you Tom. I had an ulterior motive asking you here, and as I see it, there is no easy way to get around what I have to say, so I'm just going to proceed. The proposal I am about to make revolves around a project I have been working on for many years. It is one that will extend beyond my lifetime which makes it necessary for me to find someone to take it over when the time comes.

I understand how preposterous this must sound, but I believe you could be that person. I ask your indulgence. Please listen without interruption."

How presumptuous, Tom thought. This was too much. His instinct for flippancy kicked in. "Don't tell me, an offer I can't refuse, right?"

Chaim chose, once again, to ignore Tom's sarcasm. He settled down and began his story with a directness that caught Tom entirely off guard.

"I'm a retired Mossad officer. And, I need you to do something for me after I'm gone."

"Wow … just a minute. I'm an architect and not a good one as you know. I'm not about to get myself in a jam with any spy crap. I have enough problems already."

Not to be sidetracked, Chaim continued. "What I need you to do is in no way sinister."

Tom was more than uncomfortable and made a move to get up and leave. "Look, Chaim, you seem like a nice guy, but I'm not looking for a job. A video card for my computer is all I need, and that's why I came, remember?"

Chaim smiled, "the card is yours, my friend." He went over to the shelving in the work area and came back with the item. He handed it to Tom and seemed to be looking for a way to convince him to stay and hear him out. He started with an apology.

"I'm sorry if you think I misled you and I know that you don't need a job … but you would be doing a service, not for me but our homeland. I wo …"

Tom was astounded. "Whoa! … *Your* homeland, not mine. *My* homeland is Canada, and I've got nothing to do with Israel or its problems."

Chaim countered; "Israel is every Jew's homeland and you know it. Hear me out and once you have and if you still feel the same, we'll part friends, no harm done. I'm not asking you to become a spy. I need you as a trustee to regulate the distribution of some funds which are to be used to build integrated schools in Israel."

Tom had to agree that this wasn't quite what he had expected to hear but was none the less not interested. "I'm sure there are far better-qualified people who can do this; how about the Israeli government?"

Without hesitation, Chaim came back with an adamant: "that's not an option. The Israeli government is biased and don't suggest the Palestinians because they are equally so. It has to be someone impartial without prejudice and who is honest."

Tom jumped in. "You don't know me well enough to assume I am your guy. We just met an hour ago for Christ sake!"

Chaim was steadfast. "*You* met me an hour ago, young man, but I have been watching you for weeks. I observed you working on that old motel. You worked diligently every day."

"You … you were stalking me?" Tom shouted in disbelief.

Instantly, Chaim realized that he had made a mistake. The last thing he wanted was to anger and potentially lose Tom. He had selected him to carry out his dream. "Not stalking, trying to get to know who I might be dealing with. A lot of money is at stake, and it is imperative that it is handled by the right person. I have a feeling that you are trustworthy and have integrity based on what I saw. There was no way I could have known you were an architect, but that is indeed an added bonus."

Tom decided to play along, "should I accept … what's in it for me aside from a lot of trouble?"

"That question doesn't surprise me. We all have to survive so you'll get more than enough money to retire and live in comfort for the rest of your life."

Tom decided enough was enough. It was time to go. "I think I'll pass. The whole Mossad stuff is probably hogwash. You could be a lonely old man looking for company and I ain't no babysitter. If you are that well off, hire a nurse."

Chaim wasn't easily discouraged. "What if I can prove to you who I am?"

"How or …"

"That I'm an ex-Mossad officer of sound body and mind."

"Considering your age, the body bit might be acceptable; the mind, however, is sounding less realistic. Oh what the hell, I've come this far, I'm listening."

"Oh no, sonny boy, now you can put your money where your mouth is. You questioned my sanity."

"Okay, how?"

"Fight me."

Tom couldn't believe what he had just heard. "Fight you? Now I know you're nuts. No disrespect but you're probably more than twice my age, and your bones are liable to snap like twigs."

Chaim didn't bother to hide how much he was enjoying himself. "Afraid I can beat the crap out of you, boy?"

"The only thing that scares me is calling the paramedics."

"Not to worry, I'll sign a waiver if that makes you more comfortable. Now come out on the mats, so *you* don't get hurt."

Tom followed Chaim to the center of the room and stood facing him intending to give him a shove. Chaim stepped aside and grabbed Tom's hand bending it back until Tom was on his knees. More than a little embarrassed Tom got up and smiled sheepishly.

"Okay, so you know a few judo tricks … big deal."

"Try again and this time, show a little *chutzpah*."

The old man was swift and skilled, and Tom realized

after almost an hour of hitting the mats that he was tired but most of all, humiliated. Chaim, on the other hand, was still standing and extended his hand to help him up. It was a humbling experience to be beaten by an old man. Could he be wrong about his opponent's abilities and if so was it possible that he had also misread his intentions?

He conceded defeat. "Okay, Chaim, you have my attention. What the hell just happened here?"

Without missing a beat, Chaim answered, "Merely a test and you showed me, anyone, as determined as you, can learn this."

Tom was still a little short of breath. "Is that so ... who needs it and what purpose does it serve?"

"Purpose? It serves the same purpose as a college education."

"That's the most stupid statement yet. Everyone knows damn well that an education is imperative."

Chaim nodded. "Exactly" and then out of nowhere asked, "what happened to your wife?"

This was too much. How dare he broach this subject? Tom forgot all the rules of decorum and lunged at Chaim. Fortunately, he remembered his encounter with the mats and backed off yelling, "I am trying to forget about that. Why do you bring it up and more importantly ... how the hell do you know about her?"

"I've already proven what I am so; it shouldn't surprise you that I have access to any information I want or need? Are you trying to forget because you feel responsible or what?"

"If you can get all the information you want or need, why do you have to ask me that question?"

Now Chaim was annoyed. "Give me some credit. Human nature is my field of expertise, and it is that expertise that leads me to believe you are running away from something."

Tom spit back. "For your information, my wife and baby were killed in a screwed up drug raid. The cops killed them but you probably already know that, right?"

Chaim overlooked the dig. He had regained his composure. "And, here you are alive and well."

Tom's reaction was predictable. "You're beginning to piss me off, old man! I left because I needed to decide what to do with the rest of my life."

"Aw, yes … the future … like hell! You're on the run because you feel responsible."

Feeling beaten up both physically and emotionally, Tom conceded. "Look, I don't need this. Let's each go our separate ways. I'm grateful for the lesson in humility but I'm tired and hungry, and I'm out of here."

Ever the gentleman, Chaim offered to drive him home, but Tom categorically refused saying he would take the bus.

Chaim couldn't let it end like this. "Please stay and tell me what happened on that horrible day?"

Would this guy ever give up? Probably the best solution was to tell him his story and get out. "You're bound and declared to get me to tell my story, aren't you?"

"Actually no, I'm bound and declared to have you help me save the children of Israel."

This was not quite the answer Tom had anticipated.

"So that's what this is all about? Well, for the record, Israel isn't my war, you guys fucked that up, and you guys have to fix it."

Now, they were facing each other head-on.

"It isn't the war I want you to fight. I want your help to change the ignorance and bigotry, like that of your father."

Tom didn't appreciate the mention of his father or his bigotry.

"Oh boy, here we go again and just how would you do that?"

As always, Chaim's response was calm and yet calculated.

"Still cynical, I see. I would start by showing you who you are and help you to accept the consequences of your actions; this is the only way to achieve peace."

Unlike Chaim, Tom was more accustomed to anger and shouted, "I AM AT PEACE!"

After a moment or so, Tom realized that he had over-stepped the boundaries of control when Chaim simply stated, "hardly. You are restless, vengeful and most importantly arrogant."

With this, Tom sat down on the mat and Chaim did the same. He knew that he had made a break-through. Tom proceeded to tell him about the night his family was killed. When he was finished, he said, "so you see, no matter what I was bound to lose. I followed my gut, and I want to believe I did everything possible but …"

Chaim had listened intently and more importantly, without interruption. This courtesy made Tom regret his behavior.

It became blatantly obvious Chaim did not suffer any mental deficiency. His analysis was clipped and curt. "Bad intelligence on both sides caused this disaster."

Tom listened with bated breath.

"Based on what you have told me, theirs was not updated before the raid, and yours was non-existent. The first tactical error was yours. You shot prematurely. The invader was still outside."

Tom was relentless in his defense. "I had no choice. It was pitch-dark. I could only make out his outline against the sky."

Gently, Chaim continued, "that, my young friend gave you an advantage he didn't have."

Tom defended his decision. "He could have had night vision apparatus."

Chaim acknowledged this possibility but countered. "If so, he would never have fired blindly, he would have locked on the target, you. Your mistake was not being patient enough to wait for the intruder to enter the house. If you had and once the man was close enough you could have tried to overpower him without firing a shot."

Tom's disbelief was palatable. "Me overpower a trained cop?"

"Believe it or not, yes."

Now in total despair, Tom gasped. "It was my fault. I killed my family,"

Quick to interpret his findings, Chaim assured Tom this was not the case.

"No, there was no fault on your part. As you said, you are an architect, not a warrior. Had you been one, your actions would have been inexcusable. You went with your gut like any ordinary man and almost sacrificed your own life to protect your loved ones."

Tom was now visibly shaken. The memories, the hurt, it was all too much. "Then, why this lesson? Was it just to make me feel like shit? If so, you succeeded."

Chaim assured him his actions were entirely understandable. "Ultimately you are not to blame. The police are. They had the house surrounded and should have identified themselves. In my estimation, they were an improperly trained, out of control assault team lacking proper command. Accept these facts and accept what you can't change. Put the guilt and feelings of inadequacy behind you. The dead feel no pain; it is time for you to heal."

Tom could feel the relief that flowed through him. It would take time, but he had turned a corner. Getting up from the floor Tom thanked Chaim for making him see things more clearly Again, Chaim was about to offer to drive him home but thought better of it and suggested Tom take the car and get a good night's sleep.

Tom accepted and said he would bring dinner with him when he returned the car the next evening. His gesture was appreciated by Chaim, but with a smile, he Answered.

"That is what I have a cook for, remember."

# 3

It would be an understatement to say that Tom had committed to quickly, but Chaim's tenacity and passion for his mission had convinced him.

Tom's preparedness was critical, and although he agreed with the initial plan of action, he had to admit that he had no idea what Chaim really meant by being ready, willing and able to succeed. But it didn't take long for him to find out.

The training was intense and at times disturbing. He didn't understand the importance of some of the demands; hand to hand combat was one. Tom tried to overcome his reticence to this particular aspect of the program, but it was proving difficult.

Chaim recognized his behavior, and before it could become a stumbling block, he knew he had to get it out in the open and more importantly, resolved.

He sat down on the mat and waited for Tom to do the same. There was no doubt that Tom respected Chaim, but he had something to say and voiced his concern without holding back. Chaim listened quietly.

"My boy, this isn't about fair play. So far, you have learned the necessary basics of self-defense, but now we have arrived at the point where all rules of fair play must be abandoned. This is street-fighting. It's about survival, and it's dirty and mean."

This statement was repulsive to Tom, and he said so. "You said you were teaching me the art of self-defense because it could prove useful. That I could accept because it is a confidence builder. What possible relevance does street-fighting have to do with me becoming a trustee of your financial affairs? Quite frankly, I can't see why I would have to beat the crap out of any bank manager."

Chaim couldn't contain his giggle but continued in earnest. "I can see how this might be muddling so let me try to tie everything up neatly for you. There will be times when you have to deal with people whose political agenda is in total opposition to the changes I propose. It is also an undisputed fact there are those who prefer to use brawn over brain to get their point across. If you encounter any such opposition, you now have the equivalent of a black belt in karate. Unaccredited as it may be, it is your secret weapon, and unfortunately, there may be times when you have no choice but to use it as effectively as possible."

Tom stared down at the mat contemplating what he had gotten himself into. It was entirely possible it might be better to quit now before he became any more involved.

It was as if Chaim read his mind. The last thing he

wanted was for Tom to reconsider. In an attempt to ward off any alarm he said, "but don't worry, my young friend. You will be better equipped to deal with them than you realize. You don't know how proficient you have become. Think of that first day. You were feisty but angry. You're still feisty, but you have learned that anger obscures your goal. You have become a real challenge for me. I now have to fight like hell to keep up with you. After street fighting, we will start the most intensely difficult and challenging episode."

Tom was very wary. "What can be more difficult than fighting you?" and added as an afterthought, "oh master?"

"Still arrogant, I see but more realistic now. Pitch black, my friend. This place will be devoid of any light. You will learn to operate by sound, smell, the natural sensors of your skin and intuition. Was I wrong in assuming that you were beginning to enjoy this course?"

"Well, no but …"

"I know what you are thinking. You are still hung up on the fairness of conquest. Well, we both know how effective that was when the police invaded your home. They didn't consider fair play. A hero who dies using fair play feels no glory. His admirers may place flowers on his grave, but they wilt and are soon both forgotten."

Tom had one more question.

"Is what we are doing now, really in preparation for what I promised to do for you, or is there some other reason?"

"There is. My other reason is that you have added years to my life. I haven't felt this well for over a decade."

Tom was pleased that he had helped but said that he

felt he was getting mixed messages. "Claiming to be a man of peace … you teach me to fight as if Armageddon is just around the corner?"

It was easy for Chaim to justify his reasoning.

"You and I have inherited the joys and burdens of the promised land. Armageddon is here. This may well be the last battle, not against Palestinians or Arabs but against the evils of ignorance, prejudice, and hatred of our fellow man. Like any war, there will be casualties but let them not be the children; they are the future and need protecting."

Tom couldn't let the subject go. "You're one man and, I'm sorry to say, old. You can hardly expect to do any more fighting."

Chaim was quick to say that he had no intention of fighting because he had declared Tom, his emissary and it was his job to take over whatever duties remained and carry them out.

"Why the hell did you leave Israel if you love it so much?" Tom saw that he had hit a raw nerve. A dark expression settled over the old man's face which immediately made him regret resurrecting an obviously painful memory. He didn't merely respect Chaim, he genuinely liked him. He was a friend who had guided him through personal chaos to inner peace. He rued his impetuousness, but there was no way he could take back the question. As he had been taught to do, he waited patiently for the answer. It seemed to take some time before Chaim blurted out.

"Mossad ousted me. I was too outspoken. I adamantly opposed inequality in any way, shape or form. Israel claims to be the only democracy in the Middle East, but in my opinion, it is flawed. The western democracies seem to be unbiased in the matter the Jewish and Arab conflict. Simply said, they support Israel just enough not to offend the Arab oil producers."

"If that's the case, shouldn't you have picked an American for the job?"

"No. You are Jew and Gentile, unbiased, with the heart and ability to put my plan in place."

Tom didn't want to negate the compliment, but he still had serious reservations. "How will I accomplish it all? I'm not a politician, not famous unless of course, you factor in that I am considered a convicted felon."

"Patience, my young friend, patience! The life of this … master, as you so eloquently described me, goes beyond my grave. People in high places will listen and comply."

Tom still felt a need to push. "Did I hear a silent "or else" in your last statement?"

The question went unanswered, but the dark cloud was ever evident. After a moment or two, the old man shrugged, "well let's not make too much of this yet. It is imperative that we proceed one step at a time.

You are now ready for the next phase of your training; the invisible enemy."

# 4

The intense darkness stunned him. He stood dead still and held his hand in front of his eyes. He saw nothing but could feel its warmth when it was close to his face. He listened for a sound, any sound. He was keenly aware of his breathing and heartbeat. He dared not move. This was seriously scary but exhilarating. He knew Chaim was somewhere ... but where? Suddenly he sensed something next to his ear. He immediately dropped to the floor and assuming it was Chaim reached out to grab his legs, but there was nothing there. He heard the occasional movement of his opponent but never succeeded in touching him.

"I give up," he finally said. "I don't know how you do it, but you are like a ghost."

"Perhaps I am," was the answer from across the room.

Not one to miss this unexpected opportunity, Tom dove in the direction of the voice.

When the lights came back on, Chaim was sitting against the wall thoroughly enjoying himself. "You were so intent on beating me you never once considered the possibility that my story about *the invisible enemy* was pure, unadulterated bullshit. You knocked yourself out while I sat here listening to you making all kinds of noise that in a real situation could get you killed."

"Why the charade? You just wasted a good portion of not only your time but mine as well."

"Not wasted, my boy. Fighting someone in a place as dark as this happens only in movies. In all the years I have been in this business, I have yet to meet anyone who has success-fully performed this stunt. You attacked based on what you thought you heard, and I sat here while you made all kinds of noise. I could have shot you at any time. The only thing this exercise should teach you is: let the enemy come to you."

To get Tom's mind off his defeat, Chaim took a key from his pocket and unlocked the closet doors for the first time. They were stocked with rifles, handguns, and knives among other weaponry. Tom was astounded to see such a lethal arms collection. "Do you have permits for these?"

"Yes, I couldn't take the chance and not register them. I'm a collector and a private investigator."

Tom's sarcasm was still intact, and he didn't resist taking on his self-designated mentor. "A collector? You're no more a collector than the Pope is a Jew."

Calmly and without rancor, Chaim reminded him. "It's a matter of record that your first Pope was a Jew."

Tom backed down. "Point taken."

He let it all sink in before he suggested that it was time for Tom to become familiar with this particular stash.

"No thanks. It is illegal for me to play with these toys."

"Not here. In time you will see them become second nature to you."

"Somehow I doubt that but I must admit one thing does intrigue me, your collection is unique in that there are no antiques."

"That's quite observant of you, Tom, I collect only what is currently significant. The rest is useless in our trade."

Tom clarified Chaim's statement that it was not his trade. They went back and forth on this point until Chaim flatly stated that weapons were an integral part of the training Tom had agreed to undertake. And, without any hesitation, Tom countered: "Guns are for killing, and I have no intention of killing anyone."

Chaim nodded agreement but went on to say. "The day may come when you have to make the decision to kill or be killed. If and when it does, I want you ready."

They spent a great deal of time at the shooting range. It was evident that Tom would never be a marksman.

The day finally came when the teaching ended. Chaim looked at Tom and sadly acknowledged how much he would miss his young prodigy. It also grieved him that he would never see his dream become a reality.

Without a doubt, his days were numbered. He had managed to keep his pain under wraps, but he knew that I was time to act. Chaim wasted no time explaining to Tom that he would be inserting a small capsule containing tracking program under his skin. Tom had never been a big fan of pain and wanted to know which anesthetic he would be using.

"Ah … no need, a stiff drink will do." He saw his patient pale and added "but I do have a local anesthetic, the kind dentists use. I'm sure it will keep you comfortable so don't worry."

Tom remained unconvinced and said the mere idea of this procedure made him feel queasy. He was keen to know if it could be delayed.

Chaim proclaimed it was now or never. "No, I'm afraid not. My cancer has metastasized, and I have little time left. We have to test the implant as soon as possible, and then we have to go out to sea to dump the guns and computer equipment. It is imperative there be no trace of our activity. Everything has to go."

This was a moment of genuine sadness. Tom had known about Chaim's cancer but believed it was in remission. He had grown very fond of this old man and would miss him.

He was brought back to reality when Chaim stated the obvious. "You have a job to do."

Tom had so many questions about what was in store for him, but Chaim had few answers. All he could tell him with certainty was, the GPS implant and computer programs had a ten-year lifespan. "Even I can't anticipate technology advances beyond that. For the immediate future, go on with your life. If nothing happens, I've just wasted a lot of time. That being said I would hazard a guess that a man, David Haber, will have an undying curiosity about what I have been up to all these years. He's bound to stir up trouble, but you'll cross that bridge when it happens."

Tom wanted to make sure that his plans were clearly understood. "You know that I want to go back to Canada."

It shouldn't have surprised him that Chaim had thought of everything, but Tom was still amazed by this man's intuition. "I never anticipated anything else. That's why Canada is your only safe haven. You must never be in one country for more than two weeks at a time, except Canada." He went on to explain when he had enough checks and balances in place to avoid disaster. "Nothing is without risk, you know this from your past experience."

# 5

Tom stood at the graveside and watched the coffin lowered. He didn't understand the Hebrew prayers, but it didn't matter. Other than himself, there were only two people at the burial. Tom recognized the man but not the woman. He couldn't help but notice how her youth and beauty contrasted dramatically with her associate.

Following the service, the couple approached him. "My name is David Haber, and this is my wife, Fabiola."

Tom acknowledged the extended hand, "Tom Benning." He had no intention of letting this Haber person in on the fact that he already knew who he was.

"Are you family of Chaim?"

His question seemed genuine and appeared to be accepted as such when Tom answered with a simple, "no, I'm an old friend."

It was clear that they were both in the game playing mode. This, however, didn't change the fact that neither one of them seemed willing to make the first move. Tom decided to continue the ruse. "You two go way back then?"

"Indeed we do. We served together in the war." He hesitated before going on, but when he did, he changed the subject completely. "I didn't realize Chaim had any family."

Tom didn't miss a beat. "He didn't. We were friends." He was interested to see if Haber would take the bait and decided to feed the confusion a little.

"He and I lived together for the last few years." He relished watching Haber become more animated.

"How did you meet?"

Tom wanted to keep his distance and answered casually. "Oh … in an old junk shop, it just so happened that we both liked to tinker with computers."

This led to a much more direct probe. "Computers your line of work, Mr. Benning?"

With equal sharpness, Tom let it be known that he was an unemployed architect and had been for some time. His tone also conveyed that he did not want to pursue this conversation. Haber effectively ignored the obvious and casually mentioned that he found it very unusual that Tom was unemployed with the building boom and all. Haber volunteered that he had connections in Miami and would be willing to see what he could do. His offer was exactly what Tom had expected. He instinctively knew it would not be without conditions. "No thanks. I'm going back to Canada as soon as I settle Chaim's affairs."

"You are Canadian?"

"Yes I am but thanks for the offer just the same."

Haber was like a dog with a bone. He didn't take kindly to being dismissed, so much so that he blurted out, "I understand that Chaim had a fine gun collection."

Tom was enjoying himself. He feigned surprise at the statement and answered. "Chaim made no effort to conceal his abhorrence of violence so he would have no need for a gun let alone a gun collection."

Stunned by Tom's statement, he was now more curious than ever. "You didn't know?"

"Know what?" Tom shot back.

"That Chaim worked for the Israeli intelligence service."

Tom could barely contain himself. He had this guy right where he wanted him. "Chaim, a spy?" he shouted incredulously and caught Haber entirely off guard.

"Shhhh … not so loud! He may be departed, but there are still people interested in what he was doing here."

Tom had what he was looking for. He had played his cards well. "I can assure you that he wasn't a spy. I lived in the same house with him for five years. If he had been a spy, I would've known. How ridiculous … a spy of all things."

Not to be outdone, Haber challenged with, "if you don't believe me, look in his basement. He had all kinds of mementos including a huge gun collection."

Tom willingly accepted the challenge and couldn't wait to see Haber's reaction to what awaited him. He savored the anticipation. "I tell you what, Mr. Haber. Why don't you come over to the house with me? If there are any guns, you're welcome to them."

This was music to his ears. He didn't even bother to mask his enthusiasm. "You mean that?"

Without any sense of guilt, Tom continued the charade. "Sure, you might as well take them with you. I wouldn't know what to do with them and given your old friend status, it would seem appropriate."

They each returned to their cars and left the cemetery. David and his wife followed Tom to the house. Once there, he took them directly to the basement.

"See," said Haber excitedly. He pointed at the closets. "I told you. Those are the closets."

It intrigued Tom that Haber was so familiar with the room and he asked how this was possible. He merely stated that he had visited once and Chaim had shown him the entire collection which Tom didn't believe for one minute but decided to let it go. Haber walked over to the closets and looked at the padlocks. "Do you have the key?"

"Yeah, I think it's in the workbench drawer."

Haber took the liberty of rummaging around the drawer until he found it. He opened the first door only to discover that it contained nothing but some old suitcases, a collection of mason jars and some empty boxes. He literally gasped and turned immediately to the next door. His trembling didn't help his coordination as he tried to unlock it. To his abject disappointment, it contained much of the same. His reaction was one of total disbelief. If Tom hadn't been savoring this moment so much, he might have felt some pity. The crestfallen look was well worth the charade. All Haber could say over and over again was, "I know that he had guns in these closets!"

Tom theorized that it was so unlike Chaim to possess guns but willingly acknowledged that if he had, it was possible they had been sold.

David Haber walked slowly back up the stairs, and his wife followed. He was still shaking his head. He obviously couldn't understand what had just happened.

When they arrived back at the front door, he thanked Tom for his time, took his wife's arm and led her to their car. Tom knew enough about David Haber to be convinced that although this had concluded their first meeting, it definitely wouldn't be their last.

# 6

Tom held a letter in his hand and grumbled something about it being a hell of a time for his uncle Karel to kick the bucket.

His parents had immigrated to Canada when he was a mere eight years old, and although his mother corresponded regularly with her brother, she seldom spoke of him as long as her husband was alive. His uncle was a relative unknown, so to speak.

One of the few things Tom did remember was when his father was drunk, which was often, he voiced his prejudice and called Karel a Jewish queer.

In hindsight, this hatred was probably based on intense jealousy more than ethnicity. Karel's wealth was perhaps the bitterest pill for his father to swallow and the fact that he provided the funds for Tom's education didn't help matters. Tom had always been grateful to his uncle, but their communication had been sporadic at best. The last time they had spoken was to deliver the sad news of his mother's death.

He looked up an agent and booked a return flight to Amsterdam. For the first time since returning to Canada, he was aware of his travel restrictions but reasoned the estate of a ragman shouldn't take more than a day or two to settle. As a safeguard, he decided to schedule a week to take care of any unforeseen eventualities.

He felt a responsibility to his Uncle Karel not just because he was his last relative but because he had been his benefactor. It was important to him to settle the estate properly. The notary's letter hadn't given any details other than any expense incurred for this trip was solely his. For someone with little money in the bank and who was now working for an employment agency, this was daunting, but he had no choice.

As usual, Stacey was her optimistic self. She had offered to drive him to the airport and on the way commented, "perhaps he has left you enough to at least recoup your fare. Who knows, you may even inherit enough to buy a good piece of land. More importantly, remember if there are any debts, as the sole heir you can always sign off and negate any further responsibility for the estate."

Tom's mood was anything but light-hearted. He shook his head and was downright dejected. "Not only do I not like to fly, but I'm also not looking forward to paying off a dead man's debts. The one and the only reason I am undertaking this trip is that he was good to me and never asked for anything. The least I can do is honor his financial commitments if I can."

When they pulled up in front of departures, Stacey

leaned over and gave him a little peck on his cheek before he got out of the car. He would have liked to take her in his arms and really kiss her, but she wasn't that demonstrative. He wondered if she just didn't care enough. He had hoped for more, but things weren't working out that way. An occasional kiss and holding hands in a movie weren't enough. He wasn't just looking for friendship. There were times when he had come close to telling her how he really felt. If his uncertainty had stopped him from doing this before, now definitely wasn't the time, so he let it go, got out of the car, waved and walked into the terminal.

He landed at Schiphol in the morning and took advantage of the free time to look around Amsterdam. A change of scene would do him good, and he was curious to see if he could remember any of the surroundings. As it turned out, his memories were too blurry, but he enjoyed this downtime and in spite of the time change, felt quite refreshed. When he got back to his hotel, he treated himself to beer and a sandwich, in keeping with his tight budget and turned in for the night. He slept solidly until he heard his wake up call.

His meeting turned out to be with a solemn-looking gentleman who read the details of the translated version of the will. Tom listened in shock. Uncle Karel had died a very rich man. The notary showed him the financial statements, and Tom exclaimed, "Jesus Christ, I thought he was a ragman. Mum told me that he had paid my tuition, but I never knew that he was this well-heeled."

The term was unfamiliar to the notary, and he echoed: "well-heeled?"

Tom apologized and explained its meaning.

"Oh, I see. I pride myself on my English, Mr. Benning and you have just enriched my vocabulary. Hm … well-heeled," he mused. "Now, Mr. Benning, allow me to return the favor and enrich your understanding of the rag business. Anything related to textiles is rag business. Your late uncle's weaving mills have built up excellent equity. He had a chain of fabric discount stores in the Netherlands, Germany, and Belgium but he sold those before he died. Negotiations, although now pending, were also underway to sell his mills. The prospective buyer is still eager to complete the transaction but that, of course, now depends entirely on you.

The estate is comprised of roughly 16 million Guilders in cash, mostly from the sale of the stores. If you go through with the sale of the two weaving mills at the price your late uncle agreed to, that would add another 24 million Guilders. Then there is the house and chattels with his art collection. Although not yet appraised I know that it is insured for 4.5 million."

Tom's level of disbelief was heightened with each disclosure. Juvenile as it was, all he could say was, "WOW!"

The notary smiled understandably and continued. "Yes, converted to Canadian currency it would leave you roughly 18 million dollars after taxes and fees. Now, this is only an estimate, mind you. Much depends on a good tax accountant."

Tom willed himself back to reality to ask. "What is the status of the transaction on the weaving mills?"

"Well, simply said, Karel, signed all the agreements, except the final documents. Naturally, everything is in Dutch, but translations can be made readily available to you. The possibility you might want to get a second opinion is totally understandable. Another important factor is, according to Dutch law, you are still a citizen and as such can control and run the mills yourself if you choose."

Without any hesitation whatsoever, Tom confessed to knowing less than nothing about textiles. "If the offer was good enough for my uncle, it is good enough for me." He wanted the sale finalized.

Tom left the office and spent the entire evening in turmoil. Contrary to the previous night, he was unable to sleep and paced the floor contemplating his life as a multi-millionaire. Finally, as daylight appeared on the horizon, he dozed off.

A few hours later, he was awakened by a call from the front desk. His chauffeur was waiting in the lobby. Tom's first reaction was one of panic. He had overslept. He showered and dressed berating himself for being late. He was the first person to hold latecomers accountable for their lack of respect and made sure to apologize to his driver for keeping him waiting.

He was on his way to sign papers about the sale of the mills. Settling the rest of the estate would have to wait because it involved appraisals which, the notary said could take some time. His limited knowledge about the value of art, combined with the trust his uncle had obviously placed in this elderly gentleman, made it easy to give him his power of attorney. Arrangements for bank funds to be transferred to Vancouver were already in place with the balance remaining in The Netherlands for the time being.

The return flight was as dull and as cramped as the original. Tom cleared customs in Montreal, happy to stretch before boarding his connection to Vancouver.

Only after unenthusiastically cramming himself into his seat did it occur to him. He could have upgraded and flown first class. The irony of it all was not lost on him. It was going to take some time to let go and enjoy his new-found wealth. Being a millionaire would take some getting used to. After a brief stopover in Calgary, he breathed a sigh of relief once the plane was back in the air. He was tired and looked forward to getting home.

# 7

Without warning, three men in balaclavas and armed with pistols appeared out of nowhere. They identified themselves as PLO and took control of the plane. Tom cringed and tried to become as small as possible.

"Why now?" he whispered self-indulgently. Was it possible his new life was about to be prematurely cut short? Things like this don't happen in Canada and not to me.

One terrorist, apparently the leader, grabbed a flight attendant by her hair dragging her towards the cockpit. He held his gun to her head as she knocked on the door. Whatever she said gave them access. The second and third took up positions at the front, and the rear of the plane respectively and the passengers were ordered to be silent.

Ultimately, the plane landed without incident, but Tom sensed that the worst was yet to come. The plane turned off the runway and stopped a couple of hundred yards away from the terminal. The exit door was now facing a heavily armed police force.

Two men, wearing only boots and underpants came out from behind the police line and pushed a boarding ramp across the tarmac to the plane and left. Almost simultaneously, the cockpit door opened and the flight attendant was shoved out by her captor who said something to the gunman at the front and slammed the door shut.

The attendant was then ordered to open the cabin door. Tom wondered if it were too optimistic to think their ordeal could almost be over. Perhaps, all these guys wanted was the plane. His train of thought was cut short when the terrorist at the front of the plane started down the aisle. He was halfway when he stopped and pointed his gun at the chest of the young man sitting directly in front of him. There was no doubt in anyone's mind that he was going to be executed and the woman beside him started to scream

Chaim had prepared him for any eventuality, but he was damned if he wanted to put his training to the test. Automatically, he analyzed his options. His chances of beating the odds were good, but if he had to go, he might as well take one of these bastards with him. His decision was made. His "please sir" caught the gunman off guard. Tom felt his blood go to ice when a pair of black eyes stared at him through the opening of the balaclava. "Take me. I won't give you any trouble."

"So, you like to be a hero?" he taunted and rammed his gun against Tom's forehead. "Okay, hero, now I will see if you give me any trouble. If you do, I can guarantee, you will regret it."

Tom just nodded, got up out of his seat and walked

calmly with his hands clasped behind his head. Having accepted death when he volunteered, he had nothing to lose, and he could now devote all his efforts to overpowering his captor. He was in control and ready to strike. Ironically, the captive was now stalking the captor.

Tom wasn't sure he could deliberately kill another human being, but he had no doubt he was about to find out. He knew executions carried out in plain view were ritualistic and generally staged to generate maximum media coverage.

As ordered, he lowered his arms when they left the plane. His survival improved with each step. The police would never fire as long as he, the hostage, was alive. On the ground, the gunman pushed Tom into the open, nearer to the cockpit window.

Being this far from the stairs and away from the relative security of the plane, was a daring move. Was it to taunt the police or did the killer need to be closer to the cockpit? Was it possible his radio was malfunctioning? Tom had already observed his captor repeatedly push against his left ear.

Outwardly calm and wholly committed, Tom's focus was solely on the man holding the gun against his head. The odds had improved considerably. He had room to maneuver and only one opponent to contend with instead of three.

A disturbance in the police line distracted the gunman. Tom didn't dare turn his head to see if his assumption about the malfunctioning radio was right. He had to trust his instincts. This was his moment. He took a deep breath, shouted and swung his arm up with all the power he could muster. It sent the gunner's weapon flying, and a well-placed kick to his groin left him grabbing his crotch as he stumbled and fell sideways under the fuselage.

Tom lunged for the gun, pointed it at the terrorist's head and pulled the trigger twice. The man's last words were, "I'm Mossad, Mossad, don't kill." His body lay motionless as a pool of blood spread on to the tarmac. It had all been too easy … surreal.

He hated the idea of getting back on the plane, but he knew that he could never live with himself if he didn't. As long as the police stayed where they were, it could reasonably be assumed by those on the board that the hostage had been killed and the third member was rejoining his assault team.

He prayed that the tactical team was being led by someone with enough sense to wait for his next move. The only shots fired had been his so it should be blatantly clear To the police in the distance that he knew what he was doing.

That the shots had been heard on the plane was certain, as was the chance that contact was trying to be made. His assumption that the radio had malfunctioned was now a blessed advantage.

Back at the stairs, he saw something taped to the bottom of one of the steps. It had to be a listening device; a camera would have been useless in that location. He sighed with relief and got as close to the gadget as safety permitted. "One down two to go," he whispered.

Tom quickly calculated his advantages as he crawled up the steps. The leader had no vantage point from the cockpit and, he would never leave his hostages. The terrorizing patroller was alone in the cabin.

Tom stood behind the bulkhead and rapped the gun barrel against it. There was total silence. He knocked again and started to moan and yammer, trying to simulate the dead terrorist. Someone was moving toward him but stopped short. Cautious and unsure, he called out, "Hassan, Hassan."

Tom moaned again and when he heard movement, stepped forward and dropped to one knee. He fired. One bullet caught the terrorist in the mouth, and another pierced his left eye. There was a burning pain in his left shoulder; he knew he had been hit. He wrenched the gun from the dead man's hand and stuck it in his belt. There was only one terrorist left, and he was in the cockpit. Tom motioned to the passengers to stay seated, but a big man got up and walked forward. Stepping over the dead man, he positioned himself near the bulkhead effectively blocking the aisle. He was there to help.

Facing the cockpit door, he knocked with the barrel of his gun and stepped back. The peephole went dark. It could have been one of the pilots, but Tom chose to believe it was the hijacker. He was right. His English was less than fluent, but he managed to make his wishes very clear. "Put gun down."

Tom took a calculated risk and fired point-blank through the door. After some commotion, someone called out. "Don't shoot! He fell against the door, and we are getting him out of the way. We're coming out."

Once free, the crew members started to evacuate the plane. Tom glanced back and saw the large man still blocking the aisle. He smiled and handed him one of the guns as he squeezed past and ran to the back of the plane. He tossed the second gun on a seat and jumped down the chute with the last of the passengers.

Everyone was quickly ushered to waiting busses and whisked away. Tom was distressed to see the police wrestling the big guy, his ally, to the ground. Everything seemed to be happening in slow motion. The captain was pushing his way to the top of the stairs, and finally, the police were helping the bewildered man to his feet.

Back in the terminal, it was interesting to watch the prospect of a moment of fame take hold of some of the passengers. Their eagerness to talk to the reporters seemed to cure the ill effects of their unexpected ordeal.

Tom on the other hand, just wanted to disappear. He noticed an extra microphone dangling from a cameraman's gear. He yanked it free and made his way through the frenzy. "Scuse me! Scuse me, can you tell me … can I have a moment …" he repeated all the way out the door to where Stacey was waiting. He paid no attention to what she was saying but grabbed her hand and kept right on going until they were outside.

He couldn't be sure if she knew what had happened, but there would be enough time for that on the way home. He let out a huge sigh as he slammed the door and they drove away. Only then did he take the time to look at her. She was tearing up. He had hoped she would be pleased to see him, but this seemed a little over the top.

"Good to see you and be home again. Sorry about the chaotic arrival but the trip back wasn't exactly as planned."

She didn't answer but glanced sideways when he stopped talking.

Their music was suddenly interrupted with a special news bulletin. "Damn," Tom cursed while reaching over to change the station, but Stacey pushed his hand away. "I want to hear this."

"*This afternoon a plane carrying 185 passengers and its crew landed safely at Vancouver International airport after being hijacked. A passenger who was taken and held at gunpoint managed to overpower his would-be assassin killing him before re-boarding the plane and shooting the remaining two hijackers. All passengers escaped safely ... Another bulletin just in. It appears the passenger who overpowered the hijackers is a true hero. He bargained his life for that of another passenger who is the father of two children. We have just been informed that our hero disappeared before he could be interviewed. His name is being withheld by the authorities until they have a chance to talk with him. Stay tuned. We will continue to bring you details as they become available.*"

"Jesus Christ," cursed Tom as he reached over once more turning the radio off.

Stacey pulled her caddy over to the side of the road and turned it back on, "I want to hear this. I know what went on at the airport, but I also know I will probably get more information from the media than you. And, it's about time I get the hug I didn't get at the airport." She leaned over and wrapped her arms around his neck. He winced, but she didn't seem to notice. "Let me get a look at you. I've missed you so much." With that, she turned on the dome light and immediately saw blood on his jacket. She was at first bewildered than a look of shock registered on her face. "My God, you're hurt!"

There was no use denying. "Yeah, I caught a slug in the shoulder. It isn't too bad, we'll look at it at home."

"Not likely!" she yelled as she put the car in gear and veered back into traffic. "The emergency room is better equipped than my medicine chest!"

He saw her determination. "Stop now!" His command was ignored. "Stop now, or I'll jump!" he yelled as he opened the door.

He didn't hear her response, but she pulled over to the side of the road. Tears were running down her cheeks. "What is the matter with you, Tom? You're hurt, and I want to get you to the emergency."

"I appreciate your concern, but you don't know what went on out there. I'm the one who shot those terrorists. Once the police find out that it was me, they'll come looking for me. I'm not allowed to even hold a gun, let alone shoot one, and God forbid, kill someone. The Emergency room will be three-ring circus within minutes."

"So, what do you want me to do?"

"Go home and let's see how bad it is … I think the bleeding has stopped."

Stacey started the car again but made him promise he would not object to hospital treatment if it became necessary.

At her apartment, it took the two of them to remove his jacket. She was startled by his blood-soaked shirt and carefully cut it away revealing a wound that would need more than a first aid kit remedy. She thought for a moment and picked up the phone.

"Who are you calling?"

"I know a doctor who can help; he owes me, and he will make this house call."

"It's a gunshot; he'll have to report it."

"I know but first things first." He was too exhausted to do anything but nod. He'd done his best to make her see the importance of remaining out of the limelight. He listened as she spoke to a Pascal Jim. She never once used the title *Doctor*. It dawned on him that the best he might hope for was that Pascal would at least be the equivalent of a paramedic.

Pascal Jim finally arrived, came in and put his bag down. He was a dark, stocky man of about fifty with bushy eyebrows and leathery skin. His hands looked more like those of a laborer than a physician. He tossed his hat on the couch. His salt-and-pepper hair looked like it hadn't been combed in days. He took off his jacket and without washing his hands, took the towel from Tom's shoulder. "This is a gunshot wound. Stacey! What the hell were you thinking? You, better than anyone, know that I have to report this."

She told him she was well aware of her responsibilities but also knew the gunshot report could be slightly delayed. She went on to explain Tom's reticence about going to the hospital.

Stacey explained who Tom was and reminded Pascal that she would never jeopardize his integrity, but he wasn't easily placated.

He took his instruments and shook his head. "You have to go to the hospital. Without X-rays, we can only assume that the bullet shattered and the wound is contaminated. The damn slug is probably lodged in your shoulder. I can't even try to probe for the slug. You won't be able to stand the pain without an anesthetic, and I don't have anything to give you because it's too dangerous for me to carry narcotics."

Tom knew what he was in for and said that he was used to a little pain.

"Okay, I warned you. If you're too damn stubborn to go to the hospital, you get the bottom of the barrel, me."

He finished dressing the wound and gave Stacey a prescription for antibiotics and painkillers and then turned to Tom.

"If this becomes more swollen and more painful, you get your ass to the hospital. You don't want to lose that arm or worse, your life. You need surgery; that slug has to come out. You had better get out of here by morning. I can't hold my report for long. I could lose my license."

Then he asked Stacey where she would take him, and she said she was going to the reserve. He reminded her that was about a two-hour drive which could definitely compromise his chance of recovery should Tom's condition worsen and need hospitalization. Knowing he had done everything he could, he left.

Stacey made sure he was settled and as comfortable as possible. She knew he was too tired and sore to travel right away, so she changed and told him she was going to the drugstore to get his prescriptions filled.

She worried about leaving him alone but had no other choice. As soon as he heard the door close behind her, he got up. It took him a while to get dressed, but once he was ready, he headed for the door. He got as far as the hallway before his legs started to buckle. He sagged down leaving a long red streak against the wall.

Stacey returned thirty minutes later and found him lying where he had collapsed. Barefoot, wearing only jeans and a jacket, he smiled weakly.

She ran to the bedroom and got a pillow and a blanket. Moving him was out of the question. Then she called the ambulance.

She sat beside him on the floor. The front door was open. Weak as he was, his concern for her safety was paramount. He reached out to close it but failed. He could feel himself getting weaker by the minute and before he passed out said, "there is a small capsule under the skin near my left collarbone. Don't let them mistake it for another bullet. It has to stay there. Whatever you do, don't let them give me in an MRI. If I die in the hospital, my body must be taken to the Vancouver morgue with the implant intact. My dog-tags confirm those instructions. The removal of the thing could be disastrous."

She nodded agreement, but he was adamant despite his weakening state. "Promise!" he groaned and she agreed.

With the eerie sound of the wailing ambulance approaching his voice trailed off, he was unconscious.

The surgery took several hours, and by the time he was wheeled into recovery, there were a dozen or so policemen and ten times as many reporters, hanging around the hallways. Stacey was by his bedside when he regained consciousness. He took her hand and kissed it.

"Thank you for looking after me, I'm glad you're here," he whispered and closed his eyes.

Stacey stood to watch over him, waited in a chair next to his bed and whenever she had to leave the room, a tall, muscular man took over. He stood silently by the door or sat in a chair. Whenever Stacey reappeared, he got up, and he would leave to take up his position in the hall.

The police desperately wanted to question Tom, but Stacey was one step ahead of them. She had acquired a court order keeping them out of his room until he was ready. She knew that she couldn't keep them away forever but he wasn't a criminal, and they would have to wait.

The next day he was fully awake, and his first request was for some clothes which were refused. Next, he wanted to know if the implant was intact and was assured it was not disturbed.

"They asked me about it, but I couldn't tell them anything. They said the scar was evidence of it being a medical procedure. They assumed it to be a global position locating device or some such. The surgeon was very intrigued because he had been thinking about getting them for himself and his family."

"Yeah, he came by while you away. The guy sitting near the door was ready to kick him out, but the nurse said it was okay."

Stacey, ever concerned, immediately wanted to know

if he had bothered him. Tom was somewhat confused and asked, "who the doctor or the big guy?"

"Either."

"No."

Tom knew he owed her much, not the least of which was an explanation about who he was. "It's time for me to tell you some things about myself, Stacey."

"Shhh … It can wait, you look tired."

He paid no attention. "I have not committed any crime."

"It makes no difference to me," she lied.

"Well, it does to me so let me tell you."

"Six years ago my wife, our baby girl and I had just moved to a small house outside Toronto. It wasn't the classiest of neighborhoods and lacked regular police patrols, but it was all we could afford, and we were happy.

I took to keeping a gun in my night-table. It made me feel a little less vulnerable. One night I was awakened by some rustling outside, so I took my weapon and slid out of bed. I crawled into the living-room in the pitch-dark, and someone was trying to force my front door open. I watched as the doorframe began to splinter away and the door flew open. There was a silhouette in the doorway. I fired and knew by the grunt that I had shot the intruder. The immediate result was shots spraying from front to back, through windows and doors alike. I heard Cindy scream and crawled over yelling at her to get down, but when I got to her, she was already down. I tried to cover her up but a bullet hit me in the chest, and another slug went into my back. Everything went black.

I woke up in the hospital a couple of days later only to discover that Cindy and the baby were both dead.

It turns out that it was a police drug raid. Unfortunately, their information was less than current. The drug dealer they were after had moved out of the house two months before we bought it.

To this day I don't understand police logic. On the one hand, I got a letter of apology from the chief, and on the other, they accused me of shooting a police officer.

They strongly disputed that they were guilty of any wrongdoing and to save face, the whole incident was deemed a regrettable error in communications. Case closed.

To make matters worse, my in-laws blamed me for the deaths of their daughter and baby granddaughter. They severed all contact with me and claimed both bodies and buried them without allowing me to pay my last respects.

Then, they proceeded to sue the city and police department. The lawsuit was settled out of court, and as a result, they retired to a gated community in Florida. The irony of it all is, the daughter they treated like dirt when she was alive became a means to an end. They cried crocodile tears over her coffin; the hypocrites. I, on the other hand, was charged with reckless use of a firearm and got a suspended sentence. I am banned from owning or using guns for the rest of my life.

Once I recovered, I went back to the house. There were 85 bullet holes in the walls. Cindy's blood was still on the floor, and the baby's crib was still there riddled with bullet holes and her blood on the mattress.

I immediately made the necessary arrangements and sold

the house. When everything was finalized, I headed south. While I was contemplating my future, why not enjoy a pleasant warm climate?

I got as far as Alabama and fell in love with Mobile. I lived in an old motel owned by an elderly lady. Because I planned to stay for a few months, we came to an agreement that I would work as a handyman in return for my rent.

One day while browsing in a computer junkshop, I met an old man. After a few days and some mutually interesting chats, I moved into his house.

He enjoyed telling me stories of his years with Mossad, almost as much as I enjoyed listening to them. I helped him with experiments in his computer lab, and he taught me about the digital world, self-defense and survival tactics. I was as eager a student as he was an excellent teacher and I became quite accomplished.

As a final favor, I agreed to let the old man implant his tracking device. We tested the thing many times to make sure that it would not fail.

A few weeks later I came home from shopping and found him dead on the living-room floor. The coroner concluded that he had died of heart failure.

Following the funeral, I returned to Canada with a computer, an old car and five thousand bucks in my pocket. Toronto had too many bad memories, so I decided to settle in Vancouver. I planned to wait a few years to see if anything happened. If nothing did, I would have the implant removed. I wasn't entirely convinced that it was real. It could quite easily have been the invention of a deranged mind.

"What happens if you have it taken out?"

"It's too late for that."

"For how long are you obligated to this ... this ... this thing that tells you what to do?"

"The maximum lifespan of the program is ten years unless I find a way to safely neutralize it."

"Maybe I can help."

"My God, Stacey, you truly don't understand. The implant tells the system where I am at any given time. If I leave Canada, I can only be in any foreign country for 14 days and then I have to move on. It is a cycle that continues until I return to Canada. Canada is the only safe haven for me. This isn't some science fiction thing; it's the technology of today. GPS systems are used for a variety of things, the most recognizable one being to track animals. If mine is tampered with, a lot of people in Israel are in trouble."

"Well ... let's take it one day at the time. The first thing we'll have to do is get the Toronto police straightened out and make them take full responsibility for their mistakes. You have a lawyer friend, and you can afford to sue now."

"Like hell, I'm going to lie low! I'm in enough trouble already. I had a gun in my hand, I fired it, and I killed a couple of people. The judge was very clear about the consequences resulting from any violation of the conditions of my suspended sentence."

Stacey was unrelenting. "But you had no choice and whatever you did was in plain view of the cameras. They wouldn't dare do anything now. It seems to me you want to continue punishing yourself for something that wasn't your fault. Can you honestly say that your wife and baby would be alive today if you hadn't fired that gun? You did exactly what you were supposed to do. You defended your family, and if you let me, we will prove it in court. It's about time the police and the system be held accountable."

As much as he appreciated her powers of persuasion and felt sure that she could put up a good case, he really didn't want to fight.

"But Stace, it's been six years, and the case is closed."

"The police and the crown can open any case whenever they want."

"May I remind you the crown won't open an old case without new evidence, Stacey?"

"If they refuse, we'll file in civil court for your loss. You didn't sign off did you?"

"No they came by and wanted to settle for $100,000, but I told them to stick it where the sun doesn't shine. I don't know how much my in-laws got, but it must have been about the same."

"And they didn't come back with another offer?"

"How could they; I left the country, remember?"

"Well with lots of public opinion on your side, you have nothing to worry about. You're a hero, and we all know how the public loves a hero."

Suddenly her whole demeanor changed. She seemed to relax and out of the blue asked what had happened with his uncle's estate?

"Well," he smiled. "Let's put it this way … your new client is well-heeled."

# 8

Most women dream of having someone like him, she mused. I know that I'm not the easiest person to get along with, so I hope that I haven't scared him off. He is so different, and he's been through so much. He was right accusing me of being prejudiced. I never thought of myself that way, and I never would have had he not pointed it out. My father would prefer me to meet one of our own people but seeing he doesn't want me to live on the reserve, that's highly unlikely. However, am I going to break the news that I have met a man who is not only white but an immigrant? Oh well, I'll cross that bridge when I get to it.

From the hospital window, she watched the reporters milling around on the sidewalk. "You were right about the reporters. I have trouble getting past them. Cameras and microphones follow me everywhere, and as if that's not enough, some of them are really rude."

Tom nodded but interestingly enough came to their

defense. "Yeah, but they're only doing their job like everyone else."

"I know, but I'm just not cut out for this kind of scrutiny … Anyway, I'll be gone for a few minutes, now that you're awake, I want to talk to the doctor. I'll be back in to say goodbye. I have to go home to get some sleep."

She went to the door and motioned to someone. In came the big man he remembered seeing but couldn't immediately recall where or when. He was about six and a half feet tall and muscular. His eyes were soft and kind, not inquisitive. She led him to the bed and introduced him.

"Tom, this is Billy Twofingers. He works for my dad. He'll keep the reporters out of your room. He has a cell phone to call me whenever he needs me." She turned to Billy and continued, "in the event, the police try to question him, I have put a restraining order on the nightstand." She showed Billy the document. "I know that you don't understand what this is about, Billy, but just show this paper to anybody who insists on talking to Mr. Benning."

The "friendly giant" took exception to her comment and stated bluntly, "I can read, Stacey, I ain't stupid, you know."

Stacey immediately regretted hurting his feelings. "I know, Billy. I just wanted you to know exactly what to do." With that, she pointed to a chair near the door. Billy sat down, and she left.

He sat silently and looked everywhere but at Tom, who wondered if the giant were too gentle to be a guard. The only sound in the room was the regular beeping of Tom's heart monitor and the occasional deep sigh from the big man near the door. He seemed to be in constant thought. He often looked at the wall, frowning as if there were something to study other than the green paint. Sometimes he put his head back and looked at the tiled ceiling as if it were the first time he had ever seen a ceiling. Tom watched him for a while. He looked like a child who wanted only to please a parent and do precisely as he was told. Tom caught him trying to look at him without turning in his direction. Curiosity got the better of Tom and attempted to start a conversation.

"Where does the name Twofingers come from, Billy?"

Billy didn't answer, but after some time and another glance at the ceiling he uncrossed his arms and stuck up his right hand. It had an index finger and thumb. He decided to test the waters with a distinct and yet simple statement. "So, that isn't your real name then, is it?"

Billy shook his head. Okay, Tom thought, so that wasn't an impressive beginning, but he wasn't about to give up. "Do you mind it when they call you that?" His response continued to be non-verbal. He didn't smile or show any emotion. He only shook his head and kept avoiding Tom's eyes. He wanted to know how it had happened. It was evident that the edge of the affected hand was scarred. Clearly, it was not a birth defect. "How did it happen?"

This time Billy still didn't look at him, but after a while, he answered in a low, hollow voice. "Sawmill lost them fucking fingers on a saw machine."

Tom felt vindicated. "Oh, man … that must have hurt. But, at least you have the most important fingers left."

Billy actually continued, "dint hurt too bad. Even less when they paid me fifteen thousand bucks for them fingers. The guys found them in the sawdust, but they were like hamburger so they couldn't put them back."

He was still looking straight ahead, but the lines on his face were slowly beginning to change. He wasn't concentrating on the wall anymore, but on trying to keep himself from smiling. He even bit his lip but his shoulders started to shake, and he suddenly burst out laughing. Then without warning, he was a statue again.

"You lost more than half your hand, and you laugh?" He didn't answer but stuck up his left hand, it was almost identical to his right.

"Don't tell me," Tom commented, "they paid you another fifteen for that hand?"

"Nope," he grinned. "Stacey tried, but they dint believe it was an accident the second time. I got fucked; no fingers, no money."

There was no malice in his statement, just fact. Without any warning, Billy looked directly at Tom for the first time, and to his astonishment, he got up to sit on the chair beside the bed. Tom leaned in as if he were about to tell Billy a secret. "You want to do something for me, Billy?"

He was immediately willing: "sure what?" Tom had to strike while the iron was hot, "get me some clothes and help me to get out of here."

With his eyes wide open and looking more than a little scared, he shot out of his chair. "No fuckin' way man, no fuckin' way! Stace would kill me!"

He had no sooner finished his sentence when he turned around and saw her. She didn't say a word. She stood near the door as it slowly closed behind her and stared at Billy, that same stare she had used on the police officer the day she bailed him out of jail. Then as now; no words were necessary. Her eyes said it all and Billy understood. He kept his eyes riveted to the floor, like a kid expecting to be scolded as he attempted to explain his actions. "I'm sorry Stace, but he asked about them fingers, so I told him."

Stacey maintained her silence and her stare. Billy left the room. Her expression softened as she walked over to the bed, and then she smiled, but Tom felt sorry for Billy and told her so. In his estimation, Billy hadn't done anything to warrant her harsh treatment.

"Why do I get the impression that he is afraid of you, Stacey?"

She was not to be deterred and totally justified her actions. "He isn't afraid but he has to follow the rules, and one of the rules is to keep people away from you. He couldn't do his job sitting here next to you."

Tom was not appeased. "Is this what you expect from people, blind obedience?"

It was apparent Tom didn't understand the ramifications of Billy's actions, and she certainly didn't want to upset him further. She did, however, feel he needed to know why she had reacted the way she had.

"Nonsense, Tom, he is mentally handicapped, and I know how to handle him. He gets more and more excited the longer he talks. Sometimes it can be so bad that he has to be restrained. He is on medication but often forgets to take it, and there is no one to assure that he does."

She told him that Billy rests when he feels tired but doesn't sleep. That he can sit and stare at the floor or the wall as if in deep thought. That it's his only way of relaxing. Pascal Jim says it's his way of turning off. He can have his eyes closed, but he never dreams or completely shuts down. His mother, an alcoholic, drank throughout her pregnancy and it is firmly believed this contributed to his condition. And, last but certainly not least, that his life expectancy will be negatively affected by his condition. She looked over at Tom to gauge his reaction to what she had just told him and then continued.

"He often roams the woods at night, sometimes carrying an ax. He pretends he's a lumberjack. It is so sad. He is very lonely. One morning Sam found him lying in the shed where the plumbing fixtures are stored. He had taped his eyes shut, and he was snoring. When asked what he was doing, he said that he wanted to teach his eyes how to stay closed and sleep. Sam decided Billy needed a place to call his own and set up a cot in a little room in the Quonset. It has been his home ever since. Sam sees to it that he gets some pocket money for being the watchman. He's more devoted to Sam than he is to his own mother."

Tom's concern was evident. "Doesn't anyone in his family care?"

"No. He only has his mother who, as you can imagine, is anything but nurturing. She cared enough to take his compensation money and spent it on booze. When it was gone, she threw him out. Billy did the only thing he could think of and went back to work at the mill where they gave him a job away from the machines. The rest is history, as they say."

Tom remained silent, and while looking down at him expecting another question about Billy, she realized that he had changed since his trip. He was more distant. She knew, however slight the possibility, she could be imagining it, but it still bothered her. She couldn't overlook the fact that he was still shaken by the hijacking, but somehow, deep down, she was convinced there was more.

It never crossed her mind that he was experiencing flashbacks to the loss of his wife and child and he feared history was about to repeat itself.

His actions at the airport had turned him into an instant hero, and she felt he should stand up and take credit for them. When she broached the subject of setting up a news conference, he became inordinately agitated. "No way! It would only stir up a hornet's nest and could even land me in jail."

Although she was perplexed, she continued to plead her case and told him she felt his obsession with anonymity bordered on paranoia.

He blew up. "If you would just stop and think; you might understand. The judge was very clear in his rendering. No matter what the circumstances, the simple fact of me holding a gun, could land me in jail. That seems pretty clear to me. How about you?"

Without waiting for her to answer he rhymed off the main reasons for his decision. "Even though I received a suspended sentence, I was charged with dangerous use of a firearm because of my actions the night my home was invaded, and my wife and baby were killed. As if that isn't enough, I am lying in this bed with a bullet wound which is the result of an altercation with one of three people recently killed at the airport."

He stopped as abruptly as he had started and waited for her reaction. There was none.

# 9

A new apartment with restricted access and a security camera in the lobby was Tom's first priority. He literally walked away from his old basement suite leaving almost everything for the next tenant. His newfound wealth allowed him this luxury.

In spite of the precautions he could now afford, he still didn't feel secure enough to ask Stacey to move in. There was no doubt in his mind that he loved her and when they were together he was happy, but they still met at her place, and he always left before morning.

She tried to understand his fears but the longer she knew him, the harder it was to let him leave night after night. There were so many things she didn't understand. Why did he feel safer in his own place? Was it essential to isolate himself the way he did? How long could this go on? She was ready to take their relationship to the next level but didn't dare mention it because Tom could be so closeminded on the subject.

The closest she had ever come to opening up to him was

when she asked "how long will this charade continue? Do I have to wait forever?"

She had caught him entirely off guard, but he handled it with as much grace as he could muster. "Call it a charade if you wish, but I did warn you. It will take as long as it takes. I do, however, have a hunch that things are about to happen."

"What hunch?"

"A hunch, like the calm before the storm."

"Oh Tom, the longer I know you the stranger you act. It's been two months since the hijacking and no contact. Be reasonable. Isn't it possible that it is nothing but a hoax? The old man could have been suffering from Alzheimer's for all you know."

Holding the door open for him, she bowed her head before he could see the tears. Her long hair covered her face, but as he put his hand under her chin, he saw how upset she was. He cleared his throat before speaking. "I tell you what. If nothing happens in six months, I'll consider the whole thing hogwash, and I'll have the "thing" removed."

She asked with cautious optimism, "you promise?" and was more than pleased with his answer. "Yeah, I promise, mark the calendar."

She shut the door behind him realizing that his insecurity was an integral part of who he was.

It was true, he had relaxed once the cameras and reporters were no longer parked in front of his building. His concern had always been that anything or anyone could be in one of those trucks.

Occasionally reporters still asked for interviews. He

never agreed without first checking their credentials with one exception; a reporter who represented an Israeli monthly publication. His reputation though not exemplary was well-established

Tom smiled when he saw him. He looked exactly like the picture Chaim had shown him. His name was Avi Haber a.k.a. "rat-face" because of his appearance and sleazy methods of getting information. He was often used as a *kidon,* a Mossad executioner.

Tom buzzed him in. "Okay Avi, come on up,"

"How did you know it was me?"

Tom answered blithely. "Well, you are the guy who scheduled this appointment for exactly this time, aren't you?"

"Well, Tom, I just wanted to make sure you know who you are dealing with."

Tom also saw no reason not to give Avi the same opportunity to know who he was dealing with and reined him in.

"First of all, it's Mr. Benning to you, and secondly, there is no misunderstanding. I know exactly who you are and why you are here."

Avi wasted no time. "Look, Mr. Benning. I was hoping to get your side of the story about the hijacking. There were, after all, some Israeli passengers on that plane and the public have some unresolved concerns. They are convinced that you are an air-marshal because of the professional way you handled the whole episode. Suspicions are rampant that you had prior knowledge about was going to happen, based on your readiness to offer yourself as a replacement for the other passenger. They also feel very strongly that they should have been forwarned. Do you care to respond?"

Avi reached into his pocket for his cigarettes, and with lightning speed, Tom reached over his shoulder and had a dagger pointed at Avi's throat.

"Easy, you sure are fast with that thing. All I wanted was a cigarette."

"And this is how I feel about people smoking in my pad." Tom casually added the obvious, Avi was wearing a shoulder holster, and when he reached into his shirt pocket, it looked like he was going for his gun.

He proceeded to tell Avi that he knew precisely why he was standing in front of him, and it had nothing to do with conducting an interview. "The game is over. You're here to interrogate me and may I say quite frankly, you're not very good at it. You are so transparent. Now, the truth!"

Tom settled back in his chair, put the dagger on the table beside him and waited. Avi took exception to his tone. It was not entirely unexpected but disconcerting. Tom was in control, and there was no need to continue the sham.

"Okay, the Israeli government wants to know if any of the terrorists you killed said anything before they died and what you actually knew before you got on that plane."

"Nothing to both questions but even if I did know anything, do you think I'd be stupid enough to tell you? You and I both know you're not from the government, you're Mossad. Your reputation precedes you, and you know no limits when it comes to getting what you want."

"Tales, tales … Stories old men tell when they are playing

checkers over a glass of wine, but if that is what you think, then you must believe that we have ways of persuading you to talk."

Avi was starting to show his true colors, and Tom called his bluff. "Is that a threat?"

"Take it whatever way you like, Mr. Benning."

Tom pointed to a chair. "Have a seat. Now let me tell you how I have this figured. You are here to intimidate me … hell, maybe you even want to beat up on me so let me tell you this. If you ever get brave enough to take a swing at me, be ready to be surprised. You're in Canada, chum. If any harm were to come to a genuine Canadian hero, our foreign affairs department would come down so hard on the Israeli Ambassador, your superiors would think twice about entrusting you with any future assignments."

The way he shifted in his chair, Tom knew he had hit home and Avi wasn't as secure as he tried to appear. He was probably what Mossad agents referred to as a *burn*. It was just like the old man had predicted; Avi was going to be sacrificed.

Tom decided to chip away at his confidence even further. "Get this Avi, I have enough information on you and a few other people, to bring the Knesset in for an emergency session."

Try as he might, his bravado was palatably flawed.

"Ha! I'm sure, Mr. Benning. You want me to believe you have lists of names and places that could be detrimental to Israeli intelligence?"

Tom knew it was time to strike and did. "How about, Chaim Solomon?"

Avi's eyes flickered nervously and try as he might, he couldn't camouflage his surprise. "Who?"

Tom kept up the pressure and snapped. "You heard me!"

This stopped his smirking, and he leaned forward. His body language confirmed he was out of his league.

"What about this Mr. Solomon?"

Tom didn't even try to conceal his impatience.

"Don't be stupid."

Avi scratched his two-day-old beard but didn't answer. Was it possible that Chaim had left information harmful to both himself and Mossad?

He decided to try another tactic. "You are a Jew, Tom. You could become one of us. You obviously have the training so it would be a cinch to get you in."

"What in the world makes you think that I'd be interested and who do you think you're kidding? You and I both know that you are in no position to recruit anyone." Avi was insulted by Tom's lack of respect. "We are the best intelligence gathering organization in the world. My recommendation means a lot at home."

"Avi, Avi, Avi. You are so full of shit. If you are a sample of the best then may God help your country. Do you really think that a little prick like you scares me?"

His continual ego-battering had the effect Tom intended. Avi was having difficulty controlling his anger. "I told you when I came in that we only want to know what that Arab said when you blew his fucking brains out." He made no attempt to remain calm. He shouted, "don't even try to deny it. He talked because our tapes confirm he did."

He took a deep breath before lowering his voice; he believed this made him more sinister and threatening. "Now, we can use special tactics to extract the information, but we would prefer not to have to resort to them."

"God, I love your spy talk, "extract the information." "It might be even more impressive if you were really good at your job, but you're not. As a matter of fact, you have walked right into a trap."

Avi shifted uncomfortably. "What the fuck are you talking about, Benning. You don't even have a gun; you're not even allowed to hold one let alone own one. We have such details" he said with pride.

"Now that, Avi, is a great piece of intelligence work. You see, I don't need a gun. Your Mossad ass is sitting on enough Semtex to blow your asshole right into your brain."

Visibly sweating, he barely managed to say, "more fucking bluff!"

Tom pulled a small transmitter from his pocket, and Avi turned ashen. It was hard to contain his sadistic pleasure, but he generously offered to let Avi get up and check out his claim. He almost jumped out of the chair and carefully lifted the cushion. There was an envelope. He was in no position to know whether it contained explosives or not but he was inclined to believe it did. He started to say something but changed his mind.

"Now that, my dear Avi, is what we call a hot-seat in Canada." Tom had one more card to play, and he observed Avi closely as he did. "I suggest you get your carcass out of here so I can turn the camera off."

He awkwardly looked around the room and stammered, "what camera?"

"That one," answered Tom pointing at a small decorative mirror hanging on the wall. "It's attached to a computer and all data is sent to servers as a security backup. One is in another part of this city, and one is on the East coast."

Avi was speechless. "Can you imagine how impressed your superiors will be when they review your performance here today?" While he let Avi ponder his fate, he took one last pot shot. "By the way, does Mossad know that your real name is Avery Haberman?"

"How do you know that?" he gasped in disbelief. To which Tom simply said, "oh, I know a lot, Avi."

It was evident that this meeting was over. He walked out slamming the door shut behind him. He got into the elevator like a dog with its tail between its legs. His hands shook as he lit a cigarette. He hadn't expected such opposition. Why had he been so ill prepared? He deserved better. He'd show Judah!

This was just the beginning of dealing with Israeli intelligence. It was a mystery to Tom why they had sent Avi? If they had conducted any intelligence at all, they would have known he would not intimidate easily, least of all to the likes of him.

It was now critical for Tom's security installation to be up and running. He placed an urgent call and was assured it would be done the next morning. In the meantime, he took whatever precautions he could but knew he was at risk for the next few hours.

His intention to stay alert was usurped by his fatigue,

and he dozed off only to be awakened by a needle being jabbed into his arm. He tried to fight but couldn't, and the last thing he saw before the drug took effect was a beautiful red-head.

# 10

Judah Fink supported his chin on his interlocked fingers. His relaxed clean-shaven face was devoid of emotion. His tan and brown eyes flatteringly accentuated his light grey hair. He was six feet tall, weighed 185 lbs and apparently took care of himself. His broad shoulders, muscular chest, and flat stomach made him a poster boy for health and well-being.

To strangers, he appeared distinguished. Most would have been surprised that he was close to retirement. On the other hand, those who had known him through the years were less generous and described him as tired looking and at the end of his career.

He had worked most of his adult life for the security of his country. In hindsight, he would have preferred to remain a soldier. He truly believed nothing felt more glorious or powerful than standing on a tank giving orders to his crew. It made him feel invincible.

The Golan Heights, in 1967, had been his most

memorable and last battle. But ... he was young then and gave little thought to feeling old and decrepit. Peace had been established with some neighboring countries. But this didn't stop them from waiting for a sign of weakness. There was still a taste for blood. Peace was tenuous and would only last as long as Israel remained strong. Before ever considering retirement from the army, he was spotted by Mossad. He had the makings of a prime recruit, and when the time was right, he was approached and encouraged to join. That had been a long time ago, and his assignments had taken him far afield. Then as now, he enjoyed the excitement but lately the allure of travel was beginning to wane.

He was an ambitious recruit, and his dream of becoming the top security officer became his priority. He was encouraged and genuinely believed it was within his reach. When the position became a reality, he was devastated to discover Shabtai Shavir, not Judah Fink was the new director.

He felt betrayed. He had been led to believe he was being groomed for a leadership role. In fact, this was true but just not the one he wanted. The thoroughness and excellence of his work had not gone unrecognized. He was promoted to instructor and supervisor for the younger generation of Mossad. The rationale behind this move was, all recruits have to have the aptitude, but many lack the finesse required to work in intelligence. Judah was deemed the only logical person to fill this role. It was a position directly related to future success. His impact would be felt throughout the organization and this, he had to admit, appealed to him.

His current assignment was a classic example. All of his

expertise would be tested. Tom Benning had proven himself in Vancouver and because of the status of this case, he
warranted priority handling. It mystified him why Avi had
been selected to make the first contact. In his opinion, a
female agent would have been far more effective. Avi was a
classic example of what a spy should not be. He was a sadist
who enjoyed resorting to torture rather than using a more
professional approach to interrogation. He was renowned
for this and had been censored many times. In spite of these
warnings, Avi failed to change his ways. For some unknown
reason, he unwisely deemed himself untouchable. In doing
so, he had sealed his own fate and was now scheduled to be
eliminated. The thought of delivering the news to Avi's father
troubled him deeply.

That Chaim Solomon had done such a remarkable job
with Benning puzzled Judah. Why had he broken with tra-
dition? Benning was an outsider. What did that old man
have in mind when he took Benning under his wing? Why
all the training? Had retirement been so uneventful that he
simply needed a distraction? In any event, Benning was an
extremely good student; the terrorist incident in Vancouver
was a testimonial. His demeanor under pressure coupled
with his survival instincts enabled him to control and limit
the damage. No innocents were injured. Only terrorists were
killed.

Foremost on Judah's mind was why Benning had killed
all three. He had gone over the event in his mind many times,
and each time he came to the same conclusion. The first one
could have been neutralized and held for interrogation. There

was no doubt that the other two were much more danger-ous and had to be killed; a fact that was later confirmed by witnesses.

Tom slept. Judah studied him. He had read his file and had to admit he had yet to meet a man quite like Benning. He acknowledged him to not only be handsome but fit and about half his age. He envied Tom his youth. It was another reminder that retirement wasn't far off.

Judah was in no hurry to wake him. He was well aware that the affects of a drug-induced sleep could be unpredict-able and although he sensed Tom would not cause any con-cern, he remained wary.

The time finally came, and he motioned to his partner. She was a beautiful, self-assured young woman who relished her mysteriously exciting lifestyle. She stood, placed one hand on her hip, playfully dangling cuffs from her index finger and stared at the good-looking man on the couch. Judah smiled but shook his head. "Not him, Ahuva, he is not a violent man."

"That's a hell of a conclusion" she challenged. "Just look at him and remember what he did at the airport. This man needs no weapon to kill. He will use his bare hands if he has to."

Judah would not be swayed. "I know but I also know this man reasons soundly, and he knows rage obscures clear thinking."

Without hesitation, she pursued her case. "All the same, I will keep a very close eye on him. I guess that he is as un-predictable as any man."

Judah's tone caught her off guard. "Ahuva! Think! What would you do, if you were in his situation … tell me, how would you conduct yourself? What have you been taught?" Almost by rote, she answered. "I would first assess the state of my health, my environment, and my overall situation and see if I could negotiate before acting."

"Exactly! So will he," was all he said.

Still not satisfied, she reminded him that they had been warned by Shabtai and added for good measure "besides, it's procedure. Please, Judah, we know how dangerous he is. He won't hesitate to try to overpower us even with a gun pointed at his head." Judah reassured her Tom was not reckless. More importantly, he would never make a tactical error given his training but that same fact mandated care in dealing with him.

She was not one to give in easily. "Then at least let me take the jug out of his reach." Judah smiled indulgently. "Just keep the glass filled and he will have no reason to reach for the jug."

She returned his smile. "Tell me, Judah, who was Chaim Solomon?"

"Well … Chaim was one of us … once. He was as committed to Israel as you and I or anyone for that matter. His dedication is well documented. That being said, Solomon was also openly critical of the country he so loved. He challenged any policy he thought needed to be questioned. One he was particularly passionate about was Israel's approach to the Palestinian problem. He deemed it unconscionable. Unlike many of us, Solomon was a man of conscience and lived by it. May I say a luxury unheard of in our circle?" Judah felt the need to take a moment.

Interestingly, his statement was more emotionally disturbing that he had intended. It brought back memories of how Chaim had coped with dignity when the ridicule and name-calling had been inflicted upon him. It also reminded him that he had, at times, been guilty of taunting Chaim because of his beliefs. He collected his thoughts, while Ahuva sat and waited for him to continue.

"In spite of this and in recognition of his courage and patriotism, he was ultimately offered retirement. He must have felt it was the right thing to do because he accepted and left Israel.

Once he landed, we were able to keep tabs on him with the help of Avi's father who conveniently resides in Florida. This is how we discovered Benning lived with Chaim for five years and assumed the role of Chaim's apprentice as such, he was being trained as one of our own. This is why we initiated a file on him. What is not in the file is exactly what Benning knows or doesn't know. Until the airport incident, this man was only a person of interest. Now, he could potentially be a real threat and critically important to us."

Ahuva had listened intently, and Judah knew she was weighing every detail. So, he was not surprised when she asked: "what happened to Mr. Solomon?"

His answer was simple. "Heart attack."

Her cynicism was ever evident. "We didn't kill him?"

He shook his head which seemed to satisfy her for the moment and then she turned her attention to Tom. He piqued her curiosity and Judah knew it. She found it interesting that he was potentially dangerous, yet he didn't feel like an enemy, and although he did scare her, she couldn't help but like him.

Tom groaned. It was no longer necessary to feign sleep. He'd heard enough. In an effort to control his splitting headache he slowly raised his hand to his forehead. It was throbbing as was his arm. Simultaneously, he noticed his lips were chapped and his mouth parched. The only logical conclusion was he had been kidnapped. Waiting for the fog to lift was of primary importance. This was no time to be rash.

He felt someone sit beside him. He mind was clear enough to see it was not the redhead who had injected him. A dark-haired beauty held a glass in one hand and some pills in the other.

"Here," she said holding out her hand. "These will take care of your headache and nausea. Now, you see what happens when you drink too much."

The friendly, mellow Israeli accent did nothing to change the fact that she was part of the team of kidnappers. He had every reason to suspect the odds equally favored her hand held poison as it did a cure and declined the offer.

"Here take them," she urged. "They contain codeine and will alleviate your headache within minutes. You are dehydrated which not only contributes to your headache but is causing your mouth to feel dry. Drink some water and then take the pills. Go on, it's safe." He did and inhaled deeply before finishing what was left in the glass. She instantly refilled it.

Tom lay back and let the fog continue to lift. She returned to Judah's side. She was a strikingly beautiful, young woman who was totally at ease with this older man. He slowly scanned the room and stopped momentarily at the jug beside him. She tensed but once again, Judah shook his head.

Tom gradually got up and sat on the edge of the sofa. She opened her laptop and waited patiently for the interview to begin silently acknowledging Judah definitely knew what he was talking about. This man was unlike others. When she caught his eyes drifting from her face to her legs, she slowly crossed them, carefully tucking her skirt to better cover her exposed thigh. She felt vindicated. His ogling confirmed he could be just like any other man.

Judah placed his hands, palm down, on the desk and studied them.

"Well, Mr. Benning, or may I call you Tom?"

This was the perfect opportunity for Tom to let him know that he knew exactly who he was dealing with and he took it. "Sure Judah, after all, we have been through together, feel free to call me anything you like." The fact that Benning knew his name wasn't a surprise. He might have heard it while is he was pretending to sleep, but it was more likely that Chaim had forewarned him about potential enemies. Either way, Judah knew that the best way to handle a man like Tom was with respect.

"Well then, Tom, I like a man with a purpose. It gives us a chance to get on with the task at hand … eliminating any meaningless trivialities. Avi is concerned you may have become privy to information involving our national security, while you were with Chaim Solomon."

Tom stately flatly that he didn't give a shit about Israel's national security. From there he proceeded to make it abundantly clear how little he thought of Avi as an adversary. "Surely, the decision to involve you couldn't have been based on a report written by someone as inconsequential as Avi Haberman? I didn't think that imbecile was literate enough to put a report together, let alone communicate intelligently on any subject." He was on a roll, and he knew it. He decided now was not the time to back down and pushed ahead full throttle.

"Tell you what, Mr. Fink or is it Finkelstein? I feel well enough to march on out of here. Oh, please don't bother to get up or apologize for the kidnapping. I'm a strong believer that everyone is entitled to one mistake, so I will overlook this one. Just remember, the next time I won't be quite so generous" and headed for the door.

Judah grinned as he pulled a Whalter from a holster inside his jacket. Placing it in front of him on the desk, he pointed to it. "Not so fast, Mr. Benning. I am not quite finished. You seem to take this lightly but let me assure you what might seem trivial to you, isn't to me. You already know who I am but what you may no know is that I no longer like to travel. It no longer holds any interest for me but sometimes it is necessary, and this is one of those times."

Tom knew he had no choice but to stay right where he was and argue his case. "I've got news for you. You have come to the wrong place. I am not, nor have I ever been your enemy.

So, now I would like to know what I have to do to get out of here, preferably without a hole in my back."

"Well, for one thing, you can tell us what the terrorist on the ground said to you before he died? Our lab has analyzed the entire tape, and even our specialist was unable to decipher it. The only thing we know for certain is that he said something."

Tom took exception to Judah's insistence that the perpetrators were terrorists and made it clear when he answered. "Okay, to set the record straight, all I heard was, "I'm Mossad, Mossad, don't kill" not "I'm Arab, Arab, don't kill", so you know what I think? I think he was one of your men and incidentally, if as you contend the tape was analyzed, you know damn well that he said it *after* I shot him."

"Well, Mr. Benning, it has already been established that terrorists were there to get two members of the PLO released from jail. Both were awaiting extradition following an attempt to smuggle explosives into the US."

Tom stood his ground and faced down Judah. "That is not the story I heard. They wanted two Arabs, accused of blowing up a plane over the Atlantic, released from prison."

Judah was not to be dissuaded and with equal impatience stated the problem was with the media. "Rumors, rumors, rumors. They can't agree on the facts. The case is just as I told you. It's as simple as that."

Tom didn't take kindly to being brushed off. "Like hell. It was a smokescreen. I believe "the terrorists" were Palestinians on a suicide mission for Mossad and whether you are interested or not, I'm going to explain my theory to you.

Israel has a Prime Minister who is genuinely interested in peace. Any time a candidate is elected whose policies conflict with Mossad; terrorist attacks erupt effectively derailing any possibility of peace talks. You are in bed with anyone who suits you. Sadly, I believe it is your mandate to ensure that the two sides never get close to achieving peace."

Judah didn't even pretend to be astonished at Tom's statement. He again dismissed it. "My, my, my, you sure are eloquent. Now you listen to me very carefully, if and I stress the word *if* those terrorists were indeed Israeli agents, you are now responsible for killing Israeli citizens."

"So what?" Tom shrugged. I had no such intention. Through no fault of mine, I was caught in a situation where my life was in jeopardy. It is obvious to me, if not you that I made the right decision or I wouldn't be involved in this pissing contest with you now. The entire political world knows that even before Israel's independence, there were plans to deport every Palestinian to camps. The Sinai was where they were to be built. That was what the six-day war was really about. You only took the Golan, the West Bank and Gaza to restore your borders to where they were historically.

While broadcasters aired the official line unquestioningly, the majority of the world rooted for the Jews. But little by little, they began to question their sources, and it became more and more difficult to hide the truth." He had obviously hit the nail on the head because Judah stiffened and became more formal. "What else do you know, Mr. Benning?"

Tom was actually pleased to see that he had been so successful and pushed on. "Ooooh, I see that you are distancing yourself from your victim. It isn't Tom anymore, it's *Mr. Benning*. My days are clearly numbered."

Judah reiterated that he had already given his word that Tom had nothing to fear from Israel. Without missing a beat, Tom told him he was very aware of that fact, but Mossad was something else entirely. He described them as loose cannons prepared to circumvent the laws of their own country or any other for that matter and did so without hesitation. 'How ironic" he continued "that my friend Chaim, who never had any intention of doing so, has put my life in danger. His plan was for me to live to a ripe old age while guarding his secrets. In hindsight, I wonder how much of a friend he really was."

Making no attempt to hide his concern Judah confirmed his suspicions. "So, you do have information that could be detrimental to us." Tom said he was sorry to disappoint him and elaborated. "Chaim's heart was giving up and was told he desperately needed a transplant to survive. He didn't even consider the option. He was an old man who believed the gift of life was better given to someone who still had a life to live. That was the true Chaim.

Two weeks before died, he asked me if I would do him a favor. I told him I had never had occasion to refuse him anything but this time he was uncharacteristically adamant. It was not difficult to give my promise and I did.

The day he died, I went to the funeral parlor paid the bills and stuck a pouch under his legs. The documents contained in it are a mystery, and until now, only I knew about them. I hope that you have enough respect to let him rest in peace." He paused, and Judah was about to say something when Tom snorted. "Hell … you can't afford to dig him up. That would risk another autopsy, and I'm assuming that's the last thing you want." Then, he menacingly added, "because you and I both know, he didn't die of a heart attack."

Without any rancor Judah assured Tom despite his unfounded allegations, Chaim's remains would not be disturbed and changed the subject.

"I have only one more question just to satisfy my personal curiosity. Why did you kill the first terrorist?"

Tom's answer that he had no other option failed to satisfy Judah.

"We both know that isn't true. You could have disabled him. You had a gun. You could have knocked him unconscious and saved him for interrogation. Oh well, water under the bridge. I guess that concludes our business. I thank you for your cooperation."

The first thing that went through Tom's mind was what had he missed. "That's it? You travel all this way to ask me one lousy question? If so, aside from being pissed-off at being kidnapped, I have to admit I am profoundly honored. I must be quite special to warrant such high-level attention. You, on the other hand, are probably very disappointed with the outcome of this interrogation?" Judah shook his head at Tom's assessment of their meeting.

"To tell you the truth, I had to meet you, Mr. Benning and I'm glad I did. I'm not at all disappointed. This time has been very informative … very productive indeed."

He stretched, got up and went to the door. Before opening it, he turned "oh … I … I promised Ahuva she would get some time off. Perhaps you will be good enough to show her this beautiful city?" and left before Tom had a chance to say anything.

He and Ahuva were now alone. It was obvious she and Judah worked closely so any information he could get from her would be of value. He needed to find out more about Mossad's plans and if they involved his future. Time spent with her might not be a bad idea after all.

It was as if the scene had been rehearsed. He asked her to dinner. She picked up her purse and waited for him to lead the way. Before he did, he turned to her.

"Look, Ahuva, you can understand that I'm a little apprehensive considering who you work for."

She agreed and handed him her purse. "I wouldn't have expected you to ignore the possibility that I might have a gun."

He unzipped the purse which was evidence enough that she didn't. A zipper is too time consuming and could stick at a critical moment. He looked inside anyway and pulled out the handcuffs.

"Were these meant for me or are you into kinky sex?"

Tom couldn't help being charmed by her smile. They took a taxi to the same restaurant where he and Stacey often dined. The maitre d' didn't bother to look at the reservation sheet and led them to a booth at the back of the restaurant where he had often taken this same gentleman but a different lady. Ahuva slipped into the seat, and Tom slid in right beside her.

"You don't waste any time do you?"

"Not when I have so little of it."

He put his hand on her knee. She kept smiling as she held it to stop him from going any further. Her estimation of him plummeted. He was now just another pig. She tried to push his hand away, but he resisted and whispered, "you don't want to create a scene and call attention to us do you?" He didn't wait for an answer and forced his hand up under her skirt.

"See," he grinned pulling a small caliber automatic from a clip against her leg. "That wasn't so hard now was it?"

Releasing the magazine, he removed the bullets one by one and checked the chamber. Dropping the bullets in his pocket, he gave the gun back saying, "now you can put it in your purse."

Ahuva was silently relieved that she had been so wrong about him. Her thoughts were disturbed by someone standing by their table.

"Well, well … Surprise! Surprise!"

Tom looked up at Stacey. He hadn't expected to see her. She looked even more surprised to see him, especially with another woman. She had never given any thought to the idea that he might know another woman, let alone one well enough to invite her to dinner.

"Hi, Stacey, this is Ahuva. Ahuva, this is Stacey Whitefeather. She's my lawyer."

Ahuva said hello, but Stacey ignored her. Tom instinctively moved over to make room for Stacey, inviting her to join them. She declined his offer and added acidly, "you don't need a third wheel. I can see you two want to be alone."

Tom attempted to diffuse the situation. "Wait a minute, Stace. This isn't what you think. Ahuva is here on business. She's going back to Israel in a few days, and I'm showing her the city." It was obvious she wasn't buying it.

"Well enjoy each other's company. I have to go" and left abruptly.

All the way home, she tried to figure out what had happened. She was astounded when he introduced her as his lawyer ... not his girlfriend. It was true their relationship hadn't improved. He hadn't even tried to make love to her for the last two days. Could this attractive woman be the reason? Her mind bounced from one thing to the other. It was a fact that he had needed her more when he still lived in his basement apartment. Could his inheritance be responsible? Money did funny things to people.

Much as she didn't want to, she jumped to the conclusion that he was checking what other options awaited a rich bachelor. She no longer bought his story about being hesitant to enter into a permanent relationship because of his concerns for her security. It was malarkey. Ironically, she had gone to the restaurant to make arrangements for a surprise dinner for him. Some surprise!

Much later that evening Tom called. She was already in bed but not asleep; she couldn't sleep. She deliberately let the phone ring longer than usual before picking it up. She knew why he was calling, and although she was pleased to hear his voice, she still wasn't ready to let go of her anger and disappointment. When he asked if he could come over, she came up with all kinds of excuses. Finally, Tom shouted into the phone.

"For Christ sake, Stacey, don't do this to me! I'm coming over, and I'll stand at your door until you let me in. You can call the cops, but you'll be the one who has to bail me out, so either way, I will see you."

She almost giggled with delight but managed not to and invited him over.

"Alright, alright, alright! Come on up but don't expect me to look my best." If he is that determined to explain things, hopefully, I've been a fool. She brushed her hair and let it fall loosely around her shoulders. She knew he liked it that way. She had barely finished putting on her lipstick when she heard the buzzer. She didn't ask who it was and buzzed him in. He would lecture her about it but so what, he wasn't her boss. She opened the door wide and walked away before the elevator reached her floor.

Sitting on the couch, leafing through a magazine when he walked in, would infuriate him. She couldn't have predicted it better. The way he slammed the door shut behind him, confirmed everything. "Nice touch, Stacey. You knew leaving that door open would piss me off."

"And may I say if you have come over here to lecture me, yet again, you can go right back out that very same door you just slammed closed. I'm not in the mood."

He knew it was best to come right to the point and asked her if she were angry at him for taking Ahuva to dinner. Unfortunately, her attempt at flippancy didn't quite get the results she had hoped for.

"Why should I be, you're a free man. I have no more claims on you than you have on me. As a matter of fact, I couldn't care less."

"Okay you want to be pissed-off, be pissed-off. I came to clear the air, and once I have, I'm out of here." She was genuinely worried when he said, "I'm out of here." She had expected a more conciliatory tone. She wanted to exert her independence but not at the risk of losing him, so she settled in to listen. She did owe him that much.

"I can't tell you everything Stacey, but I'll tell you this much. Ahuva works for Israeli intelligence. She and her boss were sent here to interrogate me. I may have bluffed my way out of a jam this time, but the next time these might wind up in my carcass. Here," he said, pulling his hand out of his pocket, and dropping the bullets in her lap. "I'm walking on thin ice. These are what I took out of her gun before you arrived on the scene. As my lawyer, you know that I can't buy these. This is enough proof to substantiate why I am not living with you."

He sat down beside her and took her in his arms.

"I love you too much to have you killed. If I had told her that you are my fiancée, it would have been as good as telling them how to get to me. It suits me fine if you want to call it quits but no matter what, I love you!"

He stood up again and started to pace back and forth across the room. "The shit is about to hit the fan, I know it. Here's the plan, I'll call you every four hours. If you don't hear from me, it means they've got me, and you better get your butt back to the reservation in a hurry. You'll be safe there. I'm so sorry to have put you in this predicament." He stormed out without waiting for her reaction. She stared at the bullets in her lap, dumbfounded and unable to react to his outburst. He was right, he didn't have a gun permit, and he could never have bought them without one. He was telling the truth. Even if she had wanted to tell him that she was wrong, it was too late now. He was gone.

She jumped up, rushed to the window and opened the blind. The bullets she had been holding in her lap scattered across the floor. She watched him unlock his car which was parked right under a street light. Then, for some reason, he stood still, turned and looked up at her window. Even from her fifth floor, she could see his expression change. He smiled, relocked his car and slipped the keys back into his pocket. He started to cross the street. Her heart was pounding, and she burst into tears. She hadn't lost him.

Suddenly a van came out of nowhere, speeding straight at him. "Noooooo!!!" she screamed at the top of her lungs, "oh God no!" and breathed a sigh of relief when she saw him jump back against his car to get out of the way. The van screeched to a halt right in front of him. Two men jumped out from the side door and another two from the back. He struggled, but he was no match for them. She watched as he was jabbed in his neck, before being dragged into the van. Its accelerated departure left a black streak of burned rubber on the pavement.

She stood there shaking, staring in shock into the empty street below. He was gone. She turned and saw the bullets on the floor; they were proof of how desperate things were. She called 911 and spoke to what appeared to be a dispassionate dispatcher on the other end of the line. Impatiently, she shouted the details into the receiver. She dressed quickly and by the time she had her shoes on, heard the sirens coming. She gave the uniformed police as many details as she could remember, but it wasn't much use. Without a license plate number, there was little chance of finding a white, most likely stolen van. She locked her apartment and asked the police to escort her to her car. From there she called her father to have someone bring Billy Twofingers to guard Tom's apartment. She told her dad where the extra key was hidden and headed for safety.

When she arrived, the warriors were already busy erecting a barricade. The call that she had made to her father had been intercepted. It wasn't a secure line, so she wasn't surprised. The men had been waiting for an opportunity just like this to show that their old warrior spirit was still alive.

The hours crept by. She waited not bothering to go to bed. There was no way she could sleep.

The following day reporters started calling the reserve. They were interested in the kidnapping. The name Tom Benning was still fresh in their minds, and they knew Stacey had acted as his attorney. Some news crews waited at the reserve. The warriors took any advantage they could to get on the news and stood guard at the barricade dressed in fatigues and balaclavas, strictly for effect.

The police never called. They remembered Tom Benning and would have preferred him to just disappear quietly. He had done enough damage to their image. In contrast to the news crews who had numerous trucks and vehicles parked right up near the entrance, they had two cruisers parked a safe distance away.

His disappearance was a low-level priority to them.

# 11

He heard two muffled voices as he lay half-naked shivering on the mattress. He opened his eyes slightly, not wanting to alert them that he was awake. Nothing looked familiar. He'd gone through a similar awakening not too long ago. Sadly, this time he was cuffed, and there was no pretty woman to give him pills. He tried to lie on his side to help the blood circulate back into his hands, but as he did, someone grabbed his hair and jerked him straight up. It was his worst nightmare. He was face to face with Avi's rat face.

"Hey … you dumb fuck, you're alive. I was afraid the redhead had been too generous. You've been my guest for almost two days." Tom's brain was still muggy but thanks to Avi, he was able to figure out what day it was. Now all he had to do was try to find out where he was and why.

"Oh God, I thought everything was settled between your boss and me. What is this place and what do you want this time?"

Avi's enthusiasm for his job was evident. He couldn't

help but brag and in doing so divulge too much. He was so impressed with his own importance.

"I warned you to cooperate with me, but you wouldn't listen. Now, here you are in a safe house where you will stay for as long as I want you to. We are waiting for a report from Alabama. Maybe we're too late and the worms have beaten us to the information that is supposed to be in the coffin, but we're checking anyway. We already know that there is nothing of interest in your apartment, but you did have one kick ass, first-class security system."

He had used the past tense. Tom assumed it had been stolen and was quite surprised to discover that only his hard drive had been confiscated and sent to Tel Aviv. Tom smiled. He was relieved they had only taken the drive. "You think that's funny, Benning? I suppose you are going to tell me that it's wired and will explode."

Tom continued to smile. What would happen was far more sinister than that. Chaim was all too aware of how Mossad technicians retrieved data. The drive was programmed to format and over-write without warning immediately upon its re-activation it would corrupt all recovery programs.

When Tom told Avi that he felt betrayed by his boss, he jumped to Judah's defense. "*He* won't harm you but *I* can and will, if necessary." Tom didn't appreciate the semantics and made a mental note that he would call Judah Judas from now on.

Avi, unaware of Tom's distraction, carried on. "You are enjoying these luxurious accommodations because we're in the process of collecting everything we can on you.

Your apartment has been cleaned out. Oh, and by the way, there was no Semtex, and you never did have a camera behind that mirror. We did run into a little problem though." Tom couldn't resist, stating. "Yeah, finding the keys must have been a real challenge for you with your fucked up brain." He knew he would pay no matter what he said. Avi had a ferocious appetite for vengeance, so he had nothing to lose by asking, "does this luxury hotel have anything for my head-ache?" He didn't have to wait for an answer; a vigorous slap across the face. Now he not only had a blistering headache but a bloody nose. Tom felt his warm blood oozing over his lips but disregarded it. He needed to know more. "How did you get into my place? I made sure that I had the best locks money can buy."

His cool upset Avi. He wasn't used to people taking their punishment with such aplomb. He wanted to see Tom squirm. "You did, but we were lucky. We didn't have to pick or destroy the locks which was a real time saver. There was this big, funny looking man with claw-like hands guarding the place. When he opened the door, he was most unwel-coming. Needless to say, we had to get in and his refusal to let that happen made it necessary for us to dispose of him."

Avi had succeeded. Tom exploded. "You bastard, he was retarded and wouldn't hurt a fly."

"That's what you say, but he gave my partner David, a real hard time. His strength was unbelievable. I put a slug in his chest, and he still picked David up and threw him across the room like a rag doll. Then, I put two more in his ugly skull. He went down like a ton of bricks."

That was strike one. Avi went straight after strike two. "We also went to your girlfriend's place, but she wasn't home. We figure she's at her parents' place. Unfortunate for us but lucky for her. We sent some guys out there, but it is like an armed camp. Too bad, I guess I'll have to wait a while to fuck her."

Tom was beyond furious and had to fight to regain his calm. "You know what Avi? When you were a kid, you must have been that mean little prick who pulled the legs off flies, just for kicks."

Mistakenly, Tom thought Avi was ignoring this shot when he motioned for David to come closer. "Remember the last time we met, and you were in control? Just for the record, those roles are now reversed, and I'm going to show you how I get my kicks. Your shirt has been removed for a particular ritual."

Billy had definitely gone down fighting. David was limping badly. Avi took a burning cigarette from his hand and started to smile. He was going to relish this. He brought the cigarette closer to Tom's arm. He blew on it intensifying the glow and almost salivated when he inflicted the first burn. He and David took turns until Tom's chest and arms were covered. They gloated at Tom's protest when they lit another cigarette with the butt of the first.

"See," grinned David, "it wasn't Avi who pulled the legs off, I did." He was proud to be given the chance to take some credit for this ridiculous practice. His attempt was not only sad but stupid. "It was a research project designed to show that without legs, they have trouble with flight control." He couldn't contain himself any longer and laughed. "The landings were the real hoot."

Tom's disgust was compounded by his pain. "I hope to see you rot in hell, you fat fuck. You would have been a superstar as one of Hitler's SS."

He didn't even bother to answer, but Tom's insult might have been the impetus David needed. He was on a mission. He told Avi to sit Tom up. He leered as he told Avi, "we need to round out the job."

Avi didn't need any convincing and grabbed Tom's hair to pull him up. When they finished the burning, Avi picked up a rusty nail which had been lying on a crate in the corner of the room and gave it to David. "Here, now we can play tic-tac-toe." Mercifully, Tom passed out.

When he regained consciousness, he felt colder than before, but his skin was on fire. His throat was raw from suppressing his screams during the torture. He knew it had only made them try harder, but there was no way he would give them that satisfaction. More importantly, the energy was better used to control the pain.

Slowly, he began to realize this had nothing to with Judah's trip to Mobile. This was Avi and David's planned revenge, and they were going to kill him. His priority now was not to let his pain interfere with the concentration required to survive. It took precedence over everything.

"Aw, you're awake. David sure liked beating the crap out of you, especially after you called him a fat fuck."

Tom responded in kind. "Where is that moron, anyway?"

Avi told him that he was out picking up some food and

strongly suggested he should show him more respect, upon his return. For some unknown reason, Avi apologized for causing his bloody nose saying that was an accident. With everything else that had happened, this seemed ludicrous. Tom's reaction was swift and much less civil.

"You are a Neanderthal. You torture me and may I say, you did your job well, and that's perfectly okay. You bloody my nose accidentally, and that warrants an apology. How twisted is that? I'm bleeding internally, you idiot, so unfortunately for you and David, the job you did on me was over-kill. It will be your downfall."

Suddenly Avi wasn't smiling anymore. "You lie there, barely able to move and you talk about my downfall?"

Tom knew he was more than a little worried.

"Not likely, Benning … not likely," but Tom insisted that he was dying and if Avi needed proof he only had to feel his stomach. "It's bloated because it's filling up with blood."

When Avi argued that they had hardly punched him in the stomach, Tom grinned painfully. They both knew that if this were the truth, then Avi and David had a major dilemma on their hands. Avi watched Tom as he closed his eyes. His breathing definitely was shallow. The fear that they really had done too much damage was quickly becoming a reality. He went into panic mode. He couldn't chance losing him. He had to keep him alive until Judah came back. "Come on, wake up you fucking *shaygets*."

Tom responded by making some undistinguishable sounds which only added to Avi's distress. He ran to the bathroom, feverishly looked for something that would help

keep Tom alive. He came back with wet cloth and some tow-
els. His state of mind was such that he didn't notice Tom's
hands were no longer behind his back. He draped the wet
cloth over Tom's forehead.

Because his condition was so compromised, Tom knew
he had only one chance to do what needed to be done. He
whispered again making it necessary for Avi to bend over to
hear. Calling on every ounce of strength left in his body, Tom
punched him in the face. Avi stumbled back grabbing his
nose with one hand and reaching for his gun with the other.
In total disbelief, Avi watched Tom get up with lightning
speed and kick him in the groin. He fell to his knees, and
Tom kicked him in the face. Bewildered and now in severe
pain, Avi was flat on his back. Tom stomped on his throat
crushing his windpipe. Then, he stood back and watched him
struggle for air until he stopped breathing altogether.

He took the keys from the table and removed his handcuffs. He wrenched the gun from his victim's hand and stuck
it in his belt. He removed Avi's shirt, put him on the cot and
cuffed his hands behind his back before sitting down to catch
his breath. The 'mind over matter' method that seemed so
unreal at the time of his training worked. Every muscle and
bone in his body ached. He had never experienced anything
like this before. Still, there was no time to relax. He heard
footsteps in the hall.

David walked in, went to the table with the food and
put the bag down. He had no reason to suspect anything
was amiss until he looked around for Avi. That's when he
saw Tom standing against the wall. He went for his gun, but

his opponent was more than prepared. "Uh, uh, uh David ... put your hands nice and high or a slug will go deep into your fucked up carcass."

He obeyed. Tom watched the big man cry like a baby when Tom aimed the gun at his forehead. He shook and pleaded for his life barely above a whisper. "Please don't kill me. Me and Avi, we wasn't going to kill you," he repeated over and over again.

This moron was going to be an easy target. He was so scared he would sell out his own mother.

"Who ordered my kidnapping?"

"Judah ... Judah Fink," he sobbed.

"And the torture was that also Judah's idea?"

He hesitated before answering. He seemed to be trying to figure out the best way to describe what had happened. Finally, he said, "not exactly but he knew that we would. You made Avi so mad. Avi hates you."

Tom clarified that fact with two words. "Not anymore."

David was dumbfounded when he found out Avi was dead. Tom remembered what the old man had taught him. Never let an enemy live to be an enemy again and pulled the trigger putting two shots in David's forehead. He fell without as much as a twitch. Tom wiped his fingerprints from the gun. He debated whether to keep it but decided not to and tossed it on Avi's cot as he left.

The probability that the police had found Billy Twofingers by now made his apartment a crime scene. Avi had confirmed that Stacey was on the reserve. He had no choice; he had to make the two-hour drive. He had nowhere else to go.

The ticking sound of a cooling engine had to be coming from Avi's rental car. Tom tried the keys, they fit. He thought about finding a phone booth to call Stacey. The phone call might put her at ease but the lines were undoubtedly tapped, and that was a complication he didn't need.

He drove to a quiet area of the city, turned the radio on and waited. As expected, the local news was about the unrest of the Tsakahena warriors. The police admitted to being completely baffled by their sudden hostility.

Once it was dark enough, he started the engine. The fact that it was a cloudy night didn't bother him. His only real concern was whether he would be able to withstand the two-hour drive. He was really beginning to feel the effects of his burns. It wouldn't be difficult to find the entrance to the reserve. He'd seen it when looking at the property he had intended to buy.

As he approached his destination, two police cars were parked on either side of the highway, but traffic wasn't being stopped. He passed the first patrol car innocently enough and made a sudden turn onto the road leading to the reserve. His move took the police by surprise. They set out with sirens blaring and lights flashing. Fortunately, he passed the sign, "This is Tsakahena land" before they could catch him. He sighed with relief and had to admit that previously he had found it intimidating, but today he hoped it would mean sanctuary.

Looking in the rear-view mirror, he saw the police cruisers stop at the entrance their lights still flashing. "Good luck suckers," he grunted as he cautiously drove ahead. He didn't get far. Within a few hundred yards was a barricade of car wrecks. He could see a campfire with about a dozen people huddled around it in blankets. He waited not wanting to spook anyone.

Seven or eight men with bandanas, balaclavas and assault rifles approached the car. One of them tapped on the window with the barrel of his gun and Tom lowered the window. As he did, his greeter yelled, "keep your Goddamn hands on that fucking wheel, or I'll blow your fucking brains out." He complied without comment.

In the meantime, he wanted to know what Tom was doing on their land. He told them who he was and that he was there to see Stacey Whitefeather. He was unceremoniously told to stay in his car while they checked out his story. The warrior took a couple of steps back but kept his gun pointed at Tom while another got on the phone.

It wasn't long before a white Caddy came careening around a curve and stopped in a cloud of dust on the other side of the barricade. Stacey jumped out but forgot to engage the hand brake, and her car rolled right into the wrecks. Two men grabbed her and effectively stopped her from crossing the barrier.

Tears streamed down her face while she waited for Tom to be escorted to her. She didn't care what the warriors thought or how she looked. As soon as he approached her, she jumped up against him throwing her arms around his neck. It took her more than a few moments to control her emotions. The warriors whistled and clapped their hands when she kissed him. His whole ordeal, combined with the kidnappers' sedative, was starting to take its toll and he sagged to the ground. Stacey knelt down and cradled his head in her arms. "You're here," she whispered, "and now I will take care of you."

One of the men got behind the wheel while others bounced on the bumper to free her car from the wrecks. They were driven to Stacey's home where a grey-haired lady and a huge man, stood on the veranda of the grand log cabin. Stacey pulled Tom out of the car as if she were afraid that he would change his mind and leave.

Sam Whitefeather came down to the bottom step and smiled because Stacey was happy again. Crissey remained on the veranda holding back two small girls. They wanted to join in too even though they didn't know why everyone was so happy. Sam was told what had transpired at the barricade. He shook his head when the driver pointed to the damage on the front of the car. His assessment was plain and simple. "Should be used to that by now," he said quietly. "That girl is always thinking about things other than her driving."

He went up the steps and followed the rest of the household inside. He stopped outside the doorway and sniffed the air. "What the hell do I smell?" Tom turned around and was about to walk back towards the barricade but found himself face to face with Sam. Conscious of the fact that he had not had a chance to bathe in a couple of days and given what he had been through, he readily admitted that he was "the smell." "Pardon me?" said Sam. Tom explained that he had been held captive for a couple of days, during which time he had not been given the opportunity to shower. They stood silently until Crissey called out.

"What's the matter with you, Sam?" The shower is ready for him. For heaven sake get out of the man's way and let him get cleaned up." Sam didn't move. "It's okay, sir." Tom could understand why he didn't want him in his house, but he was angry just the same. "I'll sleep in a shed with the plumbing stuff for the night, and you can be sure I'll be out of here first thing in the morning. I realize I have shown up without an invitation, and perhaps I should have called first, but I was led to believe your telephone lines aren't exactly secure." He went on to say that Sam's generous hospitality was undisputed and even took it so far as to say, "I would have hated to meet you if you happened to be in a less hospitable mood."

Sam's reaction was predictably terse. "There is no reason to mouth off at me, boy!"

"I'm not a boy! Don't *you* call *me* boy!" He pushed Sam aside. Where this strength came from, he had no idea, but it was there. He went down the stairs and headed back towards the barricade. Stacey ran after him. "Wait!" she yelled, "I'm coming with you!" She apologized for her father's behavior which she had to admit was unusual. "I had no idea he would be like this. I can't imagine what has gotten into him." As they made their way to the car, unbeknownst to them another scene was taking place.

"You damn fool!" shouted Crissey. "You get them back here, you hear me, Sam. You just get them back here right now." She rarely raised her voice, let alone yelled at him but when she did, Sam knew she was a force to be reckoned with and immediately got into the caddy. Literally within seconds, he drove up ahead of Stacey and Tom and blocked the road. He got out of the car and apologized to Tom while Stacey looked pleadingly at him.

Both she and Sam hoped that he would come back to the house but for different reasons. Stacey because she wanted to care for the man she loved and Sam because he didn't want to incur the wrath of the woman he loved. Tom accepted Sam's apology and returned to the house. His pain was worse. It didn't help that the shirt he had taken from Avi was much too small and pressed against his wounds.

Once inside the brightly lit cabin, the severity of Tom's condition was glaringly evident. He was in immediate need of medical attention. Crissey came running into the room after filling the tub and stopped dead in her tracks. She, like everyone else, was caught off guard. She stared at him and put her arm around Stacey whose hands covered her mouth to stifle her sobs. Sam cradled them both and quietly asked if anyone knew whether Pascal Jim was on the reserve. Crissey said he was and she was going to call him. In the meantime, she asked that the girls be put to bed. They had already seen more than they should and didn't need to see any more.

Crissey carefully cut away the shirt and gasped at the sight of the healing bullet wound on his shoulder. The whole house was suddenly in turmoil. Tom didn't pay much attention to what was going on. There was nothing more he could do so he tried to put himself into a trance to ease the pain.

Stacey's panic was beginning to get the better of her. "Where is Pascal Jim, mum?" Crissey tried to console her.

"He's coming, honey. You've got to get a hold of yourself. You're not going to be any good if you don't." She had no sooner gotten the words out when Pascal Jim arrived.

He put his bag on the table and came over to look at Tom. "Goddamn, somebody sure did a number on this boy. I can't tell you what they used to scratch the hell out of him, but the cigarette burns are undeniable."

"Anybody can see that you damn fool," Crissey hissed impatiently and added suspiciously. "You've been drinking again, haven't you!?"

Pascal knew better than to duck her question and admitted that he had had a couple. "Not enough to impair me, though."

With that out of the way, she wanted to know how to take care of her patient. Pascal Jim told her all she could do was clean the burns. He noted that the cuts weren't deep and would heal by themselves. His main concern was the risk of infection and to avoid that possibility, he told her to pick the dead skin away from the wounds before dressing them. Most importantly, she wanted to know what she could do about the pain. Unfortunately, he said there was nothing he could do to help her. Then she candidly asked him about a Jimmy Johnson and all he said was, "He's a dope dealer."

They took Tom to the tub and turned around to give him time to get his pants off and climb in.

Sam walked in, shook his head and started to leave when Tom said, "Sir, the car I came in is at the barricade."

Sam assured him not to worry about it. "Those guys are crazier than hell, but they won't steal it."

Tom hadn't intended to infer theft, but he was concerned about his fingerprints being all over it. Again Sam reassured him not to worry. "The boys will put it in the crusher which means any and all evidence will be gone within an hour." He turned to his wife and said, "do what you can for the boy, Crissey." This time, Tom didn't take exception to being called "the boy"; he just let it slide.

Crissey was about to head into the bathroom, but Stacey was standing in the doorway. She assured her mother she could bathe him and mentioned if she wanted to help, he needed clothes. Crissey thought for a moment. "Anna, she'll have what we need. She sells clothing at the flea market." This was a dubious source as far as Stacey was concerned and said so. "Mum! A lot of it is stolen!" This was of little importance to her, and she said so. "So, sue me. It's new, and it's clean. He needs clothes, and I know where to get them. You just get him cleaned up."

Tom sat in the tub somewhat embarrassed but feeling much better as she bathed him until she started to ask a lot of questions, none of which he was prepared to answer. Finally, he said, "please Stacey, give it a rest. I'm not quite up to discussing it. The fact that I'm here should be enough." She agreed.

She helped Tom out of the tub and asked, "you want me to dry you off or would you be more comfortable doing it yourself?"

"I'd do it, but I can't reach my back, and it feels as if the skin is cracking open whenever I move."

Crissey knocked on the door, "are you okay in there?"

When Stacey opened the door and invited her in, she saw Jimmy Johnson talking to her father. He appeared to have just declined money in Sam's hand and was on his way out the door. She saw Sam give Pascal Jim two vials He read the labels, opened one, took a tablet, inspected it and nodded.

Her mother's voice redirected her attention back to Tom. "Here try these on and see if they fit" and she left Stacey to help him dress. When they came out of the bathroom, she pointed Tom to a chair and made sure he didn't lean up against it. Crissey had the peroxide ready and started to clean the burns. Without looking at Stacey, she said, "we tried calling Billy again, the phone rings but there's still no answer."

Tom interrupted. "Are you talking about Billy Twofingers?" Stacey said they were. She had told him where to find the spare key and asked him to stay at his apartment.

Tom closed his eyes and dropped his head, cursing, "Jesus Christ!" She totally misunderstood his reaction and assured him that everything would be alright. "It's okay, Billy is very trustworthy and won't touch anything," Just when Tom thought things couldn't get any worse, they just had. Now, he had to tell Stacey more bad news.

"No. It's not okay, Stacey. I'm sorry. I thought you knew." He observed her as he told her Billy was dead. She became a statue when he continued to tell her how he had been murdered when his place was ransacked and how he had assumed the police had already found him and delivered the news to them.

"How do you know, did you go by your place before coming here?"

He told her there had been no need, his captors had been only too happy to feed him the details.

When Sam came back into the room and saw Stacey crying, he put his arm around her. If there was one thing, he couldn't stand, it was to see her cry. She had been through a lot, and he wanted to console her. He said he understood how she felt about Tom but not to worry he would be feeling better soon. Poor Sam! He had no idea how wrong his assumption was until Stacey said, "I'm not crying for that, Sam. I'm crying because Billy Twofingers is dead. They killed him, Sam, the bastards killed him."

His face turned to stone, and he was seething when he shouted, "who killed him?"

"The same people who did this to Tom," she answered wiping her tears.

"God almighty." He paced back and forth. "If those idiots at the barricade hear about this, there will be trouble, big trouble. They'll demand the right to avenge him in the true spirit of an Indian warrior. Goddamn!"

Tom assured him such action was unnecessary because the killers were already dead. It wasn't that he didn't believe Tom, but Sam was still enraged at such injustice and wanted to know where the bodies were. Tom told him he wasn't exactly sure, but he thought they were somewhere in the east end of the city.

"Look, boy, I'm an old man. I no longer have control over those hotheads out there. When they hear this, I want them to hear it from you. And, I would really appreciate it if you could try to keep them from going off the deep end. We'll tell them later."

In the meantime, Pascal Jim and Sam sat down at the kitchen table, sharing a bottle of Seagram's. Stacy glared at them both but singled out Pascal Jim. "Damn you, Pascal Jim. How can you be so self-centered? Have you forgotten you have a patient here?"

"Oh, Anastasia. … his injuries aren't life-threatening. Any fool can shove that needle in his butt."

"Well, believe it or not, I would prefer that fool be you."

That was one down and one more to go.

"And you, Sam, for God's sake take that drink away from him and stash the bottle until he has finished what he came here to do!"

Crissey tried to calm Stacey down. "Oh honey, do you think that I would let that quack touch him after he's been on the booze? I'll do it. I have probably given more injections than he has anyway."

Stacey couldn't disagree with her and thanked her. It was apparent Pascal Jim hadn't heard their conversation when he proceeded to take a syringe from his bag and cleaned the top of the vial before inserting the needle. He partially filled it, squirting out a few drops and approached Tom saying, "arm or butt."

Crissey answered for him. She pulled the syringe out of his hand and asked Tom to lower his pants a little. Pascal Jim went back to his bottle.

Tom and Stacey sat on the couch and waited for the warriors. He felt the warm sensation of the drug taking hold of his brain. As the pain ebbed, he began to feel invincible. His senses were heightened, and life was clearer and less complicated. It didn't only relieve the physical pain but the anxiety and desperation of his situation. Stacey draped a towel over the back of the couch, and he laid his head back, enjoying the high. She would have preferred everyone to leave, but the sound of Sam clearing his throat got her attention.

"What, Sam?" she barked impatiently.

He told her that he couldn't condone nor could he tolerate her sleeping with Tom under his roof. She was incredulous. "That's not what you said earlier this evening."

"Well, I changed my mind," was all he said. Crissey stood leaning against the kitchen counter. This was between Sam and Stacey, and she wasn't about to interfere.

Tom stood. He was feeling much braver thanks to the drug. "You know something, Mr. Whitefeather. I was envious of your family but not anymore. I have come to the conclusion that you are a tyrant. You are right when you say this is your house and you run it the way you see fit, but it's too bad you have to be a bully about it. I'll keep my promise and try to diffuse those morons out there, but you know what? There really isn't much difference between you and them, is there?"

He didn't answer but slammed his fist on the table in anger and frustration causing the bottle and glasses to bounce. Pascal Jim made a grab for his drink before it spilled. Sam stared at the floor. No one had ever dared to speak to him like that before and especially not in his home. He was angry enough to throw Tom out, but he knew that if he did, he would not only have to deal with Crissey but Stacey's tears. This was more than he cared to cope with in one evening.

Tom broke the silence. He had a couple of other things he wanted to say. "Once I'm done with your guys, I'm out of here. Any way you cut it, I'm better off on my own. Oh, and by the way, in case you didn't know it, there is a difference between love and control. It is very apparent to me that you don't love Stacey; you control her."

He was satisfied that he had hit a bull's eye. Sam looked like he was ready to kill him, but thankfully, the warriors pulled up, and he had to rein himself in. It was time for Tom to do what he had promised to do and he tried to make light of any potential danger. "You'd better not get too close to me when I'm out there, Stacey. John Wayne would never accept the interference of a woman."

He went outside and stood on the veranda. The pleasant feeling of his high had been driven away by his anger. Sixteen angry eyes stared at him. He stood on the top step not bothering to ask them why they had come.

"You're that white man!" shouted an angry voice. Tom ignored it. "I said you're that fucking white man!"

Without looking in his direction, he countered, "and you are a coward!" He had control. He had put his heckler on notice.

"What the fuck was that, man?"

Tom took one step down showing them his lack of intimidation. "I said that you are a coward, you're all cowards and I don't talk to cowards." He went on to say. "Men, who hide behind masks on their own land, don't deserve to be treated with respect. What has happened to you? In the old days, you would have cleansed yourselves and applied war paint. Your ancestors fought with honor and dignity. They were truly brave.

Billy Twofingers was truly brave. He was the last brave man in your band. I am here to tell you, you have lost a friend but so have I. I won't bother telling you how Billy Twofingers is gone but I will tell you he died a brave man." He raised his voice as he turned to look at Sam. "He died with honor."

One by one the masks came off, and they put them on the hoods of their cars, along with their guns. Eight angry faces were as intimidating as masks, but Tom had made some headway. He had their attention. Getting into the role of John Wayne, he slowly went down the steps and told them why Billy had died.

"In other words, man, Billy Twofingers died because of you?"

Tom couldn't quite get where his words were coming from but they were there, and that was all that mattered.

"No more than you because of your neglect. He was your brother, a brother with a handicap but you didn't care about him. He took jobs wherever he could while you stood by and didn't lift a finger. Many of you used to laugh at him, and now you cry foul and say that he was a brother who needs to be avenged. When, in reality, you are all too late. I avenged him. I took that glory away from you. There is nothing left for you but to go home."

They weren't quite ready to do that.

"I don't like the way you are trying to make us out to be the bad guys. We didn't choose to live on the reservation. We didn't choose poverty. We didn't invite the white man to steal our lands and to let us live on handouts."

He was within inches of Tom's face, and he wondered if he had gone too far. Could he wind up with a knife in his belly? It was too late to back off. He attacked, and his tone was fierce.

"BACK OFF!" he yelled. "You don't have to live here if you don't want to. You can live anywhere your little heart's desire. Why you aren't even restricted by borders. You can go right ahead and pity yourselves, but the reality is you have made your own choices. You have people who have stepped out and pursued an education. Look at Stacey. Look at Pascal Jim. Shit, look at the pile of junk right behind you. This man has built a successful business from someone else's garbage. The opportunities are endless if you look for them. Oh, I agree this option is much harder than sitting around being a shit-disturber. Just out of curiosity, have you ever heard of a tribe famous for working on skyscrapers? Their strength is simple. They have no fear of heights. They get paid big bucks. They took their skill and turned it into a money-making proposition. What's your claim to fame? Guns? Intimidation?"

"How was Billy Twofingers avenged?" someone wanted to know.

"That's irrelevant. They are dead, and that is enough." Somewhat apprehensively, Tom turned his back and went up the steps. He heard them talking as they got back into their cars. Time would tell if the situation was diffused and the barrier removed. He went back inside where Crissey was ready with dressings.

"Here," she said as she gave him the vial of Tylenol 3 tablets. "They are probably stolen, but they are the real ones."

When she was finished, Tom stood up, put a shirt on and looked for his keys. Only then did he remember leaving them in the car; that very same car that would be in the crusher by now. His resolve and determination to leave were as firm as ever, and he thanked Crissey and then crossed the room to say goodbye to Stacey who made it clear that she was going with him.

"No. Stace, it's too dangerous. Both the Israelis and our own police are looking for me. I have to turn myself in to avoid being killed by Mossad."

She didn't understand. Why if he had come to the reserve looking for a safe haven, was he now leaving? How could he just go back out there? She was deathly afraid that she would never see him again and told him so.

"Don't be so gloomy. Anyway, I'd rather be in jail in the city. At least, there, I have no illusions about who I am dealing with. And, I can't come between and your father. He can keep you safe. I can't bear the thought of you being in danger. Please stay."

As he was about to leave, Sam stepped forward. "I'm sorry, kids. I've been a goddamn fool. You were right to call me a bully. I can come up with dozens of excuses and reasons for doing it, but that doesn't change a thing. You kids have a right to live your lives." He turned to Tom, extended his hand and said that he would be honored if he would stay."

Stacey looked expectantly at Tom while Crissey sat on the couch waiting to see the outcome. Although she had also wanted Tom to stay, she hadn't interfered. Tom accepted his apology knowing full well it was a rarity. Stacey could see how tired he was and she took him to her room. He lay down, and she pulled off his jeans. She noticed that his face was a little redder than it had been. At first, she thought it was modesty, but when she kissed him, she felt the heat of his skin.

"MUM!" she screamed at the top of her lungs. Crissey was there in an instant and saw Tom's condition. It could only be one thing, an allergic reaction. It was either to the drugs or worse, the drugs were dirty. She dismissed the latter. She knew the source and Jimmy was known to deal in clean drugs. She looked towards Pascal Jim, but he was already asleep, slumped over the kitchen table. She knew this was serious and told Stacey.

"We don't have a choice anymore, honey. He needs a hospital, or he could die. This is an allergic reaction. His face is beginning to puff-up. He'll start scratching soon. We need help now."

Standing in the doorway, Sam heard every word. He went to his office and picked up the phone. A van arrived at the front door, and the driver kept the engine running. Sam yelled orders to the crew outside. He felt young again, a leader.

Six men came in and grabbed the mattress. Tom tried to get up, but they pushed him down and squeezed the mattress, almost folding it in half to get it through the door and carried him out. The back doors of the van were open, and the mattress was pulled inside. Stacey and the crew of six jumped in as the doors closed behind them. She knelt down beside him and made up her mind that if he died, he wouldn't be alone. She held him as they rolled around the curves towards the parking lot near the warehouse. Searchlights and lanterns flooded the area. It could easily have been the middle of the day.

Shortly the sound of rotor blades from an approaching helicopter drowned out the sound of the searchlight generators. Everyone looked up, and their eyes followed the helicopter until it landed on the pavement. A paramedic jumped out and walked towards the mattress. Instead of putting Tom on a stretcher, he first took his blood pressure and pulse giving the information to his partner who, in turn, relayed it to the emergency doctor at the hospital. Too tired and sore to object, Tom had to leave all decisions up to Stacey. She gave them the vial of the injected drug. They inserted an IV, put him on a stretcher and rolled him to the helicopter. One attendant walked along the stretcher holding the bag of glucose. Stacey followed and set her foot on the skid to get in with them.

"I'm sorry, ma'am, we can't take you with us."

There was no way she wasn't getting on that helicopter.

"I'm his lawyer and fiancée," she objected. This didn't seem to carry much weight with the paramedic.

"I'm sorry, but there isn't enough space for you."

She was equally unrelenting. "Then one of you will stay here." They went back and forth for another minute until she lost it. She told him in no uncertain terms that either she would be allowed to board or she would seize the plane.

"Now that would be really smart. You would need a pilot because our pilot won't fly without us."

By now they were surrounded by sixteen dangerous looking men, some had picked up the guns they had earlier discarded.

"CHARLEY!" yelled Stacey, not moving her deadly eyes from the paramedic. A lean man of about fifty came running towards her. "Can you fly this thing?"

"Damn right, Stace. Just get him out of the seat, and we're off."

"Okay," said Stacey no longer negotiating. "Get Joe Lightfoot and Steve Parsons. The others will take the pilot and the paramedics. Take them to the highway and let them go."

It became clear to the crew that this lady meant business and she had the backup she needed to put her plan into action. The paramedics quickly changed their minds. Stacey knew that she could be arrested for air piracy but not until after they landed. There was still time to strike a bargain, and she started before the helicopter was off the ground.

"Do you know who the patient is?"

"Makes no difference, ma'am, what you did is a crime."

She was a practiced negotiator, and these skills were about to come in very handy. "Perhaps, but Mr. Benning here is a wealthy man who can make life very difficult for you. Neither one of us really wants any bad publicity. You know how merciless the press can be."

She told them that if they insisted on having her charged with air piracy, it would be their turn to sweat. She had the advantage and set it right out there for them to see. "There are three of you in this thing, but I have over twenty people from my band who will say anything I ask them to. Twenty eyewitnesses are a lot of power in court. You know as well as I do, even a whiff of prejudice against native people can cause quite a stir."

The two paramedics and pilot nodded to each other. Sam watched from the sidelines and smiled as the rotor blades started picking up speed "damn," he mumbled quietly. "I done something right with that girl, she puts a lot of men to shame."

# 12

Tom remembered the helicopter take off but not the landing. The smell and sounds helped him figure out that he was back in a hospital, but he had no way of knowing how long he had been there. Was he a free man or a prisoner? If his memory served him right, he was on thin ice both with the cops and Mossad. He let his mind ramble. If he found himself in police custody, he knew he would live to stand trial. And, if there were a trial, he could now afford the best lawyers money could buy. Mossad, however, had their own swifter way of meting out justice. Either way, his future looked bleak.

He was brought back to reality by a man standing in his doorway. Judah, the man he feared more than anyone else; the man who had ordered his kidnapping and torture was smiling. A chill went down Tom's spine. A smile can usually be defined as friendly or cool but Judah's telegraphed nothing.

Tom knew that Judah had instigated his torture and then made sure that he was in Mobile when it took place. This was his way of technically keeping his hands clean. Tom feared Judah and with good reason but he wasn't about to admit anything of the sort him. Without hesitation he attacked.

"You son-of-a-bitch! How dare you come back here?"

Judah's smile never wavered, and his tone was unmistakably condescending. "There is no need to be so hostile. I have a perfect right to be here, not that it is any concern of yours, I have some unfinished business to attend to."

Tom was insulted by his arrogance but didn't back down. "Coming here is probably one of the biggest mistakes you have ever made."

It was clear that Judah was not about to let him have the last word and he cautioned Tom about his accusations reminding him, he had an alibi. He had been in Mobile.

Tom snapped back that he wasn't being told anything he didn't already know. "In spite of your promise to let Chaim rest in peace, you dug him up. Well, I can take some satisfaction in knowing that you took the bait, went on a wild goose chase and came up empty-handed. Not only that but I would venture to guess you have taken a lot of flack and now you are here to either conduct another interrogation or blow my brains out. My, how things have changed since you tried to convince me how important I was during our first meeting."

Things had definitely changed, but more than even Tom could imagine. He had been right about Judah returning to Israel and being met by a barrage of questions. What he didn't know, nor did he probably care to, was the reason for Judah's return. He would probably be less than thrilled to find out that Judah's mission was to persuade Tom to return to Israel. This order had been issued as a result of a webpage popping up on the internet. The message referred to a study, done by an Israeli researcher, into the impact of integrated schools and a small trust fund that had been established to facilitate a further study of this issue. It went on to identify Thomas Avery Benning as trustee.

To the average person, this would appear like a PR announcement, but in Israel, this information instantly caused raised eyebrows and put Tom on their radar. To make matters worse, an additional piece was sent directly to certain members of the Knesset. It stressed the importance of keeping the trustee of this fund alive at all costs or the political fall out could spell disaster. The nature of this transmission and mystery of its origin raised concern to a new level.

Judah's proposal that Tom goes to Israel completely caught him off guard. "My superiors have requested your presence in Tel Aviv, and I'm here to make the necessary arrangements; not interrogate or shoot you, as you suspected."

Tom stared at him. He was dumbfounded. This was outrageous! He had no intention of going anywhere, least of all into that hornet's nest. Judah mistakenly took the silence as one of contemplation, and when Tom smiled, he breathed a sigh of relief. The success of this mission stood to bring him high praise and perhaps even lead to the fulfillment of his dream. It was long overdue, but he still yearned to become Mossad's "big boss."

This faint hope was not only short-lived but irreversibly dashed when Tom said "you've got to be nuts? I thought you had more sense than that."

Although Judah was burning with rage, he ignored Tom's comment. Undaunted, he continued to explain that there was nothing to fear and went so far as to say Tom's safety was better guaranteed in Israel than anywhere else in the world. It would be accorded the highest priority.

It was also true and irrefutable that Tom had accepted a responsibility back in Alabama and owed it to Chaim to follow through. Unlike previous encounters, this time Tom was taking an interminable amount of time to speak. Judah knew he had made some progress. He studied Tom closely. Finally, with nothing more than a nod, Tom complied with Judah's request. It was now a matter of working out the details.

Tom explained he could not be in any country, other than Canada for more than 14 days, adding that his death on foreign soil, should it happen, would result in dire consequences for Israel. He reminded Judah, the genius responsible for these complex programs was now a ghost, leaving mere mortals to deal with his legacy.

Once the arrangements were made, the operation was set in motion. The entire trip was to be veiled in secrecy. No passports, luggage or goodbyes. Tom knew Stacy would never go along with this decision and he felt like a traitor skipping out on her like this.

He made himself a promise that if he survived, he would bite the bullet, give her a full accounting of his actions and graciously take the verbal lashing she would invariably dish out. She deserved that much, and he was convinced she would forgive him even if she didn't forget his actions.

# 13

Judah held the door open to let Tom's escorts into the room. Ahuva, he already knew as Judah's partner-in-crime and a pleasant dinner guest. The red-head he remembered only as the jabber. He recalled Avi and David referring to her as the "Ice Lady," and he had to admit that she did nothing to make him think this moniker was unwarranted. She barely nodded when introduced. He couldn't help but reflect upon the fact that they were equally beautiful. Laura Koben's hair framed her face and effectively highlighted her flawlessly, fair complexion. Her bangs fell to just above her eyebrows accentuating her generous mouth. She deliberately stood still and took in her surroundings, before selecting a chair next to the door. Again, unlike her counterpart, she didn't cross her legs and even adjusted the hem of her dress to just below her knees.

Ahuva had already picked up a magazine from the nightstand and was leafing through it. Without looking up, she

asked Laura if she would like to take a break. She justified
her offer by saying, "everything's under control here."

Laura's reaction made it clear there was friction between
them. Her tone left nothing to the imagination. "Oh my
God, Ahuva, don't be so bloody transparent! I'm not leaving
this room so you can hop into bed with him. Judah knows
you well, doesn't he? No wonder he assigned two of us to
this job. Let me remind you why we are here, in case you've
forgotten. Judah's orders are crystal clear. We are to protect
him not sleep with him." Ahuva glared at her.

Both stayed out of sight as much as possible especially
when Stacey came by. They illicitly used their radios but did
so sparingly not only to avoid any interference with hospital
equipment but the very real possibility of someone picking
up their frequency.

When she was around, Ahuva more than made up for
Laura's unwillingness to interact. These women were definitely polar opposites. Laura only spoke when it was abso-
lutely necessary and then, with as few words as possible. She
was very observant and always on her guard.

Eventually, a new face was added to the mix. He introduced himself as Josef Panetti. He did his utmost to appear
officious but failed miserably. He was surly. His mannerisms
were effeminate, and he made no attempt at civility. He announced he was in charge of arranging transportation to the
airport and inexplicably felt the need to inject his uncertainty
about this whole "caper."

None of these factors ingratiated or instilled confidence
in Tom. He was so unimpressed, he considered pulling the

plug on the whole deal, but ultimately, his sense of duty prevailed. He looked at the tube in his arm and sighed. "What the hell let's do it ... what about these tubes in my arm?"

"Not to worry," squawked Panetti. "The Ice ... Laura, the nurse will take care of everything. This is how we will proceed. Nothing will take place until after your visitor leaves. Tomorrow you will be in Israel."

"Shut the hell up, you little faggot. The whole world doesn't need to know." Panetti bowed his head and took his licking. He remained quiet after Laura's outburst.

Tom revisited the idea of telling Stacey about the trip but decided against it. The less she knew the better. A mere whiff of suspicion that she knew anything at all would be enough to put her in danger.

That evening after Stacey left, Tom got ready. Flanked by his escort; dressed in jeans, a tee-shirt, sunglasses, and sneakers, he could have passed for a rock star leaving the building. Josef sat in a limousine nervously biting his lower lip. He hurried everyone in and slammed the door. Opening the glass partition, he shouted to the driver, "go ... go, get the hell out of here!" Josef only began to relax once they had turned the corner.

The tension of the moment left Tom feeling a little vulnerable, and he said so. Ahuva pulled her skirt up high enough to show her gun and smiled broadly. "I thought that you would never ask." An eternal flirt, she couldn't help herself.

Tom glanced over at Laura. He still couldn't figure her out. She was an efficient and professional nurse. She removed his intravenous expertly but at no time, even in that proximity, did she make any eye-contact with him. He had to admit he found it disconcerting. Most women generally gave him at least a second look but not this one.

He shifted his attention to Joseph and his ever-present briefcase. He was more than curious to know what it contained and asked Joseph to open it. He did so without any hesitation. Given his previously officious behavior, Tom found this unusual. "Easy … now … Joe. I don't know you all that well, and I'm very suspicious of bags and purses."

"Really, Mr. Benning," exasperation was evident as he pulled out a magazine featuring Tom's photograph on the front cover. The picture had obviously been doctored to make him look like a terrorist surrounded by images of war. It was more like a kid's comic book than a bona fide magazine.

He stared at it, mystified. Where did the picture come from and who was responsible for this farce? It frustrated him that he couldn't read it and that no one seemed prepared to even hint what the article was about. He decided to soft-peddle his curiosity.

"Not a very glamorous shot but that's of little consequence, I'm more interested in the article and what it says."

"I can't help you there, Mr. Benning, the magazine is one of those Palestinian rags, and I don't read Arabic. All I was told is it's about you and how you killed Palestinian martyrs … and how Palestinians have to avenge their deaths. The one thing I can tell you is it has a large readership in the Arab community."

"Well, I can tell you it sure isn't the way to welcome a guest to your country."

Joe didn't miss a beat and replied. "Well, Mr. Benning, I for one don't consider you a guest, merely someone who can be used to achieve a goal. If however, you are a guest, it is of Mr. Fink and therefore, his responsibility to answer any of your questions. At this point, I am not authorized to expand on the matter."

Ahuva had trouble suppressing a smile and looked out the window as they drove on in silence.

Josef made it clear he resented the way Tom had insulted him. In spite of his self-inflated opinion of himself, the reality was he was no more than a low-level diplomatic corps employee who had a penchant for pettiness. He had a secret up his sleeve. He hadn't bothered to explain why they wouldn't be going to the regular passenger departure terminal and felt a rush of delight when they drove right past it, and Tom shouted. "Hey … what the hell is going on? Where are you taking me?"

"Relax," gloated Josef. "We are going to the cargo terminal where there are no scanners or metal detectors, just speedy departures."

Tom's anxiety fuelled his skepticism. "And, no flight-plan I suppose?" He wouldn't bet on it, but it seemed that after Josef assured him it was mandatory, he deliberately wanted to heighten the tension and said offhandedly, "but it can always be revised after take-off."

A small, private jet stood ready to board, but Josef stayed

in the limo. Tom turned around in disbelief, "isn't that joker coming with us?"

It was Laura who answered his question. "No. He is going back to Ottawa. He works at the Embassy." It was as if a plug and been pulled and she couldn't stop talking. "I don't know him, but you are right; he is a joke. I don't like him. He makes my skin crawl. I feel like he is hiding something. And, most of all I dislike him because he thinks he is better than we are, with his diplomatic immunity and all, the little faggot."

Tom smiled.

Ahuva had other things on her mind. She was like a cat on a hot tin roof. She frowned and kept turning around and looking over her shoulder, over and over again until they reached the plane. The vast expanse of open space they had to cover made everyone uneasy, except Tom. He preferred open spaces. It gave would-be assassins less place to hide.

A cargo handler was halfway between the plane and a hangar trying to start his stalled tractor when it backfired. He was close enough that they could hear him cursing.

The pilot hit the pavement. Two guns came out from under the skirts and cartridges fell into the chambers. Ahuva knelt with her back to Tom covering the area below the fuselage and Laura stood in front of him, facing the hangers and the tractor. It had only taken a second or two at the most, and his 360-degree perimeter was secure. It was just as Judah had said. These two beautiful women were a top-notch professional team.

Laura was focused on trying to find the shooter. Tom

started to laugh. He couldn't miss the puzzled look on her face and she explained. "I don't blame you. It would have scared me too if I hadn't seen that guy out there trying to start his tractor."

She lowered her arms, unloaded her gun and put it back under her dress. With the crisis over, Ahuva got up and brushed the dirt from her knee only to discover a hole in her pantyhose. "Oh … fuck! They were brand new!"

Tom and Laura boarded the plane in front of Ahuva, and the co-pilot closed the door behind her. Tom stopped to take in the sheer luxury. This could hardly be in the Mossad operating budget, but Tom knew that legally or for that matter illegally seized material was a benefit. It was deemed a low-cost acquisition and disposable without consequences.

"Oh boy," enthused Tom. "I love it. Where did you steal it?" The co-pilot was quick to ask why he thought it was stolen and Tom was equally quick when he answered because such a plane was probably worth close to seven million dollars. The co-pilot quipped "eight and a half to be more precise but what is a million more or less at this level?" and took his place in the cockpit.

Tom took a seat across from Ahuva. She made eye contact with him whenever he looked at her. It was as if she were reaching out to him. He realized that this flirtation would be hard to ignore. He couldn't afford to be impulsive. The fact was that as a bodyguard employed by an enemy, she was the enemy and a professional seductress. He had to keep a clear head. It was imperative to find out whatever he could from these two women before they landed.

He studied her face. Her beauty could not be easily equaled. He wondered what had drawn her to this type of work. She had orders to protect him but should that change, she could kill him in an instant. Chaim had warned him that female agents were as deadly as men and in some cases, more so.

He had never contemplated the possibility of killing anyone, let alone a woman but it was a fact that he now found himself directly responsible for the deaths of three men. So it was not unreasonable to find himself in a similar situation with a woman.

It did seem impossible that Ahuva could be lethal but readily recognized that this was what ultimately made her so dangerous. He had to concentrate on the reality of his situation. It was his only way to survive and get back to Stacey. She was the whole reason for him being on the plane in the first place. He picked out some magazines from the table beside him and started to read. This was going to be a very long flight.

After an hour or two, Laura got up and said something to Ahuva. It was evident she was annoyed, and she left to talk to the crew. Ahuva didn't respond to the outburst and pulled her legs under her onto the seat. She and Tom were alone. He didn't know how she felt about it, but he found it disconcerting and pulled the Arab magazine out of his pocket and handed it to her. "Would you read it to me, please?" To his surprise, she abrasively referred him to Laura. He deliberately ignored her tone. "She's not here, besides I trust you more. You won't lie to me."

Ahuva had made a grave mistake. She was getting too close to her subject, and it was impairing her judgment. This had never happened before. After an uncomfortable silence, she spoke. "I'm afraid. This attraction I feel for you could get me killed." What she said next literally floored him. "This is the end of my career." She was caught in a personal battle. Her upbringing, her training, her entire lifestyle for that matter, had always been about being the best Mossad agent.

Now she had to acknowledge that since Tom had come on the scene, she felt more like a woman than an agent. She worried because she had never felt like this before. She couldn't shake the feeling that there was more to discover and she was determined to find out everything there was to know. With total abandonment, she flew out of her seat, threw her arms around him and kissed him. Tom couldn't deny his arousal.

He was entirely taken aback when she broke away and asked him how it had felt to kiss a whore.

"I don't know whether you are whore or not, but it's of little importance. What is, however, is that my feelings are personal and none of your business."

She was almost jubilant. "Ahh, just as I suspected. You just can't admit it, but we both know you kissed me back."

He was on thin ice. "Well ... not to destroy any illusions, I will admit it was pleasant."

She wasn't about to let him off the hook that easily.

"That's it? A sensitive man like you can only describe it as pleasant?"

He told her he had no intention of misleading her. He

was carrying enough baggage as it was and it would be better for all concerned if she just forgot about this whole episode. Instantly and emphatically she replied. "I don't want to forget it, it was special."

Ahuva reached for her gun. Every muscle in his body tightened. She had just proven she could be unpredictable, but this was too much. The only thing that helped him to stay calm was that he knew how valuable he was to her superiors and it helped him to relax enough to address the consequences of firing a gun in an aircraft cruising at 30,000 feet.

She smiled, blew him a kiss and said her only intention was to give it to him to show she was no longer a threat to his life. Whether she realized it or not, she definitely had a flair for the dramatic. "Considering how I feel about you, "I'm finished as an agent, so I don't need it anymore."

"Your gun might not be much protection to me in Tel Aviv. The possibilities of being shot down by some Arab terrorist or even a stray bullet are high."

She laughed and told him that Tel Aviv was as safe as Vancouver.

"Then why are you and Laura here to protect me?"

Given these circumstances, he thought it was a real question as did she. Although what she said was true, she stressed things had a way of changing quickly. He didn't miss a beat. "That is why I need you to translate this, Ahuva." She took the magazine and sat on the floor beside him. He couldn't stop himself from reaching down and touching her hair. He didn't do it to please her or for that matter, to flirt. It was an urge he couldn't resist.

She had indeed succeeded in seducing him. So much so that he had to fight the urge not to take her in his arms and kiss her again. She was not oblivious but continued to read. What turned out to be a little propaganda article written by a Palestinian journalist, took some time to translate.

She didn't get up when she finished but stayed put and relished his touch. She felt a warmth, she had never felt before. It was addictive.

Tom was now the one in a quandary. He, in turn, was enjoying the warmth that emanated from her. He fought to block his feelings. He needed to remind himself that Ahuva wasn't why he was on his way to Israel, Stacey was. Had this decision been a terrible mistake? He couldn't help but worry he might never see her again. Ahuva rested her head on his knees. She looked up at him and whispered, "I never knew that I could feel this way. I'm afraid I need you so desperately that if I can't touch or hold you, I will stop breathing. Wanting you is unbearable. I have had sex with many men, but I have never known love. Now that I have, life without you has no meaning for me."

He had to diffuse this and fast. Not only was it unfair to let it go on, but he also couldn't knowingly continue to deceive her. "Oh, Ahuva ... we are thousands of feet in the air. By the time we land, we will both feel differently."

She was quicker on the uptake than he expected. "You speak of *we*, so I know you feel as I do. In my work, there are no tomorrows. I live for today, and I want to love you today."

He told her in no uncertain terms that he was in love

with Stacey and wanted to marry her and he intended to do so with a clear conscience.

"If we do what you want, you and I will both know what we have done. Cheating is cheating. It's wrong, and it goes against my beliefs."

In spite of and with total disregard for his words, she pulled his face to hers and kissed him passionately. There was no frenzy, no wild groping. There were only soft sounds of their mutual delight. Finally, he gathered the strength to push her away and headed to the bar at the back of the cabin.

Although the plane had started its descent, the pilot had not yet issued the order to prepare for landing. Tom hoped the pretense of making a drink would give him a chance to catch his breath and come to terms with what had just happened.

She was not a fighter for nothing and followed him to the bar wrapping her arms around him. He saw her tear-filled eyes in the mirror and realized that he had taken advantage of her feelings and indulged in her beauty. He turned, put the glass aside and held her.

Without warning the plane banked sharply to the left and went into a steep dive before climbing sharply. The cockpit door burst open, and Laura tumbled out, crashing into Tom and Ahuva who were still wrapped in each other's arms. The pressure of the ascending speed kept them all pinned against the rear bulkhead as they heard the desperation of the pilot.

"Mayday--mayday--mayday! Enemy missile! Mayday--mayday …"

The captain's military experience was no match for this attack. He had managed to successfully evade the first missile but a second one forced him into this steep dive. Instead of increasing speed to pull out of the dive, he reduced it in an attempt to lessen the impact with the water. The tail touched the water causing the fuselage to break in two. The wings were torn off, and the cockpit continued on for a few hundred yards before it sank with the pilots still strapped in their seats.

The tail went down with the open end exposed to the sky. Tom and Ahuva grabbed Laura and attempted to climb up to get out of the sinking wreck, but her limp body didn't respond. The cabin sank before they could reach the opening.

Ahuva came up first, and then Tom appeared. He was still holding Laura by her hair. He unsuccessfully struggled to maintain his grip, but she sank slowly below the surface. He went after her only to reappear gasping and alone. They grabbed some of the floating debris, held hands and waited to be rescued.

It seemed like hours before helicopters buzzed overhead. The sound of their menacing blades was most welcome. Fighter jets screeched by while divers were dropped from the helicopters. Life rafts inflated on their way down, and minutes later, they were safely out of the water. The jets continued to search for the missile launch site as a zodiac roared up to take them to shore. The two survivors held hands as the waves pounded the hull and they remained locked throughout the trip. Because they were in shock, they literally had to be pried apart so that they could be taken off the boat and onto the dock.

Tom lost consciousness before he could be put in the ambulance. Ahuva wept. She had failed to protect him.

# 14

Judah pulled the curtain across to separate the two beds and sat in the chair next to Tom. He pulled out a book to jot down notes, a practice he had recently adopted. He had watched his father's memory deteriorate, and now that he was older, his concern the condition could be genetic was worrisome.

Seldom was he challenged but when he was, he never underestimated anyone and never contested a wrongful accusation. Later in private, he would refer to his notes which usually confirmed his memory was still as sharp as ever. This check and balance system gave him comfort and was his silent ally.

Tom stirred. Judah put the book in his pocket. There was no particular reason for him to be there, except for the fact he liked and admired this adversary. Tom was an understated type who never flaunted his abilities or his knowledge. This intrigued Judah enough for him to consider Tom an assignment worthy of his personal attention.

When Tom opened his eyes, the first words out of his mouth were, "Jesus H. Christ, Judah …" An amused Judah replied, "yes, yes, he was one of us, but that was a very long time ago."

Tom was feeling testy and didn't want to talk to anyone least of all, Judah. "Why is it every time I wake up in hospital, I am confronted with your damn face?" Judah wasted no time in setting the record straight. "You are on my turf now. I call the shots, so don't you forget it."

Tom was not easily intimidated and demanded to know where Ahuva was. Judah smiled, pulling the curtain aside. "Right here beside you. She only had a couple of scrapes and bruises, but you had a concussion and a nasty gash on your head."

"And, Laura?" Judah shook his head. He seemed genuinely sad. "No, you two were the only survivors, but the divers did find her body. Contrary to our suspicions, she didn't drown; her neck was broken. She died instantly, most likely even before the impact with the water. Thank you, by the way, for your heroic attempt to save her."

Tom dismissed the accolade, but Judah insisted it was justly deserved and he was only giving credit where credit was due. He went on to say that Ahuva, who usually had an uncanny ability to remember details, was experiencing difficulties. He explained why he had come to this conclusion. "She remembers seeing you dive down for Laura but nothing prior."

Judah smiled his smile and presumed Tom would be good enough to fill in those details when he felt up to it. Tom looked at Ahuva. She trained her eyes on him. He got the message. He would not be filling in any gaps, any time soon.

Judah stood watching them. "She looks okay, but we will keep her here for observation. We are more than a little short-handed, and she is still willing and able to continue her duties. Rest assured she can still shoot a gun."

Tom had more important things on his mind. He demanded to know where he was. Judah confirmed he was in Tel Aviv. Tom couldn't resist taking a jab at Judah, mainly as he had just expressed Ahuva's prowess with a gun. "Tel Aviv ... Is that the Tel Aviv that is supposed to be as safe as any city in Canada? Correct me if I'm wrong but were you not the one who was so sure you could protect me? I want you to explain why we are here and what the hell the good is of being here? God ... you call this safe?"

Judah answered, "it is."

Tom continued to push. "Then get her out of here. I don't need protection."

Judah didn't take the bait. He told Tom whether he needed Ahuva's protection or not was a matter of opinion and it was his call. Tom would remain in her care until he deemed it no longer necessary. He headed through the door with a final warning. "In the meantime, it would be better for all concerned if you talk to no one and I mean *no one* about who you are or why you are here."

Judah had not overlooked Tom's limited time frame and was already making the proper arrangements.

Ahuva hadn't said a word. Then again, she seldom interfered when Judah spoke. This time, however, there were other reasons for her silence. She had more important things on her mind, not the least of which had to do with being a Mossad member. She was the first to admit this limited her chances of being anyone's lover, let alone Tom's. She clearly recognized she was about to enter into the toughest fight of her life. The cultural and moral differences existing between them would seem insurmountable to most, but she took a pragmatic approach. It was a major battle to be fought and won.

Tom also had some soul searching to do. It seemed like only yesterday he had been with Stacey. At home, everything had been so easy. She was always on his mind. Now she seemed to be slipping away. At first, he thought it was because they were so far away from each other, but it was more than that. As preposterous as it seemed, he wondered if he could be in love with two women at the same time. It occurred to him that if anyone else ever tried to justify such a position, he would have judged them harshly. He had always believed himself to be a moral man, but if the truth were known, he had never really been tested.

Ahuva was the first to break the silence.

"You're very quiet, Tom."

He nodded. She went on to ask him if his back still bothered him. He just shook his head and turned to her. He wanted to know how she was and most importantly, was she really suffering from memory loss. She told him that she was okay and feigning memory loss seemed like a good excuse not to tell them everything. What had happened between them was much too private to discuss at a debriefing.

"I wanted to talk to you first so we could get our stories straight."

He signaled for her to be quiet and mouthed most likely the room was bugged.

She continued to throw caution to the wind.

"I don't care if this room is bugged or not anymore. I love you, and I don't care if the whole world knows. We were almost killed out there, and I now want to live for me. I have given enough to my country."

He was not comfortable with her declaration.

"Get over it, Ahuva. We're not exactly the ideal couple. In case you haven't noticed, we are very different. We got caught up in a moment that never should have happened. I'm sorry."

She didn't accept his rejection and spoke about how she had thought about it, and she was convinced that she was in love. She even went so far as to announce she felt her loyalties were compromised and there was no other option but to resign whether she ever saw him again or not.

When she finished, he said that it was a decision only she could make and that it didn't affect him one way or another.

Without flinching, she stared right at him. "Do you believe that I have been honest with you?"

Again he nodded. "I have been honest with you all along as far as this is concerned and anything else, well quite frankly, isn't any of your business."

"So what you are saying is that what happened between us means nothing to you?"

"Look, Ahuva, get this straight. I didn't say that, nor did I mean to. Christ! Stop trying to put words in my mouth."

He turned away. He didn't want her to see how affected he was by this exchange. He had deliberately hurt her, and that was not only cruel but wrong. He needed to apologize and somehow set the record straight.

"I'm sorry. I guess I wasn't completely sincere. I do find you very attractive, and yes, I am a bit infatuated with you. Mostly though, I am flattered that a young woman with your looks would give me a second thought. What I can't handle is who you are and what you do. There, satisfied?"

She had hoped for more and told him so.

"Ahuva, please, you must understand there is no way I'm pursuing this. I'm in love with someone else. I grant you we have gone through a lot and that may well have something to do with the way I feel, but once I get home, things will be back to normal and hopefully I can pick up where I left off. I want to forget about this insane nightmare."

The nurse entering the room stopped the conversation and Ahuva from getting out of bed. Although annoyed by the interruption, she took advantage of her presence and asked to have the needle removed from her arm. "It hurts like hell!"

The nurse tried to explain to Ahuva that she still needed medication, so her hands were tied. She had to deny the request. She did, however, recommend that Ahuva speak to the doctor when he made his rounds the next day.

Not used to being rejected, she angrily started to peel away at the tape and said acidly. "I survived a goddamn plane-crash so I sure as hell will survive without this thing in my arm!"

The nurse rushed over to her and by agreeing to remove

it, calmed her down. She went into the hall and came back with a tray. She removed the needle in spite of the protocol involved but not without trepidation. "I sure hope that I won't get in trouble over this, I could lose my job."

Ahuva smirked, satisfied that things had gone her way. This was one of the few times Tom had witnessed how cold and dismissive she could be.

# 15

**D**ays later they were driven to Mossad headquarters on King Saul Boulevard. Ahuva went to one part of the building while Tom was led to a room where seven men sat around a table. As he was sizing them up, one took the lead.

"It is good to see you doing so well, Mr. Benning. If we had lost you in an airplane crash, this meeting would have had a very different agenda. It is a mystery to us why your death could have such relevance, but we hope you are here to shed some light on the subject and most importantly, why it would have such an impact on Israel."

Tom took a seat at the table. "The word "impact" sounds so warlike, don't you think Mr. Haber?" and left it at that. He waited. It took but a minute before the next question.

"Do you know anyone else in this room beside Judah and me?"

Tom confirmed that he knew everyone but might have some difficulty recalling some of their names. He went on to explain it could be an after effect of the crash.

Judah called the meeting to order.

"For security reasons, we are trying to keep this group as small as possible. It should be noted that we didn't have to resort to using force to get your participation. You have saved us a great deal of trouble. Thank you."

Tom wasn't about to let such a stupid statement go into the records without some retort. "Did you mean that as a threat? Come on … was it really necessary to add that piece of useless crap?"

Judah pretended not to understand. "What do you mean?"

Tom was not amused and said so. "The crap about having to use force, if necessary is what I mean, and you know it. I am well-versed when it comes to your ruthlessness and you, more than anyone else, should know it doesn't impress me. The rest of the world may equally fear and justify your tactics because Jews have suffered so much in the past but please, spare me your rhetoric."

His stubbornness and stamina were well known and respected by everyone present but now took on an added perspective. He was fearless.

"We're not here to impress or scare you. We merely want to stress how urgent this matter is. No matter how antagonistic you feel towards us, Mr. Benning, we want you to feel at home here."

He was feeling feistier by the minute. "As a matter of fact, I feel very much at home here because, at one time, we also had a Canadian group of seven, but they were less lethal and far more creative."

Judah was in a hurry to get the meeting back on track. He mentioned that he was glad to see that events of the last few days haven't diminished Tom's sense of humor and followed that statement with, "the article in the Palestinian magazine, however, wasn't quite as humorous. It was disturbing inaccurate and detrimental to Israel. We believe that you have information that could prove even more troublesome and I now ask you to tell us what you know about the webpage that was published."

"Nice speech, Judah," answered Tom clapping his hands. "Somehow your concern for my well-being doesn't put me at ease. You and I both know that the moment I am no longer of any use to you, you will dispose of me like you do of any other enemy. Whenever I hear the word Israel spoken by you, the hair in my neck stands on end. You claim to love your country, but you don't use the name Israel with love. To you, it refers to duty, war, oppression, and security.

My old friend, Chaim, spoke of Israel with love, peace, and coexistence for all its inhabitants. He spoke of its history, its landscape, and its architecture and it led to his expulsion from your organization because he was mistakenly interpreted as soft. Okay, I have had my say. Let's not waste any more time; on to the next item on my agenda."

He knew this surprised his audience. They had believed they were the only ones with an agenda. Tom continued to hold the floor.

"Before we leave this room, your group will consist of six members. I happen to know there is a traitor among you and he must be dealt with and expelled, or I will refuse to tell you anything more."

"Mr. Benning, this is preposterous," Judah protested. "We have all fought for the same cause for many years. Don't you think that we would be aware of any security breaches within our ranks?"

Tom was as irreverent as ever. "I don't know what you know. Hell, I don't even know if he is the only traitor, but this one can be confirmed not only by me but by your own organization."

"You have watched too many spy movies, Mr. Benning." Judah's attempt to make light of Tom's allegation failed to dampen Tom's eagerness to have his say.

"Is that why I am here? Is that why you have spent all this money for my protection? Is that why the plane was shot down killing three people? It is inconceivable to me that you would think I could buy such a ridiculous explanation. You insult me, sir!"

"It was not my intention to insult you nor do I believe we have wasted the money invested in your protection. What I do believe is you have probably become a little paranoid considering the circumstances of your arrival here. That, to me, is understandable."

Tom went on to say time would tell whether he was paranoid or not. The mention of time gave him the opportunity to address the fact that it was of the essence. He could only stay in a foreign country for 14 days which meant he had to be out of Israel by midnight of the fourteenth day. He cautioned that dragging out this hearing was a luxury they couldn't afford and stressed the need to identify the traitor in their midst so they could get on with business.

"Does this have anything to do with the GPS gizmo inside you?"

The question had some relevance to what was currently being discussed, but it was asked by someone Tom did not recognize.

"I see that Judah has informed you about the little instrument, Mr ... I'm sorry, your name escapes me."

"Burman, Isaac Burman and I head up the computer department. I am also very involved in internal affairs." He added defiantly.

The face and name had eluded Tom, but his recall was instant with the introduction. He knew Burman to be distrusting and ruthless. His rimless glasses intensified his beady little eyes, and his thin lips held an ever-present sneer. He was one of those individuals who held himself in high esteem and didn't hesitate to show his distaste for those he deemed less intelligent. His arrogance was evidenced by the way he had interrupted Judah and usurped the meeting by asking Tom where the GPS tracker was located.

Tom was not only annoyed but disappointed in Judah who appeared to hand over the meeting so easily. In deference to him, Tom waited for some sign. This courtesy was not lost on Judah. He looked directly at Tom and acknowledged the gesture. Then and only then did he reply. "Your guess is as good as mine. It could be anywhere in the world. Chaim's program can send shockwaves trough the publishing media, all controlled by his program in cyberspace. Chaim had more knowledge about modern-day computer programming than you could ever imagine. I was his apprentice for five years. So, what are your thoughts about me now, Mr. Burman? Am I a hoax or the real thing?"

Typical of those who choose to skirt any direct query, he played the evasive card. "Well, … we thought you might be a grandstander who got lucky neutralizing the three terrorists but then, there was also the possibility you were working for the other side."

Tom particularly noticed that although he had asked him for his opinion, he had delivered a generalization.

"God, I love that spy talk, neutralizing, the other side and stuff like that. It seems to say a lot and yet nothing."

He had hit a nerve. Tom's cynicism and open hostility were an issue for Burman, and he took exception. This had been what Tom was waiting for, and he jumped at the chance to explain his attitude and did so in no uncertain terms.

"Well, let me tell you just why that is, Mr. Burman. I'm forced to deal with the likes of you."

Judah was studying his hands, a habit he used to compose himself. Instinctively, Tom understood he was setting the scene and about to take back control of the meeting. In doing so, he would make it clear to Burman that he merely was second in command unless it came to matters of security. His approach was impeccable which reasserted he was in charge.

Judah stood and said with conviction. "We, in this room, have a common goal. I speak for all of us when I say if your allegation of a traitor is true, we are unified and committed to guarding you. You must believe this, Mr. Benning."

It wasn't that Tom didn't believe him, but there was one thing that bothered him.

"That sounds good, but allow me to clarify that you speak for everyone *except* the traitor."

"Who do you believe is the traitor, Mr. Benning?" It was a simple question, as Judah had intended it to be. Tom knew that answering it would put him jeopardy. Before doing so, he addressed the fact that everyone in the room except himself was armed. He proposed all weapons be placed in the center of the table thus minimizing the likelihood of a bullet between his eyes once he identified the culprit.

Haber's vehement objection was no surprise. He argued this act of disarmament put them all at risk. What was to stop Tom from grabbing a gun and shooting any one of them? He was effectively overruled when Judah put his weapon on the table. One by one the others followed his example which left Tom with no option but to identify the culprit. His pause only added to the tension in the room. Finally, he said, "David Haber is your traitor." He waited to let that fact sink in before he added, he was responsible for Chaim Solomon's death."

Haber gasped. "*Oy … the chutspah!*"

Tom ignored his protest. "You are American by birth but carry dual citizenship. This fact has benefited you and lined your pockets well. I became one of your assignments because Chaim was already under surveillance. Your paranoia related to your double-agent status kept me on your radar even after Chaim's death.

I find it interesting that you just assumed I knew you were a double-agent and based on that assumption, got tired of waiting to see if I would spill the beans. When you found out about my trip to Europe, it was then you hatched the plan to hijack the Canadian plane. You wanted me dead. A direct hit would have been too suspicious, but death in a hijacking would have been perfect."

David Haber slowly got up from his chair. He leaned forward and rested his hairy knuckles on the table. He was livid. His eyes were barely visible beneath his bushy eyebrows he glared at Tom over the top of his glasses. An actor to the end, he was silent for a moment while the others awaited his rebuttal. He set the stage well. He started quietly, slowly building to a crescendo.

"I was wounded fighting in the six-day war. I have given 34 years of my life to the Israeli cause, and just recently, I lost my only son in a field operation."

He reached for some water and proceeded. "This man, who accuses me of being a traitor, is the person directly responsible for my son's death. This same man is deemed a threat to our national security!"

He turned to Tom and shouted. "How dare you! How dare you expect the people in this room to believe your absurd accusation? Where is your evidence?"

He fell back down in his chair. His nostrils flared, and his breathing labored.

Tom took his time to observe the six men around the

table. Haber's outburst had left five of them uncomfortable. The sixth, by contrast, sat calmly inspecting his hands, looking quite relaxed. Unbeknownst to Tom, rumor had it Haber was next in line to become the director of Mossad. With him out of the way, Judah had reason to believe his chances of getting the nod were considerably improved.

He raised his eyes and calmly asked Tom if he had any proof of the allegations. This was more than Haber could stand. "Of course he doesn't!" he shouted in a booming voice. "The *shaygets* didn't have anything on him when he was fished out of the water!"

"David … David … David. There is no need to be derogatory. We started as gentlemen, and that is how we will continue."

Haber resisted.

"He didn't call you a traitor. Let's face it, Judah, this guy is a phony, and he killed my son. We missed the boat when we didn't dispose of him the minute he set foot in Israel."

Tom jumped up and pulled his shirt up over his head. It had the effect he expected. They all stared at his scarred body. Some of the wounds were not completely healed, and they started to ooze. He looked unflinchingly at the man who had just admitted wanting him dead. "This is the work of your beloved son. The bastard tortured me. He had me caged like a fucking animal, and then he tortured me. Both you and Judah know this is the truth, you son-of-a-bitch. He would have tortured me to death if I hadn't broken the little fucker's neck!"

Judah interrupted and in doing so not only confirmed

his involvement but accepted any blame for mishandling the situation and asked if they could let the matter rest for now. He knew Tom's dramatic gesture was unplanned but couldn't deny its impact.

Tom pulled out his agenda which brought the meeting back to order.

"Okay. Item number one: I misled you about evidence being in Chaim's coffin. It was never there."

He went on to explain. "Chaim knew he couldn't trust any of you not to dig him up if you suspected he had taken documents to the grave with him. So he set a trap. Whoever opened the casket triggered a series of events which ultimately led to the infamous page appearing on the website. The information about David Haber's treachery is actually under the headstone.

Chaim instructed the monument maker to hollow out a cavity between the headstone and its base. That is where the sealed, weatherproof pouch remains. It contains the evidence against David Haber, his CIA contact and his Palestinian cronies. You see, Chaim knew that he was going to die and he left nothing to chance. He had cancer and only had a few months to live. So David, how does it feel to know you killed him for nothing?

The second item on the agenda pertains to evidence concerning the downed plane. This was anything but a random attack. David and a few of his followers planned it. One of them is Josef Panetti who is a little nothing working at the Israeli embassy in Ottawa. Supposedly, he was in Vancouver to coordinate transportation from the hospital to the airport.

His cover gave him free rein to gather and transmit information at will, not the least of which was the actual flight plan and time table. He relayed the information to David Haber who arranged for a fishing boat equipped with missiles to be strategically situated and ready for action.

These facts can easily be verified by reviewing the communication logs. David Haber wanted me dead because of my association with Chaim, and he wanted Chaim dead because he suspected him of being a double agent. With us both dead, Haber could stay in Florida and carry on as usual."

Judah had another question. "Why did Chaim go through all this cloak and dagger stuff to hide evidence under the headstone?"

"Chaim loved Israel. He wanted political changes but not at the expense of anyone's safety. This is why he wanted me to agree to that chip under my skin."

David Haber threw his head back and put his hand on his forehead exclaiming, "*oy-oy-oy*! What a story. This *shay-gets* is even better than Baron Munchausen."

"Adds up, David. It won't take the boys in communications long to verify some of this … if it's true."

David was astonished that Judah would even consider pursuing this. "Judah … please. He's got *chutzpa* but you don't believe this *chozzerai*, do you?"

He shrugged. "Well, he did come here of his own free will. We didn't have to force or threaten him. This seems reason enough to give him the benefit of the doubt."

David was purple with rage. "That's it! I've heard enough, I'm going for lunch."

Judah told him that lunch was going to be served in the room and with some devilment added, "Besides, if you go for lunch in the cafeteria, we will have to send Ahuva along, and we all know how Fabiola would like that." He sat back down dejectedly subjecting himself to Judah's smile and the others outright laughter.

While they waited for lunch to be served, Judah summoned someone from the communications department and asked for a trace to be put on all calls made David Haber over the past few weeks.

There was no discussion about the accusations made against David during lunch, but two armed guards arrived before everyone had finished eating, to escort him away. He was searched, and his telephone and gun were confiscated.

That evening Judah arrived at Tom's hotel room with a nurse. She carefully examined, cleaned and dressed his wounds. When she was finished; he thanked her, commenting on how much better he felt. His relief accentuated just how much pain and discomfort he had tolerated until now. He credited her with the calm he felt. He was standing on the balcony overlooking the city when he heard her prepare to leave. He turned and smiled, and she winked at him before closing the door behind her.

Judah had always found evenings to be the most beautiful time of the day, and he loved sunsets. He told Tom he hoped to enjoy them for at least another few years.

"I wouldn't worry, Judah. You have a lot of mileage left on you. You look like someone who works out regularly."

He confirmed he did but feared sometimes he overdid it.

He had been experiencing some back problems lately, and it concerned him. He seemed to want to hang around and talk, but Tom found this a less than an enticing idea. This was the man who had him tortured and left him scarred for life. He could never forgive such barbarism.

Judah must have sensed the resistance because when he did speak, he just wanted to know where Tom wanted to go.

"We need time make the arrangements for your security."

Tom told him he would actually prefer to go home but knew that wasn't an option. He had to finish what he had started. He took time to think and then said "Egypt. I want to go to Egypt. I hear it is beautiful and I have never seen the pyramids. Correct me if I'm wrong, but Egypt is no longer your enemy, right?"

Judah confirmed they were no longer enemies but said security would be a real challenge there.

"Well, I guess we have a real problem then. The whole idea is not to be on Israeli soil Judah so what do you suggest?"

Tom had to give Judah his due because he came up with something Tom never would have thought of. "Well, we have a yacht. You will be just about as secure as you are right here. You have seen our capabilities."

Tom questioned this reasoning but told him to go ahead and make the arrangements. Judah nodded and took a phone out of his pocket. He said only two words and he put the phone back in his pocket.

Tom looked at Judah. He had to feed him bits of information to keep him ahead of the others. He was the *katsa* (case officer). Judah knew that he was about to receive another piece of the puzzle and waited patiently.

"Okay, Judah, find the word: "*moichel*" on your computers. It is one of the programs you can use to monitor where I am and if I'm alive. Your technicians may want to try to alter or copy the program, but I would strongly advise against it. Any tampering will instantly destroy the copy on your computer and any capability of monitoring me." Judah had to admit that he found it all fascinating but a little too dramatic for his taste.

Tom seemed to have decided to settle in and gave no indication of going home. He looked over at Tom and asked if he would like some company on the yacht. Tom said no thanks, the less he saw of him, the better he liked it.

Judah laughed. "No you *putz*, I meant Ahuva."

They sat in silence for a while longer before Judah spoke again. "One thing puzzles me, Thomas. You weren't raised a Jew, but you use a lot of Yiddish terminologies, some of which is only used within our organization, why is that?"

Tom told him about Chaim stressing the importance of knowing as much as possible about their ways. "He believed Mossad's behavior and language needed to be second nature to me. It became part of my daily training for the five years I spent with him. He was an extremely thorough man."

Judah changed the subject and told him that Ahuva had asked for her release and it had been granted. He said he mentioned this because he thought Tom would be interested. He praised her as an excellent soldier to whom he would entrust his own life and how unfortunate it was for all concerned that she had now become a liability. He said it in a way that made Tom feel responsible for her downfall, and he turned away.

Eventually, Judah left, and Tom went into the bathroom to wash up. There was a knock on his door, and he came out dripping wet. He had a towel in his hands as he opened the door. He had half expected to be Judah again but was more than pleasantly surprised. Ahuva stood in the hall with a magnum of champagne in one hand and a travel bag in the other. She looked down at her feet and giggled, "c-f-m's."

She came in and kicked them off once the door shut behind her. He was about to say something, but she kissed him before he could. Then she put her finger to his lips, indicating that he shouldn't speak. He watched as she took a scanner out of her purse and checked the room. "Okay, it's all clear now." He told her that he had randomly picked the room and Judah had been the only visitor.

"I wouldn't put it past him to leave a bug or two," she said, "now I'm sure that we can spend the night alone. I'm so glad I'm with you. The debriefing took hours, but they finally gave me my discharge." She was bouncing around the room with excitement. "I'm a free woman."

Tom questioned her about going with him. He wanted her along but didn't quite accept that she was no longer Mossad. The whole story could be a ploy. She could still be an operative. She didn't want to hear any of his apprehensions. She was in love and wanted to be with him. She was footloose and fancy-free, especially now.

"Look Ahuva, if we do this you have to understand that I

have no intention of screwing up my relationship with Stacey and when the times comes for me to leave, I will, and this will be over."

She told him she would stay with him for as long as he wanted. It was as simple as that for her. She loved him. Then she proceeded to set him straight about why she felt the way she did.

"For a smart man, you sure are dense. Listen to me. I'll explain everything in very simple terms so you can understand. Contrary to what you may believe, I came here because for the first time in my life I have fallen in love. It is something I have read about but have never even come close to experiencing and I don't know how to handle it. I may not behave like most women, but I'm not like most women. If I were, you have to admit you would be less interested in me. I cannot pretend to know how to play the game or dance the dance, whatever you call it and I don't want to, but I do want to spend every moment I can with you. I'm a realist. I know that you will never marry me and you will eventually leave, but I live in the moment, I always have and can honestly say, at this moment I love you."

She had certainly been direct and honest, and it left him floundering. Her candor was unnerving, but he knew he had to pull himself together and be as honest with her as she had been with him.

"I don't know how I really feel about you. I do know I want sex, but every man wants to have sex with a beautiful woman. I am fighting to hold on to my principles. I'm not willing to sell out for a night in bed with you."

"Let me tell you something, Mr. Righteous! Contrary to what you believe, I hate sex. Most men turn me off. They make my skin crawl. This is undoubtedly because any sex I have had, until now that is, was in the line of duty. Now let me explain why this is different. For one thing, just the touch of your hand sends a warm glow throughout my entire body. An accidental brush against you gives me an indescribable feeling. I want to be one with you. Does that explain it?"

He couldn't deny it did, with great clarity for that matter but it didn't explain how it could work. He sat very still trying to come to terms with, and find a reasonable compromise to this situation.

Within moments, Ahuva set the tone for things to come. She definitely was a woman used to decision-making. She sat down next to him, held his face in her hands and kissed him tenderly. His fate was sealed. He caressed her lovingly. He wanted her as much as she wanted him. She gently pulled herself away and gazed into his eyes while she undressed him. She was sensual but painstakingly careful. His wounds, although dressed, were still extremely sensitive.

It was as if his emotions transcended any pain and he got up and carried her to the bed where they continued their disrobing ritual. When he finally slid inside her, she smiled and closed her eyes. Later, they lay in each other's arms silently content.

"Thank you, thank you, thank you," she whispered in his ear. "The beauty that I feel inside will stay with me forever. No matter what lies ahead, I will always remember this night."

# 16

Ahuva was proving herself to be a woman of no shame. She stood naked on the bed laughing down at him. She didn't have a care in the world.

"I want you to look and then remember you have to wait a whole day before we're alone again," and with a grin, she announced, "okay, that's enough ogling" and playfully hopped off the bed and headed into the bathroom. "Now get up. I'm hungry, and you have some shopping to do so let's get going. I want to board the yacht as soon as it arrives."

The yacht comment surprised him. He had assumed it was already in the harbor but learned it was arriving from Haifa and would dock around noon. Divers would inspect the hull below the waterline to ensure there were no explosives after which, they would be free to board. Every precaution possible was being taken to guarantee Tom's well-being. He was now a top priority.

She knew he was feeling vulnerable. He was edgy and

snapped at her about not being the only one who was hungry. She was not going to let him upset her. She giggled happily and answered flirtatiously. "Now you know why I pranced around naked. You need to eat if you intend to make love tonight like we did last night. You wouldn't want to find yourself saying something like your mind is willing, but the flesh is weak, now would you?"

Silence.

"Say something … Tom … why don't you answer me?"

Ahuva stuck her head out from the bathroom. He was standing in the middle of the room with her gun clenched in his fist, pointed towards the curtain.

"What are you doing?" she squealed.

He shushed her and pointed to the balcony. A man was sitting, smoking a cigarette.

"Oh Tom," she said pulling on her robe. "You really are a worry wart. Just so you know, there is another one in the hall. They'll both leave when they know we are awake. She drew the curtains back all the way and opened the sliding door. Instantly, the man leaped on top of the railing and grabbed hold of a rope. Ahuva greeted him.

"Hi Herschel, you might as well come through here it's easier than the rope."

Tom was surprised to see that "the man" was in actual fact little more than a boy, twenty maybe.

His fatigues enhanced the fact that he was tall and physically fit. He was the picture of a fearless soldier as he jumped down from the railing. "Thank you, captain, but I'm not supposed to."

He was ill at ease and blushed when he added: "I didn't mean to scare Mr. Benning, ma'am."

She made light of Tom's paranoia and enquired if he had been cold during the night. Understandably, Ahuva's comfort level far surpassed Herschel's. She was a high ranking officer and he a soldier. "No, ma'am, it was not bad at all. I stayed in the corner, out of the wind." She said she was happy to hear it and adopted a more formal stance.

"Well," she said moving slightly aside in the doorway, "I know you have your orders, so I won't tell if you come through here." Then, with a smile, added, "consider it an order."

"Yes ma'am," he said and stepped inside and went straight to the door.

Tom couldn't believe what he had just witnessed

"How did he get there?"

"A rope."

"That rope?" He pointed outside. "Yeah, down from the roof. Their orders are not to interfere with your normal routine, but they have to make sure you are safe. As a matter of fact, there are probably another couple on the roof."

She crossed the floor from the dressing room back to the bathroom. "Tell me what the "H" stands for in Jesus H Christ?" He was beginning to find this was a habit of hers. The best way he could describe it was that she seemed to think in shorthand. Not that she had anything close to attention deficit, quite the contrary, she absorbed information inordinately quickly, and this allowed her to move from topic to topic with ease and speed.

"Holy," he called back.

"Holy?" she replied in mocking disbelief.

"Yeah," he said "Jesus Holy Christ. Will you please hurry up, I have to pee." She laughed uproariously and wondered aloud why he was so puritanical all of a sudden and magnanimously offered to share "her" bathroom with him.

He peed, showered and was in the process of brushing his teeth when she reappeared. She was breathtaking. He stared at her reflection in the mirror. She was smiling when she acknowledged his appreciation. "Cruise-wear, we are going on a cruise, are we not?" and struck a pose she knew he wouldn't be able to resist. She was right but reminded him there was no time and went to stand by the door leading to the balcony.

The view was undeniably beautiful, but she hardly seemed to notice.

Her eyes wandered to her right and over the sea towards the horizon, but she didn't see it. Seagulls drifted above, but she didn't hear or see them either. She was deep in thought. She had never loved a man before, she had never loved anyone, not even her parents. She had only read about it and seen it portrayed in movies. She had always theorized that people just didn't care about each other. But she had been proven wrong. People did care. She had proof. She was in love; heart-stopping love.

Her eyes filled with tears. She closed them and saw his face. No matter what, his face would be there forever. She would follow him to the ends of the earth if he wanted her to. They would be one. She clenched her fists until her nails dug deep into her palms. She felt no pain, only his presence. She made a silent oath to fight anyone who dared to even try to take this God-given gift from her and to kill anyone who tried to harm him. Tears streamed down her face. She was devoid of reality and screamed at the top of her lungs, "Y-E-S-S-S-S ... HE'S MINE, MINE ALONE!"

Two guards instantly burst into the room their uzis ready, as did Tom, his shaving cream effectively camouflaging his ashen face. She saw only him and raced into his arms. Once it was clear there was no danger, the guards retreated to their post. To put it mildly, Ahuva had had a moment of weakness. In time, this would be a funny story, but at the moment, it was extremely embarrassing.

Tom returned to the bathroom to finish shaving convulsed with laughter. His reaction could have been attributed to nervous shock, but deep down he knew that had nothing to do with it. The scene, once defined, was funny. He and the guards recognized the humor simultaneously but managed to maintain their composure until they left the room. They all knew Ahuva's dignity had to be protected.

When he finally came out, she had changed her outfit. Tom knew it was because the other one was covered in shaving cream. He noticed her putting her gun and knife into her purse. She looked puzzled when he asked her why there and not under her dress as usual. She explained that she was under the impression he didn't like her wearing it there. He shook his head, knelt down in front of her and strapped it against her leg while smiling as he did. He told her he found it reassuring to know where the gun was if he needed it ...

aside from the pleasure of lifting her skirt. The knife wasn't as important. He had learned that a knife as a weapon got him closer to the enemy than he preferred to be. He liked a little leeway.

As was her habit, she changed the subject. "I'm hungry. We'll eat breakfast first and then go to the boutique to do our shopping. After that, we'll head over to the marina and board early and relax, perhaps even before the divers are finished." He made some comment about her taking control. She just smiled. He wondered aloud, why they would be allowed to board before the hull inspection was completed.

"Are the Palestinians considerate enough not to blow it up in the marina?"

She said it had nothing to do with consideration. It was easier for them to blame someone else if it happened at sea.

She set him straight on the subject of Palestinians. "They are not all bad. The militant factions of the Palestinians are evil but on the average, they want what we want, peace."

He marveled at her calm. She talked about bombs and shootings with such ease. Tom knew it was part of who she was, but he had to admit it that she was more informed than most people.

Two hours later a car with two guards was waiting to take them to the marina. As they left the parking lot, their tension heightened which did nothing for Tom's confidence. They were ultra vigilant looking for any hint of danger. Tom recalled Ahuva telling him that Tel Aviv was a secure city but this behavior more than confirmed the threat of terrorism was an ongoing concern.

The driver brought Tom back to reality. "Why go out to sea when we have many nice places in Israel to visit? Our beaches are beautiful."

Tom looked at Ahuva for assurance. She was becoming his trustworthy advisor to the reality of being in Israel but, she seemed preoccupied with what lay ahead.

"Well, it is a little too complicated to explain but take my word for it; I would prefer to be at the beach or visiting Cairo and the pyramids, but the sea is easier for you guys to control."

This answer seemed to satisfy his curiosity. The driver went on to say, obviously Mr. Fink knew what he is doing. Before he could say another word, they arrived at their destination. It turned out, only to be minutes away.

This was no ordinary day at the marina. There were guards, zodiacs with divers and a captain dressed in white, watching the inspection which was already underway. Ahuva walked straight to the captain and asked if they could board and he granted them permission. "We don't think there is anything down there, but we have to check it out to be sure."

Ahuva led the way. The captain smiled as he watched Ahuva and Tom go straight into the lounge.

Ever the architect, Tom admired the woodwork. Ahuva infinitely more interested in their sleeping quarters went down to check them out. Halfway back up the stairs, she announced the accommodations were far better than she had hoped. There was a double bed in the stateroom, not bunks.

He looked down at her and winked devilishly.

# 17

The Mediterranean was at its best; bright, and picture perfect. The smell of the water combined with a slight breeze, caused by the yacht distancing itself from the shore, was hypnotic. They stood hand in hand on the deck and watched the coastline slowly disappear. The Goliath was aptly named. It was big and powerful but glided gracefully through the water.

He looked at Ahuva. She was radiant. It suddenly dawned on him why, in spite of so many obstacles, he was so drawn to her. She had rekindled feelings he had only felt when he was married. This was both miraculous and disturbing.

Until now, he had given their association little thought beyond the fact that he was her assignment for a limited time.

Now he was faced with reality. She was turning his life upside down. They were polar opposites which only heightened her appeal. He felt he could open himself up to Ahuva in a way he had never been capable of doing with Stacey. This revelation was liberating. He could almost physically feel the load lift from his shoulders. He was going to settle back, cruise the Mediterranean and put any thought of Judah and his cohorts on indefinite hold.

Ahuva let go of his hand and slipped her arm under his and snuggled closer. She didn't look at him when she spoke, and perhaps that was because she sensed it was in no way close to what Tom would expect to hear.

"You hate Israel, *Tsatske?*"

She had been right. He stiffened and remained still while carefully weighing how to answer.

"No ... not really, or maybe it would be fairer to say not any longer. Hate is natural for some, but it is not innate. Chaim put it most eloquently. Babies aren't born with hate; adults plant the seed. This is why we must attack hatred and indifference before it takes root in the children."

Ahuva looked around to see if they were being watched and when she didn't see anyone, she kissed his cheek and headed up the stairs leading to the bridge. He turned around to follow. His timing could not have been better. A gust of wind caught her skirt. She made no attempt at modesty; Tom would appreciate the view. He did indeed but had anyone else? To his relief, he saw one guard was positioned on the diving platform, too low for him to even be aware of what was going on and the vantage point of the two on the upper deck was no better.

She moved closer to the railing. He knew she intended for him to look up and predictably, he did. Mission accomplished, she turned around and started to come back down.

Her knee bent as her foot touched the first step. She smiled, fully aware of what she was doing. So was he and decided not to give her the satisfaction she was so overtly looking for.

When she was back beside him, he nonchalantly asked when they would drop anchor. She was miffed that he didn't play along and just shrugged. He kind of liked having the upper hand and ignored her snub. "Are these guys staying on board?"

Her look and tone made it crystal clear, she was not amused.

"What do you expect them to do, swim back to shore? The stateroom is ours. We will close the curtains and lock the door." He reined in his self-indulgence and surrendered.

"I know, but after your performance on the stairs, I want the whole boat." She melted, and they stood holding each other as the Goliath slowly came to a stop.

The arrival of a helicopter was imminent based on the accelerated noise of rotor blades. Tom saw the captain pick up his receiver, but the noise level was such that it made it impossible to hear, let alone decipher the captain's conversation with the pilot. The helicopter circled a few times and returned to shore. The captain cradled the receiver and came down the stairs with two guards in tow.

It was almost noon, and he extended an invitation to join him for lunch. It was a pleasant enough gesture, but Tom's need to be alone with Ahuva pre-empted any socialization. The captain's courtesy appeared to go unacknowledged as Tom knelt down to tie his shoelace. Irrational or not, he sensed this was as good a time as any to make his move and went directly for Ahuva's gun. It was so spontaneous; it caught everyone by surprise but not enough to stop Tom from starring down two Uzis. As if they didn't exist, he calmly pointed his gun at the captain who was already returning the favor. Tom seemed totally unperturbed by the odds and stood his ground.

"Give it up, Mr. Benning.," the captain ridiculed. "A twenty-five caliber isn't a bargaining tool against these odds."

Ahuva behaved as if this were an everyday occurrence. She playfully leaned on Tom's shoulder and looked at his face. He was tanned and his hair blonder. Even his eyes were bluer than when they had first met. He was more handsome than ever and looked like he didn't have a care in the world. In fact, his smile was quite wicked. She knew without a doubt, he was determined not to back off.

To complicate matters even further, a third guard positioned his gun with the barrel resting on the bulkhead. Tom saw him from the corner of his eye, but he didn't seem to care that a fourth gun had joined the fray.

He nodded to the captain, "I agree that the odds are a little unbalanced, but you already know how reckless I can be."

Gently he moved Ahuva away from his side. "Taking out three Arab terrorists was more than risky, and here I am trying to beat the odds yet again."

"You caught the terrorists by surprise, Mr. Benning and it was easy for you to be brave. You had an entire police force to back you up. We both know that you aren't a fighter."

It gave Tom great pleasure to say. "You are grossly misinformed, captain. For the record, those terrorists were very much on their guard. It may interest you to know that I have survived astounding odds, but today I am happy to say, I don't have to prove my superiority. I have the advantage. Right now, I'm like God, omnipotent. You guys can't fire a single shot at me even if I were to kill one, or all of you. My safety and survival is your priority. If you did anything to countermand your orders, you would be in deep shit."

The captain confirmed, "it is true, we have those orders, but if you shoot us without provocation, you will still have to face the music in Tel Aviv. Besides, what reason do you have to kill us?"

Tom assured him he had no intention of killing anyone. All he wanted to do was get them off the boat. Tom had counted four fishing trawlers in their immediate area, and it was plain to see they didn't have any nets in the water. What they did have, however, were rubber rafts ready for action. He was willing to bet that all four were there to guarantee his security. So, in his humble opinion, it made the captain and his guards unnecessary. Had Judah Fink not told him that they would be as secure at sea as on Israeli soil?

The captain saw that he was fighting a losing battle. He took a radio from his pocket and spoke to someone in Hebrew. Moments later a zodiac came bouncing across the waves to the yacht and pulled alongside. The first two guards got in, but when the third one threw his leg over the railing, Tom put the barrel of his pistol to his head. The young soldier trembled visibly and looked like he was going to vomit. When Tom ordered him to hand over his gun, his grip tightened, and his knuckles turned white. He was a well-trained professional who would never willingly surrender his weapon. He stood his ground, but he looked apprehensively to the captain for direction. A simple nod of the head was all he needed. Tom had the gun and extra ammo.

"Thanks," was all he said when the last of the crew was gone, and he gave Ahuva her gun. It was then she reminded him that he had forgotten to chamber a cartridge, but he hadn't forgotten.

"At no time did I think that wanting to be alone with you was reason enough to shoot anyone." She moved closer to him and whispered. "Can I put my cruise wear on now?"

She took his hand and led him into the lounge where she took the scanner from her purse. She went over the room and found two bugs which she pitched overboard. Tom sat down and saw there were newspapers on the coffee table and asked where they had come from. She said that the captain had put them there when he came on board and that more than likely, they were a gift from Judah.

Tom hadn't seen a Vancouver paper since his whole ordeal had started. He picked up the first one from the stack and discovered that the mysterious disappearance of Thomas Benning dominated the first page. One of the main points of the article was that the Israeli secret service was suspected of masterminding the kidnapping. He tossed that paper aside and picked up the next one. It announced that the plane transporting the kidnap victim, Thomas Benning, had been shot down over the Mediterranean Sea by Palestinian terrorists. It went on to say there were no survivors and only the bodies of the pilot and co-pilot had been recovered. The

Israelis were still searching for the bodies of the passengers and the flight recorder.

While most of it was true, the lie shocked Tom. Evidently, there was still some doubt whether he was to live or die. The latter would be less problematic if the public already believed him dead. Judah had effectively covered all his bases.

Ahuva uncapped a beer and walked over to him. He was wiping his eyes, and she couldn't tell if he were just tired or whether he had read something upsetting. She put the glass on the table and sat beside him. "What is the matter, *Tsatske*, bad news from home?"

"No, bad news *for* home; I never thought this would get international coverage, let alone that Judah would lie."

Ahuva, ever intuitive, knew precisely what he was thinking. Stacey would have either read or seen the reports, and he knew she would be devastated. When she said as much, Tom literally bolted to his feet. He had to call her and set the record straight. Ahuva remained seated but took command. She calmly but forcefully made the observation that he wasn't thinking rationally. Once she had his attention, she proceeded to rhyme off all the reasons why his idea was a bad one. He sat back down dejected. He had to agree and this only compounded his feeling of helplessness.

"I brought you a beer, but under the circumstances, I think you need something stronger. Wait here." She went to the bar and opened a bottle of Canadian whiskey and poured a double on the rocks and brought it to him. She noticed that he had folded the papers and put them aside. She made a mental note to gather them up later and put them in the trash.

He leaned back and closed his eyes. He needed time to reconcile the loss of Anastasia. There was only one option open to him. He had to store away anything that might interfere with what he still had to do. When he opened his eyes, Ahuva knew that he had resolved his problem. He downed his drink and asked for another. It did the trick. He was beginning to relax.

Ahuva made herself a drink, picked up her scanner and methodically went over every inch of the Goliath. It was a profitable search. She collected seven more bugs before she returned to the lounge with her harvest. Tom thought it fitting that they drowned like their predecessors. She agreed and motioned him to follow her outside where she methodically lined them up on the railing. With two fingers in her mouth, she whistled with eardrum-splitting clarity. As if that weren't enough, she ceremoniously took off one of her shoes and systematically smashed them one by one before tossing them overboard. The offending mechanisms sank like rocks, and they burst out laughing.

For the moment, they didn't have a care in the world, and it felt good. Ahuva glanced over at Tom. "I have never seen you laugh like that, *Tsatske*." He was still chortling when he said "I couldn't help it. Just imagine the reaction of the guys at the other end." The thought still tickled him enough to bring on a new round of laughter.

It had been a warm day, but with the sun gone, the breeze off the water was cool. It was a welcome change for Tom, but he wondered if Ahuva, who was barefoot thanks to her ear-lier antics, might be chilled. He asked her if she wanted to go inside, but she said no; she just wanted to watch the sunset. It was spellbinding, and she knew it was because she saw it through the eyes of a woman in love.

The waves seductively splashed against the hull as he carried her to their stateroom, laid her down and caressed every inch of her body.

# 18

They sat on the deck enjoying a leisurely breakfast. Both were relaxed if not well rested and to anyone observing them, it was beyond question that a dramatic change had taken place in their relationship. Their newly minted bond needed neither church nor state approval. If his declaration of love had been easy, it could in no way be called spontaneous. It was, however, true and finally free of encumbrances.

During his self-examination, he had come to the conclusion that not only did he deserve some peace of mind but so did Ahuva. They were good together and right now that was all that mattered. Deep down, he knew that sooner or later he'd have to face Stacey. He owed her that.

Ahuva brought him back to her by saying. "You and I have a lot in common, *Tsatske*." Puzzled he asked what she meant.

"We are both totally alone in the world. We have few true friends and no family. We live dangerously; spend most of the time looking over our shoulders; you more than I and we are about to be forced to give up our new found freedom. Your twenty-four hours are up. The crew and divers will be here in a little while to take us back."

Her insight was uncanny, but he detected a touch of pessimism which was uncharacteristic. True, he didn't like the hotel and all the guards but apparently, neither did she. Without any forethought, he made up his mind to stay a while longer. He knew this would annoy all concerned, but he didn't give a damn. He had the upper hand. When he told Ahuva of his decision, she was both delighted and apprehensive. "They will be furious, *Ttsatske*."

This was not his problem, and he made it clear that nothing would stop him from getting his own way. There were ample supplies on board so they could quite conceivably extend their stay to a week. They discussed their options and decided one more day would be a reasonable compromise and far less difficult to negotiate.

Besides, a week could mean undue hardship for guards whose families expected them home on schedule. Tom didn't want to be unreasonable or selfish in the extreme, but he reasoned the state of Israel owed him. Had he not already endured enough at their hands?

"Okay," he said. "When the captain arrives, I'll tell him that we're staying and he can come back tomorrow."

The decision made, they sat back to take in the sun and relish the prospect of another day of freedom. She reached out across the table, and he cupped her hands gently between his own. The moment was short lived. They could hear a boat approaching. The closer it came, the more the tension rose.

Tom told her not to worry. There would be no trouble. He would let them know the change in plans, welcome them to inspect the hull and then leave. No one would be allowed to board until tomorrow, and he was sure that his loaded gun would be enough to discourage any attempt to do so.

He turned and asked her for life jackets. She had no reason to question him. She silently got up, took two out of a bench seat, strapped one on herself and put the other on him. She knew him well. He would never harm her or unwittingly kill anyone. He was the only man whose judgment she trusted implicitly.

When he asked if she had her gun ready, she didn't answer. She wrapped her arms tightly around him and rubbed her knee up and down his leg. He put his hand against it without taking his eyes off the fast approaching zodiac. He smiled, but he couldn't allow himself to be distracted, and he told her to stop. There would be plenty of time for that later. She blew softly in his ear and backed away.

The zodiacs came alongside. The captain dismissed any protocol and categorically stated he was coming on board.

Tom was ready and waiting and wisely or not, actually feeling quick cocky.

"Permission denied."

The captain stopped dead in his tracks when he saw Tom pointing the gun at him and blustered. "For heaven's sake … Benning! You are already guilty of mutiny. Is that not trouble enough for you?" He went on to say that he didn't believe Tom would harm anyone adding "you may be a reckless, arrogant, son-of-a-bitch but you're not a cold-blooded killer. We're finished playing games. I'm coming aboard," and started to do just that. Tom calmly agreed that he wouldn't shoot anyone, but he had no problem shooting the boat. He turned sideways, cocked the bolt and emptied the magazine, splintering away a large piece of railing. The once perfectly varnished teakwood railing was now shattered. Menacing daggers of wood littered the deck, and some bobbed on the water. The powerful stench of gunpowder hung in the air as he inserted another magazine.

"In case you're wondering, the next salvo will go straight through the deck and pierce the hull below the waterline, and I will continue to fire until the last bullet is spent. How do you feel about being the captain of a sinking ship?"

The captain, as officious as ever, felt it was his duty to informed Tom that he would also have to abandon ship. Tom mimicked the captain's tone and told him not to worry. "I will be the first one rescued, and I will be taken to a nice hotel, where my wishes will be everyone's command. While you, sir, will rot in jail awaiting a court-martial. You can see that Ahuva and I are prepared. See, our life jackets?"

It was obvious to everyone's annoyance that Tom was enjoying himself much too much.

"Allow me to remind you, captain, your orders are to unconditionally protect and keep me safe." He silently congratulated himself on his ingenuity and watched the captain for any sort of reaction. There was nothing unusual.

Tom had no way of knowing, but he had grown in the captain's estimation. His actions had caught everyone by surprise. They were well conceived and had earned him re-spect, however begrudgingly.

"The divers have to check the hull. I have my orders." Tom nodded his assent.

The captain had one more question the simplicity of which was very telling. It concerned a mission he feared. "What will I say to Judah Fink?"

His outburst was so violent it left him breathless, and the captain stunned.

"Fuck you!" he yelled at the captain, tossing the Uzi over-board. "Fuck them all! Fuck Judah Fink and all the others who are making my life miserable. Tell Judah that I will come tomorrow. Tell him that a *shaygetz* from the other side of the world cares more about his people than he does. All I want is one more day before I surrender to his goons. Tell him that if you dare. You have the men and the power to take this boat. I won't resist you, but I ask you not to."

Tom put his arm around Ahuva, and they walked inside. He didn't wait for the captain's answer but hoped that his outburst and his plea had not fallen on deaf ears.

The captain, who still had one leg over the railing, pulled it back. His decision was made. He reached over and took a gun from one of the guards and left it on the seat near the bulkhead. The zodiac circled the yacht and waited a few yards away from the stern. When the last diver surfaced and was back in the zodiac, it roared away.

The captain stood erect. He felt empowered for the first time in a long time. He had made a decision without any outside consultation and if need be, was prepared to face the consequences. His dignity was restored. He felt no anger only envy. That man on the yacht was a free man.

The next morning right on schedule, he peaked over the bulkhead happy not to see a gun there to greet him.

"Hello, Mr. Benning, do I have permission to come aboard?" Tom came out dressed only in jeans. He walked out to the middle of the deck and stood there with his arms crossed. He had a big grin on his face and nodded. "Permission granted, captain. It is time to see dry land again. I hate fucking boats. The captain was curious. "If you hate boats so much, why did you fight so hard to spend another night on one?"

"Judah promised me a vacation, but because he is renown for breaking his word, I made sure that he kept this one. Once in a while, I have to have it my way. It makes me feel alive."

He extended his hand to the captain, who eagerly took it and then went about getting the Goliath ready to return to port.

Tom and Ahuva stood holding hands and watched the first zodiac lead the way. It was about a mile ahead of the yacht, with another trailing them at about the same distance. Everything seemed under control until the lead zodiac yawed. The evasive action was too late, and it exploded in full view.

The captain yelled down to the guards, who shoved Tom and Ahuva into the lounge and threw a couple of life jackets at them. "Put them on, now!" was all they had time to say. The yacht made a complete turn and zigzagged away in the opposite direction. The remaining zodiac zoomed by at full speed and headed directly to the burning debris.

Two helicopters appeared almost instantly. One hovered above the burning debris, and the other continued to follow the yacht. Two fighter jets screeched across the sky and fired two missiles which left smoky trails until they became fireballs in the distance. Their target instantly became a cloud of black smoke that could be seen for miles.

The captain was given the all clear to return to his former course and headed at full speed towards the harbor. The helicopters flew shotgun.

Two divers and a guard were already standing on the dock as the yacht pulled into the slip. They had been rescued by the second zodiac after managing to jump overboard just before their boat exploded.

Judah stood beside them but stepped forward to hold his hand out to Ahuva. She took it and stepped easily onto the dock. He made no comment about the attack. Instead, he concentrated on the damage to the Goliath. Judah was not his courtly self. He was surly and rude. He completely shunned Tom, reserving his anger for the captain.

"What the hell happened?" he shouted at him and was astounded when he was referred to Tom for the answer. "You'll have to ask Mr. Benning, sir."

Tom made a point of ignoring the conversation and went to talk to the three, soaking survivors. He could play Judah's game.

"Jesus Christ, that was a close call."

They were modest to a fault about their experience,

acknowledging their training was so intense, it almost guaranteed their safety. Tom didn't know if they were programmed to toe the party line or not, but he was impressed with their acceptance of the inevitability of danger.

Judah signaled him it was time to leave and ushered Ahuva and him into his car. The ensuing silence was powerful, but eventually, he couldn't refrain from asking, "what the hell was the idea of forcing the crew to leave the yacht? They were there for your protection! What were you thinking? And, what was the idea of staying any longer than necessary?"

Ahuva looked at Tom trying to anticipate how he would handle these questions. Tom ticked them off one by one; intentionally setting the tone and precision of his delivery to irk Judah.

"First of all, no one was there to protect me; they were there to protect your investment."

"Second of all, screw you! I'm not your property. You said that I should consider it a vacation so I did just that. I didn't need an entourage, especially one handpicked by you."

Judah responded in kind.

"You are arrogant and reckless and worse, you are obstinate. Each of which might be enough to lead to your downfall but in combination, it is inevitable. I strongly recommend you get yourself under control before it's too late."

"Contrary to what you think, I'm very much in control but thank you for your concern."

"Perhaps you are now, but surely, you couldn't have been when you decided to use the yacht as target practice. What was the idea of that?"

They bickered back and forth for most of the short drive back to the hotel. It was the first time Tom witnessed Judah lose his cool. Judah knew it was not in his best interest to continue this verbal barrage because Tom was gaining the upper hand, so he disengaged himself, became quiet and tried to regain his composure.

As they pulled into the hotel, Ahuva leaned over and whispered something to Tom. So surprised to overhear her call him *Tsatske*, Judah said. "Oy … *Tsatske* already … Is it that serious with you two?" Tom confirmed it was and told him in no uncertain terms that it was none of his business.

Judah was anxious to defuse the hostility that had developed and saw this as his chance. He took Ahuva's hand and kissed it and then extended his to Tom. It was plain he wanted to not only ingratiate but declare peace. He smiled at them both. Much to Tom's surprise, it was unlike his usual smile, it was genuine and warm.

"Well, let me be the first to congratulate you lovebirds and make arrangements to have you moved to larger quarters."

# 19

Tom entered the room with an air that belied his uneasiness. He was relieved to see that his welcome, by the remaining six men around the table, was devoid of the cynicism he had previously experienced. In contrast, the atmosphere was now one of respect. Tom took the time to smile and nod acknowledging everyone individually around the table. As he had hoped, his courteous manner was reciprocated. He had cards to play and wanted to do so in his own good time.

Memorizing the bios of each participant had improved his confidence level which would hopefully give him an advantage, however slight. He didn't have to wait long to see he was right. Shoran-Lemone was the first to speak.

"We were all sorry to hear about another attempt on your life."

Tom thanked him for his concern and added "well, Mr. Lemone, as I was told, "that's Israel."

And, "that's Shoran-Lemone to you, Mr. Benning."

Tom was now two for two. Maybe this was going to be even easier than he thought.

"Yeah, okay, just as soon as you start calling me Sir Benning. I'm well aware of your affectations, Izzy Lemone. It may or may not be common knowledge, but I happen to know that you added that Shoran shit to your name when you married."

His sparring partner was furious. He turned to Judah and ranted. "Must I listen to this *meshuggener*? He calls me arrogant! We are the ones who had to wait for his highness to return from his cruise and to top it off, discover the *smuck* purposefully damaged the yacht. He respects nothing. His actions have put this whole project in jeopardy. So? We have to take this?"

Undoubtedly, Judah's response was not what he wanted to hear.

"Yes, unfortunately, we do. He is in the driver's seat, at least for now but you do have the option to leave if you so choose."

Izzy slumped down in his chair embarrassed that he had let Tom get to him.

Judah went on to defend his position.

"This man has been traumatized, threatened and tortured. What's next? Who wants another piece of him before we know what we must know? Come on, he is one of us, a Jew. This whole situation continues to be an ordeal for him.

He could have walked into any medical facility and had the GPS removed without any repercussions to himself. To his credit and out of respect for his promise to Chaim

Solomon, he chose not to. He is a man of honor, and his decision favors us. He is here for us."

Judah had made his point and used his diplomacy to deflate a potentially explosive and unproductive session. Tom not only appreciated but respected this expertise. He thanked Judah for his remarks.

Then, he addressed the fact that he had been intentionally difficult and would make a concentrated effort to modify his tone and be civil when dealing with the members of this group.

Discussions began anew. Within minutes, the resolve for civility seemed futile. Everything started to rapidly go downhill. One thing led to another culminating in Judah calling for order by banging his fist on the table. Some of the accusations and comments thrown across the table had unsettled Tom. They renewed his apprehensions about ever leaving Israel alive.

"There is no need to be so paranoid," interrupted Judah. "I gave you my personal guarantee that we would not harm you and that you can go on with your life in Canada, once this is over."

Tom was not mollified.

"Right, your guarantee, but there are five other guns around this table. Life is cheap here, and that was confirmed today when you used your own people as decoys."

Judah remained unflustered.

"Easy, Mr. Benning; let's not get carried away. We do not believe any life as expendable. After those boys volunteered, they were briefed on every eventuality of the mission before accepting it. Their expertise made them excellent candidates, and they knew it. They are trained to the nth degree and were anxious to put that training into practice."

Tom's assessment was somewhat different. "You could have sent in an unmanned, remote-controlled decoy which would have been equally effective and without risk."

"Well, Mr. Benning," Isaak Burman's interruption was intended to redirect the conversation. "Contrary to your belief, you will be free to leave. I will also guarantee it."

Menno Rozman, who had said nothing so far, became the third to guarantee his safety but not without taking a pot shot at Tom.

"I tell you what Benning, I agree with Isaak, you are paranoid. You see too many traitors and too many guns pointing in your direction."

Tom pushed back his chair and stood almost in one motion. His fists were clenched and his good intentions short-lived.

"Okay Rozman, I tell you what, you obviously don't know your ass from your elbow. We were all here when I exposed David Haber."

Rozman protested. "I resent that, and I demand an apology!"

Tom scoffed. "Hey man, demand all you like, you won't get it from me. Only an asshole would make a stupid statement like you just did. I've had more attempts on my life, than probably all of you together."

The meeting had deteriorated to a level not only beyond unproductive but potentially damaging to all concerned.

Judah had to put an end to these escalating hostilities once
and for all.

"Gentlemen, gentlemen, please! Fighting amongst ourselves resolves nothing. We need to move on without rancor."

Tom held the floor and summarized. "Judah knew about
the GPS, so there is a strong possibility Josef Panetti did too.
A logical conclusion would be this information was fed to
your enemies by him or David Haber. This would account
for the fact that the Palestinians could zone in on the signal
and target the yacht." Burman was the first to speak.

"Well, it is most concerning, Mr. Benning but on a positive side, we have reason to believe their equipment isn't as
good as they think it is. They went for the stronger signal on
the decoy, without analyzing it."

Tom continued. "What about the next time? They obviously suspected that I was at sea and will be looking for
their next shot."

He was assured this had already been taken into account.
The yacht would be back out at sea by tomorrow and would
stay there as a permanent part of the landscape. Inexplicably,
Tom's humor resurfaced. "You mean seascape, don't you?"

His attempt at humor fell flat. "Okay … seascape. A
fishing trawler will take you to and from the yacht. Don't
concern yourself with any of the details; we have thought this
through very carefully."

Tom knew what he was about to say would disappoint
them. "I am not in the least bit sorry about having little or
no faith in your intelligence; it is my life on the line. If the
truth be known, I actually see you all as a bunch of ruthless

killers who know the score. You deal with this crap all the time. It makes you feel alive, important and invulnerable." As abruptly as he had taken the floor, he sat back in his chair.

"Well, I think you have made yourself perfectly clear, Mr. Benning. In the meantime, we will continue as planned. I hope you will ignore the condition of the yacht. Quite frankly, it looks like someone used it for target practice."

His sarcasm didn't miss its mark, but neither did Tom's. "I will pay for the damages as soon as I get back to Canada."

They still had a lot of ground to cover, and it wasn't going to happen unless there was unanimous approval to avoid further outbursts. There was a momentary silence and Judah proceeded.

"Help us sort out this mess, Mr. Benning."

Tom agreed to do the best he could. "It is, after all, my reason for being here and I am as anxious as anyone to live in peace."

Someone muttered "nobody lives in peace anymore," which Tom politely refuted.

"We do, in Canada. Now bear with me and let me tell my story without interruptions. It is long and will take time, too much of which has already been wasted."

He began.

"I met Chaim Solomon while I was bumming around Mobile looking for computer parts; something I regularly did because I was trying to build a machine on a shoestring. I heard about a computer junk shop and set out to find it. When I did, I coincidentally found an old man rummaging around in a bin of sale items. It just so happened that we reached for the same item at exactly the same time. The old man looked like he didn't have two cents to rub together, so I backed off. That is how I met Chaim Solomon, a man I very soon realized, I had completely misread.

As it turned out, he lived in a big old house, while I lived in an old motel cabin paid for by me doing repair and maintenance work.

To make a very long story short, Chaim asked me to move in with him. I did, and we enjoyed a five-year friendship. I am proud to say his trust in me was such that he eventually told me about his career in Mossad. He liked that I showed an interest in his life and took delight in training me in self-defense and hand-to-hand combat. I found him extremely intelligent and astute for a man his age, and it astounded me that Mossad could let him go. His technical knowledge alone was far greater than the average individual, and now I discover, more advanced than anyone of you could have imagined.

When Chaim knew that he was dying, he took me further into his confidence. There were documents relating to a planned invasion, the six-day war, and ultimate deportation of every Palestinian. There was a pre-requisite however; this couldn't be done without more land to accommodate the required camps. The Sinai Peninsula was deemed the optimum solution. Chaim Solomon vehemently opposed this operation, and when there was no chance of any resolution to his dissent, he was retired by Mossad."

Judah corrected his last statement. "But, this is not news,

Mr. Benning and just about everything he told you is inaccurate. Besides, there is no such proof."

Tom was adamant that proof did exist. It consisted of documents, maps, names, and budget costs. Chaim had assured him that the information contained in the documents was damaging enough that Israel would have to cede all occupied territory. The hush in the room was so noticeable it seemed like everyone had stopped breathing. Again only Judah spoke. "Have you seen this evidence?"

Tom confirmed that he had seen some of the hard copies before Chaim burned them. Everything was now digitally stored in various locations around the world.

Tom continued to list two of the most relevant and diverse studies undertaken by Chaim. Not only did he become an expert hacker but most astute in international finance. He needed money to activate his plans, so he figured out how to access it. By hacking into bank computers, he could transfer funds whenever he needed them. He justified his actions by saying it came from Swiss banks and to quote him: "Those bastard Swiss bankers know that it is Jewish money and won't return it so, I take it."

It was time for a break. Judah stood, went to the door and signaled the refreshments could be served. Tom was tired, and it showed. Everyone took advantage of this time to get up, stretch and answer nature's call. The session was proving to be more intense and draining than anyone could have imagined. Judah took Tom aside.

"Do you know how to get at these programs?" Tom shook his head.

About twenty minutes later, they were back at it. Tom had to admit that the break had been a good idea and that although he was tired he felt refreshed enough to continue.

The device under his skin had been inserted by Chaim. The surgery had been done in his kitchen but only after Tom had downed a half bottle of rye whiskey and a local anesthetic had been administered. It took a while to get it regulated because it needed to be programmed exclusively to Tom. Perfectionist that Chaim was, he tested everything more than once before closing the incision. Tom confessed it hurt for a few weeks, but now he was hardly aware of its existence.

Judah wanted to know why he had allowed Chaim to do this to him and what was his ultimate goal.

The first reason was that Chaim was a good friend who rarely if ever, asked him for anything. Another was Tom didn't have any plans or family so, no obligations and it didn't hurt that he was angry with the world. Last but most importantly, he would receive enough money enabling him never to have to work again. Chaim's cash offer was a hell of an incentive. He reminded everyone that he had been a poor man then and all he had to do was look after the little gizmo.

He went on to say Chaim's goal was peace. It was his consensus this could never happen as long as the children of Israel were taught hatred. He wanted to establish totally integrated schools with Jewish and Palestinian children sitting side by side, learning to embrace their similarities and differences in a constructive, nurturing way. He believed that equal involvement of both communities was mandatory to ensure any degree of success. Chaim took the money from those Swiss bankers for the sole purpose of giving it back to the children of Israel. Tom's role was to wait to be contacted by a banker and to release the funds bit by bit. They were to be used to build integrated schools.

He seemed to have satisfied the curiosity about Chaim until "what was your relationship with Chaim?" was asked.

Tom smiled. "Does it matter? I can see your twisted mind is wondering if our relationship was homosexual."

Josef Melo hadn't expected such a redress. He picked up a pencil and started drumming on the table and when he caught everyone looking at him, stopped.

The questions kept coming. Tom was asked why he had traveled to Holland before arriving in Israel.

He started off by saying that he didn't believe it was anyone's business, but in an attempt to keep things cordial, he was prepared to explain that trip.

His uncle's death and his responsibility to settle the estate made this trip necessary, and he was only away a week.

"What purpose did the hijacking serve?"

Tom shrugged and countered with questions of his own.

"Could it have been one of your own operations? Did David Haber have anything to do with it?" His questions, it appeared, were ignored which didn't surprise him in the least. These people were good at asking, not answering.

He knew the session wasn't finished, but he took advantage of the lull in conversation to say he was exhausted and quite sure the others were tired as well. He sighed with relief when everyone agreed it would be a good idea to call it a day.

He pushed his chair back and was about to leave when Judah asked him to wait. He sat back down and watched everyone else leave the room.

After a few surprises, Judah did just that when he handed him a gun.

"I know that you are responsible. I think it might be wise for you to have this. There may be the odd time when Ahuva isn't with you, and that could be just the time you might need one. Please don't get it wet; saltwater does such ugly things to a fine weapon."

He winked and smiled one of his real smiles which showed he approved their relationship.

"You think it is necessary? I mean really, Judah, you want me to *shlep* an Uzi?"

Judah nodded. "Yes and a colt in your jacket."

Tom accepted the guns.


They had lived in the bungalow for almost four months. The surroundings were barren and inhospitable but Tom liked it, and that was reason enough for Ahuva to set aside her preference, for city living.

She stood on the veranda, phone in hand and scanned the road as she did when he was due to arrive. A dust cloud confirmed his car was near. Its trail obscured everything including the security vehicle following him. Invisible as it was, she felt easier knowing it was there.

He had changed; he was happier now. In spite of this, his daily trips to headquarters concerned her. It was then he was most vulnerable. To add to her apprehension, Judah had finally given in to Tom's badgering to drive himself if he accepted extra security.

One evening after listening, yet again, to the same harangue about the ineptitude of the lab techs, she asked a simple question. "Why not see if you could work alongside them?" The die was cast. He waged a campaign to make it happen.

His single-mindedness immediately caused problems. The staff did not appreciate his interference, perceived or not, and complained about him to the department head regularly. He, in turn, became increasingly intolerant of their unwillingness to follow his lead. But all things considered, he admitted it was still better than twiddling his thumbs at home.

Tom's car skidded to a halt at the end of the driveway. The soldiers in the car behind him waved their berets, turned around and headed back to the city.

"You forgot your guns again!" she called out.

It had taken him a while to get used to carrying them, but now it was second nature. He opened the car door, took the guns from the seat, put the Colt in his holster and casually slung the Uzi strap over his shoulder. He smiled at her coming down the steps to meet him. He waited halfway down the path for her to eagerly put her arms around his neck and kiss him with a tenderness that was impossible to describe. It never failed to take his breath away. As was his custom, he savored the moment and said. "I don't envy those guys eating my dust. I sometimes wonder how they can even see where they are going."

As part of her welcome, she always asked him about his

day, and he usually answered with a perfunctory okay. This time, however, he said okay but added, "I have a secretary now, a blond, blue-eyed beauty. Judah picked her out for me because he thinks we make a good pair."

He enjoyed teasing her as much as she did him. They walked toward the house, and she made some vague comment about the weather before asking if they had to leave the following week again. He nodded. "Oh, *Tsatske* … if it wasn't for you. I would just as soon stay home; where to this time?" He said he didn't know.

"I guess I shouldn't complain, but I'm getting kind of tired going to the same place all the time. I know we haven't had any problems, but surely there must be somewhere else that is just as safe as the sea."

"Yeah I know," he sighed wiping the perspiration from his forehead. "They never tell me anything beforehand. The only certainty is that we will be on the move. To be honest, the sea doesn't hold the same attraction for me anymore either. I'll never forget how mad the owner of the yacht was after I shot the hell out of that railing. From what I hear, it still hasn't been fixed. It might be fun to get that boat back, but I don't think Judah will agree. He keeps swapping them around for security reasons. Which reminds me, I'll have to tell him I didn't like that last one at all, it stank of fucking fish."

Her effort to stop his use of profanities, as she called them, didn't seem to be making much headway. "You have to stop that bad habit, *Tsatske*."

He knew exactly what she was getting at but asked which

one she meant. She had uncovered so many since they had been together, he was having a hard time keeping track.

"That's not true," she said. "I just want you to stop saying fuck before the baby is born." He gave in gracefully. "'Kay, I promise."

He no sooner had the words out of his mouth when she also reminded him that he had a very bad habit of farting in the house and worse still, in bed. He took the line of least resistance because he couldn't deny her accusation. "See there's another thing you want to change. Tell me, do you expect me to head for the door every time pressure builds?" She said no, but she did expect him to go into the bathroom.

"I can't help it if one pops out when I'm sleeping."

Now they were both laughing, but she managed to forewarn him. "If another one pops out, you will wake up very fast because you will be on the floor."

They walked arm in arm up the steps. She brushed his hair back with her hand and stroked his beard. "I like it tsatske, but don't let it grow too long."

She continued into the house to get him a beer and called out from the kitchen. "So, Judah didn't even give you a hint about where we are going this time?"

"Nope, but I've got a funny feeling he may finally give in and let me go where I want. I decoded another message today so that might be my reward." She was curious and asked him where he wanted to go.

"Cairo, God knows I've asked him often enough. I even offered to pay my own expenses and this time, he didn't say no ... so maybe."

She came back out and put the cold beer on the table beside him. "Does that mean that you finally got your inheritance out of Holland?"

He told her that some of the funds were deposited in Vancouver a while ago; in fact, before them settling into the bungalow. More recently, he had instructed the notary to transfer some of the money still in Holland, to Tel Aviv. He had given strict instructions regarding the confidentiality of this transaction and had entrusted him to select the highest security process available.

Ahuva was a little hurt but mostly annoyed that he hadn't bothered to tell her anything about these arrangements until she stopped to realize it really wasn't any of her business and let the matter drop.

She instinctively put her hand on her belly. He had moved for the first time yesterday. It had taken her a few minutes to realize exactly what had happened. The squiggle was unlike anything she had ever felt before, but it was a happy experience, and she would always cherish its memory.

Tom was anxious to know what the doctor had said that morning, and she happily told him the baby was fine. "Did he tell you whether it is a boy or a girl?" A rhetorical question at best. She had already made it clear the surprise of it all would be magical.

She nestled up beside him and told him she had gone shopping after her doctor's appointment to buy some maternity wear. He leaned over and offered her a sip of his beer, but she shook her head and got up. "It's not good for the baby."

He still had both guns with him so she asked which one he wanted to keep and she would put the other inside. Because he balked at constantly having guns around, she made the decision and said she would leave the colt. He knew it was futile to argue, but at times he couldn't help himself.

Defeated, he stood to let her take the holster from his shoulder and grumbled. "You're even more paranoid than Judah. I can see all the way to the bottom of the hill from here. No one has ever, nor could they ever come up here without being spotted. This is not like the West Bank."

He looked into the distance. The heat was rising from the dirt road and the desert that surrounded the property.

Ahuva came back out onto the veranda.

"You like it?" she asked with a smile and some hesitancy. She was wearing a dress much too big for her. It fit her like a potato sack. "It looks great," he lied.

Ahuva had tried to discourage his belief that sooner rather later they would have to stop making love until the baby was born. She assured him that her doctor had said there was no need to stop. It was healthier not to abstain as long she was comfortable. Tom remained unconvinced, and her maternity wear was a stark reminder that time would come.

"Let's just sit for a while. This is the nicest time of the day." He kissed her forehead, and she thought she heard him mumble something about one good surprise deserving another. She looked puzzled until he reached into his back pocket, pulled out an envelope and gave it to her. How she knew what it was, he'll never know, but she was ecstatic.

"Oh … *Tsatske*, you bought the house. You didn't have to do this. I know you don't like Israel."

"Yes, everything you say is true, but I thought it was about time to put down roots. Besides, I didn't like paying all that rent to that miserly Arab."

They laughed, and he pulled her closer. "I love you, now let's go in and have dessert first, shall we?"

No sooner had she gone into the house when

Tom called out. "Wait … wait, Ahuva … SHIT! I see Judah's clunker coming. He sure picked a hell of a time to visit."

He parked his car, got out and put his hat

on the roof which is what he usually did before wiping his forehead and face with his handkerchief.

"It sure has been a hot one today!" he yelled towards the veranda. "Glad to see it is cooling down. We might even get some rain tonight!"

Tom invited him into the shade of the veranda and as he approached could see Judah was excited about something.

"News, I have some good news!"

Ahuva looked at him and smiled, "not as good as I got when Tom came home!"

He'd reached the bottom step and looked up at Ahuva's glowing face. "Well I won't rain on your parade, you better go first."

She told him that Tom had bought the house and showed him the deed.

"Well," he said "in that case, my surprise will complement yours, Tom. "It looks like we have the relay transmitter installed at our embassy in Ottawa. If we've got it right, the program will falsely indicate you are in Canada which means you can stop moving around and stay put."

Ahuva was over the moon and said so. She excused herself and went into the house to get Judah a beer.

"It's risky testing the project. The satellite will send a signal to you, and we will tap into it as we have done before. The difference being, this time when we tap in and let GPS follow its normal pattern, we will deflect a copy. The relay transmitter in Ottawa will then send it back to the satellite. It will generate a second signal with the copy arriving a fraction later.

Now, this doesn't change the fact that you will still have to leave, in case we are wrong."

"This is good news, Judah! It looks like I will finally get to Cairo after all."

Much to Tom's disappointment, Judah apologized saying this was only the first breakthrough. The process had to be tested.

Tom shouted at Judah and asked him how he expected him to tell Ahuva there would be no Cairo trip. The commotion brought her to the door.

"You two aren't fighting again, are you?"

Judah grabbed his hat and ran down the stairs yelling, "goodbye you lovebirds." His escape was quick.

"What did you fight about?" Tom hung his head.

"Well, that *shmuck* just told me that we can't go to Cairo next week."

She put her arm around him. "Oh come on, *Tsatske*,

everything will be okay. I turned down the bed, and the air-conditioner is on. Here, have a sip of your beer and come in. It's an attitude adjustment time."

He got up, kissed her and told her he would have bolted long ago if it hadn't been for her. She kept him sane. Without missing a beat, she reminded him he had also told her she saved him from going blind and that now was as good a time as any for an explanation.

He laughed with abandon. "Well … eh … it's a long story."

"Oh come on," she encouraged "we have all night."

They settled into bed. "Okay, but I'm going to make it short and sweet. Once upon a time, my father caught me playing with my wee-wee. He spanked me until my little butt was glowing and the next day, marched me off to confession. The priest told me that masturbation was a sin and as if that weren't bad enough, he averred it caused some boys to stutter and some to go blind. Shit, until then I didn't even know what masturbation was. I just played with it."

Ahuva wanted to know if he had believed the priest and if he had continued to play with it. Tom answered yes to both questions. "Weren't you scared to go blind?" she teased. It was impossible to contain himself any longer, and he just roared while barely managing to stutter: "N----n-n-n-o, I-I-I-juuuust li-li-li-li----ke t-t-t-to t-t-t-tell the st-st-st-story."

They both collapsed into the kind of laughter that is so contagious it takes a long time to ebb.

"You are so bad," she said, "but so funny."

Eventually, she became more severe and was curious to

know if Tom hated his father. He said he didn't. If anything, he pitied him because he had forgotten what it was like to be a boy

Her next question was more poignant. "Did you love him?"

Tom thought about it and said he certainly feared him, but he had been raised under the "love thy father, regardless" rule which left him no option.

# 20

The relay transmitter in Canada was working, so the bi-weekly trips were no longer necessary. The lab technicians saw this as the opportunity they had been waiting for. They were chomping at the bit to get their hands on Tom's GPS, but their eagerness was tempered by Judah's caution. Chaim's programs were the next priority. The school funding transfers were running smoothly. The fact that Tom didn't know whether the money was actually being used as Chaim had stipulated didn't seem to concern him. The sums being released were minimal. The majority was to be held in trust until peace was established.

The first school was slated for Gaza. The building had been on schedule until the site was vandalized and the materials stolen before the walls were high enough to install the rafters. This resulted in all future projects immediately being put on hold, and all construction halted until the threat of looting was resolved.

His efforts were concentrated on the search to help find

the computers that held the files they so desperately needed. Chaim had promised him he would know when the job was complete, but he wasn't prepared to wait for it to run its course. He wanted this episode of his life over, sooner rather than later.

Weekly tests concluded transmissions were still being received. When this stopped, only then could the gadget safely be removed from his chest. The apparent lack of success was frustrating, but Tom had come up with a theory that he believed could escalate their progress and there was only one person, he was prepared to share it with.

It had been some time since he had seen Judah. He decided to take a break and head to his office. Judah was dozing in his chair but the instant he heard someone at his door, grabbed a book. He was pleasantly surprised to see Tom and signaled for him to make himself comfortable. It was interesting how their relationship had gone from bitter adversaries to respectful friends.

"Well, to what do I owe this pleasure?" Tom wasted no time and told him he had a theory about Chaim's programs and needed to bounce it off, someone. Judah was instantly wide awake. "I'm always interested in new ideas. So far, we've hit nothing but brick walls. Let's hear it."

Tom suggested they return to the lab and share the information with the staff. Judah disagreed. He wanted to hear the theory first.

"Like I said, it's only a theory, but I believe it's worth investigating. I have watched the lab technicians. They, like most people, tend to look for the most complicated way to solve a puzzle. Chaim was an exception. His genius was his unconventional way of thinking. It would never have occurred to him to resort to complicated programming. My theory is that he hid it in plain sight.

I think the computer is here, in Tel Aviv, right under our noses. Who, other than Chaim, knew your equipment and people better?"

Tom continued, and Judah listened intently. He was a sponge absorbing every word. His eyes scanned Tom's face as if he were reading a map. When Tom was finished, he leaned back to see what, if anything, would be Judah's reaction.

First, there was silence then Judah whooped. "Wow! You know something, my friend … you could be right! Well, well, well … this puts a whole new twist on things. A revelation like this could cause a lot of turmoil." He paused and then in a conspiratorial whisper asked. "You haven't mentioned this to anyone else have you?" Tom shook his head. "No … not anyone that matters."

"Who, my boy?" He asked with obvious disappointment. "To whom would you go with something this important?"

"Danny."

"Danny Yatom?"

"Yeah."

"When did you talk to Danny?"

"Yesterday, we had lunch at the hotel."

"Ha, haaaa … you *smuck*. You're not as good at lying as I am, Danny is out of town … Seriously?"

"Naah, you're the only one."

"Then, I have a favor to ask." He began to smile and quite

simply without shame, asked Tom to let him take full credit for his idea.

Tom was well aware that Judah was close to being forced into retirement and when that happened, he wanted to go out with a bang. In the meantime, such innovative problem-solving could delay the inevitable. He gladly accepted the role of a co-conspirator. Judah was jubilant.

"Do you mind waiting here, Thomas?" He sat back down to await Judah's return. He had combed his hair, taken a few deep breaths and gone downstairs. He was surprisingly calm and composed. Tom knew that he was going to give the performance of his life.

When he entered the lab a hush fell over the room. He'd planned to show more restraint but was so energized that he walked straight over to the chief programmer and grabbed his writing pad. He tore off a page covered with programming notes, scribbled down the date of the computer upgrade and demanded to see every old drive that had removed from the machines after the date specified on the pad.

"But sir," the programmer gloated, "I thought you knew they had been destroyed."

Judah couldn't have asked for a better reaction if he had tried. It gave him the opportunity to rant, and it felt good. He demanded to know when they had been destroyed, who had ordered the action and why. His questions were answered, and he proceeded to methodically belittle the decision, the work and the person responsible. The fact that the order had been issued by Burman was icing on the cake. "What a fool! You mean to tell me he never even considered the possibility they would be needed? That shows how short-sighted he is because it just so happens, I need them to verify if there are any discrepancies between the old and the new drives."

His tirade got the results he wanted. He was told there were no discrepancies. The entire content of every drive had been copied to the new system and checked. Then, any redundant files were removed as well as bits and pieces left over from deleted programs, put on floppies and stored in the vault."

Judah was enjoying himself immensely. "I want copies of those floppies."

The technician protested. To get what he wanted would be very time-consuming. Judah dismissed his objection and told him to do it anyway.

"I'll sign for them, and you damn well keep it in the logs as signed out by me personally."

Tom saw the sparkle in Judah's eyes the minute he came through the door. It hadn't been there when he left, but it was definitely there now. "So, what happened?" Judah told him he had ordered everything copied to disks and sent to him without delay. Tom was less than enchanted when he realized Judah wanted him to scan it and get back to him with anything he found. They both knew that there was probably nothing worthwhile on those disks, but he did put up a good show. Tom protested he was not a programmer and voiced his concern about the possibility of material being discovered on his machine which could lead to accusations of espionage. These were summarily dismissed by Judah.

The next day Tom went back to see Judah. He wasn't

sleeping this time. His eyes were glued to the monitor, and he was shaking his head mumbling to himself. He had been expecting Tom so had left his door ajar. He looked up and smiled. "You have something for me, Thomas?" He signaled for him to close the door. "There's no need to let them know what we are up to until the time is right."

"Come here, come here and see this," he pointed to the screen. "There is a repetition factor throughout this document, like this one ELPMET and YREVA. I have tried to decipher it, but it doesn't appear to be any sort of computer language."

Tom found this amusing but most of all very relevant and asked Judah if he remembered how Chaim behaved after a couple of glasses of wine. He said he did; sometimes he would sing but more often than not, he fell asleep.

Tom probed further. "And, just before he fell asleep?"

Judah's mouth dropped open. "Jesus Christ, Thomas! Backward, backward, the *shlemiel* used to talk backward. So elpmet must mean temple and Yreva must be Avery, your middle name. My God, Thomas, it is so simple. It's all beginning to make sense." Tom laughed and took a jab at Judah.

"Yeah, *schlemiel* or not he was smart enough to keep you in the dark."

Judah wondered if the whole program could be made up of reverse language. Tom strongly doubted it. He suspected Chaim wanted to bait them with a few words here and there with the actual program written differently, but he felt confident they were on the right track. Chaim had succeeded in proving their vulnerability to hacking.

Judah was still licking his lips, already savoring the moment of truth, yet to come. "Well, well, well, I surely have a surprise for that asshole, Burman. He will have to be a bit more respectful of old Judah after this." He so wanted his moment, he needed reassurance.

"You haven't tipped them off, have you?"

Tom pretended not to understand the question. "Who?"

Judah rose and rested his hand on Tom's shoulder. "You're a *smuck*, you know that? But there is one thing for sure, Thomas Benning, I owe you a lot." He dropped his hand and went back to his desk.

"I'd better get busy. I have to write my presentation. How's this for starters?

> *I have asked you here today to present a discovery; identify the diligence and ingenuity it took to achieve and last but not least, to substantiate the adage that with age comes knowledge and wisdom."*

As quickly as he had started he stopped. "Enough bullshit for one day! Go call Ahuva and tell her you're on your way home."

# 21

Ahuva stood in front of the mirror. "Do you think I still look sexy, *Tsatske?*"

He had been watching her, waiting for the inevitable question. The further along she got in her pregnancy, the more reassurance she seemed to want or perhaps, need. He hadn't quite figured that out, but he always tried to make sure she felt good about herself. It wasn't difficult because he found her irresistible. She had that glow only pregnant women possess; a glow that enhances a woman's sexiness. He reminded her how many times they still made love and he was happy to admit that she had been right. She was only days away from giving birth and still a more than willing participant in their lovemaking.

He asked her if she remembered the day she had gone shopping for her maternity clothes. She nodded and said she also remembered that they were way too big and now when she looked at herself, they were almost too small.

"The clothes you bought months ago are now beautiful."

No matter what he said, she was in a funk and not ready to come out of it. "I look like a tank."

He contradicted her. He said he couldn't help how she felt about herself, but to him, she was stunningly beautiful.

"But I don't look sexy," she pouted.

"I am so proud to walk downtown holding your hand, but I have noticed that you seem to want to hide. How many times do I have to tell you that you are glamorous?"

Her eyes welled up, and she stretched her arms out to him.

"Come here and just hold me, I need to feel you. I need to know that you love me even this way."

He went to her willingly and smiled down at her. "You sexy, little vixen."

They both laughed.

"I can't wait for this baby to be born as a matter of fact, right now would be perfect! I have had enough of this; I want to be un-pregnant again."

Tom was a little taken aback by her bluntness. She had never complained during her pregnancy.

"Oh … you'll feel better once the baby is born" he told her. She held him as close as she physically could and thanked him for being so tolerant and declared her love over and over again. "Can we go to bed for a while; just to have your skin against mine?" She was over her pout and led him into the bedroom as he protested. "It's the middle of the day. You really are a vixen."

She felt so secure. She had heard of so many women being left to raise their children alone. She knew this would never happen to her. She touched his face.

"I still like your beard, *Tsatske*." At one point, he had thought about shaving it off, but she convinced him not to.

Ahuva had been very open about her concerns, wishes, and plans throughout her pregnancy. Tom, on the other hand, had not.

For one thing, he had wondered how to broach the subject of circumcision if they had a boy. The baby was due any day and his need to discuss it was more urgent than ever.

"What will we do if it is a boy?" The question caught Ahuva entirely off guard. She had no idea what he was talking about and said so.

He told her he had been thinking a great deal about circumcision and had decided he was against it. It didn't seem fair to him to inflict such pain on an innocent, little baby. She agreed the procedure was painful but argued in its favor. That pain would be far less than the pain he would suffer if he were not circumcised. Her justification was that he would be different from other Jewish boys and would be subjected to teasing and ridicule.

Her remarks intensified she wanted to raise their child in the Jewish faith, which surprised him. Until now, she had been an avowed non-believer in organized religion. When he questioned this new position, she said she simply wanted the child to have a base. It was all so logical. He wanted to kick himself for waiting so long to have this conversation. He should have known Ahuva would have thought everything through. He felt relieved and leaned over to rub her back.

"Have no fear," she purred. "I am as Jewish as this child

will ever be but I would like him or her to wear the Star of David and … um, a *mezuzah* at the door would be nice."

He agreed but with one condition; "as long as you don't put it near the bedroom door."

"What does the bedroom door have to do with it?"

He explained. He didn't want to miss out on any of her kisses, and if the *mezuzah* were outside their bedroom door, she would have to kiss it every time she went into the room.

"You are lucky that I know when you're kidding and when you aren't. Otherwise I would smack you."

They lay quietly for a while, enjoying the tranquility that surrounded them until she broke the silence.

"You know what would make me very happy, *tsatske?*"

He said he thought he had already made her happy. He had stopped saying fuck, hadn't he? She giggled, said she had noticed and really appreciated his effort to reform but asked if he could be serious for a moment.

Ahuva reached under her pillow and opened her hand. She was holding the Star of David on a chain. "Would you wear this?" There was no answer necessary. He raised himself up on one elbow so she could place it around his neck. She saw him close his eyes for a moment. When he opened them again, he looked at her, took her in his arms and whispered; "only to please you." Her tears were ones of joy

Later that afternoon Ahuva asked him when he planned to have the GPS removed now that it was safe to do so. He told her not until after the baby was born. He didn't want to be in the hospital with some unexpected complication while she was giving birth. He promised he would talk to Moishe Cohen after the baby was born.

"You think that there could be a problem?" she asked apprehensively.

He said he really didn't think so, but he wanted to play it safe. Ahuva didn't question him any further on that subject. Her surprise at how easily he had accepted to wear the Star of David, however, got the better of her. His explanation was simple. "Think about it," he said in mock horror. "Men will be envious of me when they see how beautiful my wife and baby are. They will say that it is wasted on a *shaygetz*." He paused for effect and then pointed to his neck. Perhaps it was a good thing she had given him the Star of David, it could be his saving grace. She smacked him playfully, as she had so often threatened to do and doubled over.

"Oh my God!!" was all she said. At first, Tom thought she was teasing, but it became clear she wasn't. "oooh … oooh … OH F..U..C..K, if this isn't a contraction, I don't know what is!"

# 22

"What brings you out to our hacienda at this time of the day? Ahuva went to the market earlier this morning, and as you can see, I'm babysitting. She must be having a good time because she is later than she thought she would be. She probably ran into a friend or came across a great sale and has lost track of time."

# 23

Judah didn't smile nor did he go to the playpen to kiss the baby. He literally dropped down in a chair. There was sadness in his face, the likes of which Tom had never seen before.

"You look like the devil, man. What's happened? I know I haven't seen you for a while but don't tell me they have found an unexpected problem."

Judah was shaken, but it had nothing to do with anything Tom referred to. He had devastating news, and after much soul searching, he decided there was no other way to handle it but to tell Tom and hope for the best.

"No my friend, I wish that it were that simple ... I'm sorry to be the one to bring you this news, but then again, I am the only one who can. This morning, a suicide bomber blew himself up in the middle of some people in the market. Ahuva was standing next to him. She and four others were killed."

I took a moment for it to sink in and then he grabbed the

veranda post and stared at Judah in total disbelief. He was ashen and motionless until he slowly slid down against the post, his face contorted in agony. He closed his eyes and told himself it was a mistake; a nightmare that would end once he opened his eyes. His anguish was excruciating to watch.

Judah didn't want to be there, but he had no choice. He stood by while Tom cursed the God that she believed in, the God she praised for giving her a son. He pounded his fists on the cement floor until they bled. The tower of strength, the man he had so often admired, envied and considered indestructible, wept like a child.

This wasn't the first time Judah had carried out this duty, and it probably wouldn't be the last, but he never got used to it. It left him feeling so helpless. All he could do was be there.

Tom finally stood up. He held onto the post for support, and he spoke to no one in particular. He said it was their wish to go at the same time. Neither he nor Ahuva wanted to have to experience what he was going through. Tom turned to Judah and asked him to take their son.

Judah knew exactly why. He told Tom that although he would do most things for him, helping to make the little one an orphan was not one of them.

Their pact had been made before he was born, in fact before they ever considered the possibility of a child, rendering it no longer viable. In an effort to shock Tom back to reality, he reminded him of his obligation to Ahuva. She would never have wanted anyone but Tom to raise Benjamin. To reinforce his argument, Judah asked a redundant question. "In the event, you should decide to carry out your plan, would you want Benjamin to be raised by his grandparents?" He was partially successful. Tom was adamant that this should never happen. If he decided to die, the boy should be taken to the kibbutz where Ahuva grew up. She was happy there.

Judah explained that Ahuva's parents had already been told of her death and if Tom were to leave, they could claim his son and would do so without hesitation. They had never made a secret that they always wanted a boy. If they were awarded custody that would effectively negate him going to the kibbutz.

Tom was inconsolable. He kept repeating that it would be better to be dead than to live without Ahuva. Judah told him reason had to prevail. "A promise made in the heat of passion is hardly reason enough to abandon your son. His conception changed the rules."

Tom wept silently and asked barely above a whisper. "What will I do now?"

Judah put his hand on Tom's arm and told him the funeral had to be the next day. He would make the arrangements. He looked directly at Tom and assured him he was not alone. "We will sit *shiva* here."

Tom straightened and said that he wanted to see her body, but Judah dissuaded him.

"There is nothing there. Two of the other victims haven't even been identified."

Tom wasn't easily convinced and pursued the hope that it was a horrible mistake; that it wasn't Ahuva after all. He questioned how they could be so sure. Judah simply handed him her mezuzah.

"We found her purse and she was wearing this. As you already know, both your names are engraved on it. I am so sorry to say there isn't anything else. Her remains have been placed in a closed casket."

Tom leaned up against the wall and moaned. "God, I gave this to her when Benjamin was born."

A short while later, he looked at Judah and said he respected the fact that she had to be buried the next day, but he wouldn't sit *shivah*. Judah told him there was no need.

"Mourn her in your own way. Take Benjamin, go on a trip. In two weeks everything will be finished, and you can return if you want." Tom just nodded, and the two men sat in silence for the longest time.

Their mourning was cut short when a car pulled up to the house. At first, Tom didn't recognize it nor did he care who its occupants were until they stood at the foot of the stairs. He instantly went from distress to extreme anger and shouted at them.

"Go away, you are not welcome here! You will not sit *shivah* in her house, and you will not cry tears over her coffin! She was a child of Israel, your child and yet you called her a whore! I don't know if God exists, but if he does, I hope that he curses you as I do. You will never hold her son who, when he is old enough, will know what you did to her. I look at you, and I see evil. Go away, get out of here and don't ever come back."

The old man was undeterred and pointed his finger at Tom. He yelled there were laws and courts that would give them the boy because they were citizens and he was not.

Tom stood his ground.

"I make you this promise before that happens, I will go to where you live, and I will slit your throats. You will never have him as long as I am alive."

Tom told them honestly that until they had arrived, he felt absolute despair. Then, with all the sarcasm he could muster, he thanked them profusely for helping him find the answer to his quandary; to see the most important reason of all for him to go on. He needed to make sure that they never had anything to do with their grandson. He told them they would never have even the slightest opportunity to diminish Ahuva in Benjamin's eyes. More importantly, Benjamin would hear how his mother had lived and died for her country.

"We have the right to mourn our child," they lamented, but Tom was unmercifully gruff.

"You had no child! Now, FUCK OFF!"

Judah who had stood beside his friend, wordlessly offering moral support. When they had gone Chaim said, "you were hard on them, Tom."

Tom was unrepentant. "Not more than a few minutes ago, I found out that my wife is dead. What the fuck do you think I should have said? They swooped in like a couple buzzards to pick over what was left."

They watched the old couple walk away arm in arm and Tom summarized their idea of parental love to Judah.

"The only thing they did was give birth to Ahuva. When times were hard, they sent her to a *kibbutz*. When she returned home after her military service, they no longer treated her as their child. They didn't approve of her clothes or her work in Mossad. They called her a whore. A child is always a child, and a parent's love should always be unconditional."

He said he knew them to be cowards and he was convinced his warning would be enough for them to leave Benjamin and him alone. The fact that they had sent Ahuva away was proof positive they didn't want her around.

"I know, and I am sorry I didn't have a chance to spare you that confrontation. I should have expected it, but you don't have to worry, I will make sure that they don't bother you again."

Tom broke down and sobbed. "Jesus Christ, Judah! What the hell am I going to do without her?"

Judah knew it would take a long time for Tom to get over his sorrow, but he had no doubt it would happen. "You are strong, and you will get through this. Actually, if you think about it, you have no choice. You must raise your son."

Tom was still grappling with the reality of it all. He rambled something about revenge against the bastard who was responsible for his sadness, but Judah cut him off. "Nothing will bring Ahuva back." As an afterthought, he asked. "Would you like me to send over the rabbi who married you? He is certainly more adept at offering solace and advice than I?"

Tom slowly shook his head. He was exhausted and needed to be alone. Judah had to make the arrangements, but before he left, he told Tom he would be back later to take him to a hotel.

"No … thank you. I've changed my mind. I'm staying.

I will honor her my way, and although I don't know about this *shivah* stuff, I believe the right thing for me to do is be here."

Judah nodded his agreement and did something he had never done before. He embraced Tom. Then he kissed the baby and left.

Tom looked around. Nothing seemed to have changed but little by little he began to realize the immensity of it all. The thought of never seeing her again was unfathomable. He picked up his son and made a silent vow that he would always love him enough for both of them. First, they would mourn her and then they would honor her by making her proud of them.

Tom stayed home throughout the entire grieving process. When it was over, he sat for hours on the veranda. There were still times he half expected her to come out of the house to sit beside him. If a car came down the road, he still hoped it was her, and it could take him a moment or two to realize it wasn't her. She was never coming back.

There was an ironic parallel that often came to his mind. He'd married twice. Both women were from dysfunctional families where love was not part of growing up. In spite of this, they were each capable of unconditional love. They were young wives and mothers, and their lives were tragically taken in violent, unforeseen circumstances. Tom had loved them and found it difficult to rationalize such injustice.

Judah came by often. Sometimes, after a couple of glasses of beer, he could even get Tom to smile. He hoped it was an indication that he was beginning to accept life without her. Tom knew that Judah worried about him because he was a young man and lonely.

Judah had finally been put out to pasture, he had a lot of time on his hands. Tom found it amusing that he filled some of it with the enjoyment of having little Benjamin bounce on his knee. The more he thought about it, the more he realized this part of his life was definitely over, and he would leave Israel. Judah had come to the same conclusion. He was of the mind that as long as Tom remained in Israel, he would never get on with his life. After careful thought, he decided he would encourage Tom to return to Canada; maybe even find his former fiancée.

He parked his car in the driveway as he had done so many times before and came up the steps.

Tom called out. "Problems, Judah?"

"Yes … well no, not really a problem but someone is inquiring about you."

This irked Tom. "Goddamn! I thought all that crap was behind us."

Judah said he had thought so too, but there definitely was someone very interested in him. Tom wanted to know how he had found this out, and Judah explained that although he was officially retired, he still kept in touch with certain people. "The men in the technical division happen to not only respect but like you, so they still keep watch over you. They believe it is the least we can do. As a matter of fact, I have something for you from all of us."

Judah reached in his pocket and gave Tom a chain with a little canister attached, and Tom protested he was not the religious type.

"This is different," Judah said. "We took what was left of Ahuva's Star of David and put it in this capsule with a Hebrew prayer. It's for you and your son."

Tom was moved. "This means a lot to me. I will wear it every day until Benjamin is old enough to understand its meaning. Then, he will wear it. Please thank the boys in the lab for me." Judah was pleased with Tom's reaction and knew that everyone involved would be too.

Judah asked Tom what he wanted him to do about the snoop.

"Okay, Judah ... shoot the bastard or invite him here for a beer, and I'll kill him or hang him from the olive tree in the back."

"You don't have an olive tree, you *smuck*."

"I'm sure there is one out there if I walk far enough."

They sat laughing for a while, but Tom knew that the "somebody" looking for him had to be dealt with, sooner or later. Why would anyone be looking for him? He asked if Judah thought the Arabs could still be interested in him, but Judah told him it was too late for that.

This was probably as good a time as any for Tom to let Judah know that he had been thinking more and more about returning home. Judah agreed this was a good decision and asked him if he had given any thought to when he wanted to leave. Tom was perplexed that Judah took his decision in stride and told him he had been speaking with the Arab who sold him the house and interestingly enough, he wanted to buy it back. It was to be a wedding present for his daughter.

"I think I'll call him tomorrow and close the deal." Ever cynical, Judah surmised. "Knowing him, you'll be selling at a loss."

However long Judah had known this decision was inevitable, he was sad to see it become a reality. "So when will you be leaving us?" Tom thought it wouldn't be too long. He said he was actually homesick so as soon as he could get some money out of the Bahamas, he would book his flight. Judah was going to miss Tom but Benjamin even more. He had become an integral part of his life.

"What will become of Benjamin?"

His question stunned Tom. "He will come with me of course."

Judah laughed. "I know that you *smuck*, I meant his education."

Tom's promise to Ahuva to raise their son in the Jewish faith was a given.

"He will have his bar mitzvah, and I will find a rabbi to see that he graduates as a Jew with full honors."

Judah clapped his hands, a move entirely uncharacteristic for him.

"His mother would be so proud."

"Never mind that, I'll be proud but there is time for that yet, he is only four."

They both knew this was goodbye. Judah set the tone.

"I hear that British Columbia is very beautiful this time of the year. Shalom dear friend, I shall miss you."

# 24

Anastasia was about to leave her office when a delivery man came in. He put a package on her desk and without saying a word, handed her a clipboard that read "sign here please." She wasn't expecting any deliveries and neglected to check whether the package was indeed for her before she said she wasn't in the habit of signing for unsolicited parcels. Her reaction was probably unexpected because the courier was anything but courteous.

"Well, Miss, I don't care. We hold the goods for thirty days after which they get to be shipped back to the sender."

He picked up the package and added, "in this case, The Netherlands" and turned to leave.

"Wait, did you say The Netherlands?"

"Look, lady, I get paid by delivery so make up your mind. You want it or not?"

She grabbed the board, signed the delivery slip and the courier almost ran out the door. He was obviously trying to make up for lost time.

She was tempted to leave it on her desk but glanced at the waybill. There was something familiar. The return address, "H.B. Mulders. Notary, 29 Koningsweg, Amsterdam, The Netherlands; it gave her an eerie feeling. She remembered Tom had business dealings with a notary in Amsterdam, but she was almost sure his name wasn't Mulders. To the best of her recollection, it was Schoenenberg, or something similar. She took off her coat and threw it on a chair. She reached into her desk drawer for her letter opener only to toss it aside when it didn't cut through the tape and resorted to scissors to open the package. A letter attached to what appeared to be legal dockets read in part:

*Dear Madam,*

*We are sorry to inform you of the passing of Notary Albert Schoenenberg. We have been assigned to close his practice. There were specific instructions …*

The contents were impeccable. For each Dutch document, an English translation was attached. It took quite some time to read through everything, and when she did, she rested her head in her hands. Why had Tom left instructions for her to handle his estate in the event of his death? At no time had he ever mentioned anything of the sort.

Something else nagged at her. She reviewed one document in particular. It referred to funds being transferred to Tel Aviv, but the transaction date made no sense. It was long after Tom had gone missing. There could only be two reasons for this. One that someone had managed to access the account or two, TOM WAS ALIVE.

She needed to calm down and think rationally, so she did what she always did in such circumstances, she locked her office and drove to the beach. It had become her refuge.

It was almost deserted for which she was grateful. She kicked off her shoes, walked across the sand to the hard packed mud and stood barefoot letting the waves lap at her feet. The water was cold but refreshing.

This was her favorite time of day and she especially liked to spend it standing right where she was. The setting sun cast an orange glow against the clouds above the horizon. A sandpiper busily pecked in the sand and except for the occasional melancholic cry of a lonely gull the only other sound was a fishing trawler's engine.

She shook her head in disbelief; she had been doing this for five years. At times, her loneliness tended to blur her sense of reason. She often tried to imagine how different things might have been. If only she could have mourned at his graveside. She wanted to believe things would have been easier, given her closure.

Tom's body had never been found so there were still times she questioned his death. What is it they say, hope springs eternal? It never failed, if someone reminded her of him, she would go out of her way to take a second look. It was easier to be disappointed than miss a chance encounter.

She had, of course, met other men but no one measured

up. Unfair as it was, she compared everyone to Tom, making any relationship impossible.

Today, her world had been turned upside down. She was now faced with the possibility that he was alive. It was difficult to keep a level head. Would getting on a plane and going to Israel make it any easier to get answers? Would it give her better insight into what had happened? Or, was she merely looking for a chance to walk in Tom's footsteps? A better plan might be to call the bank in Tel Aviv to see what information they would release, if any, before making any rash moves.

The recollection of Tom discussing Mossad's covert tactics sent her off on another tangent. Could he be imprisoned? Was it possible that the crash never occurred; that it was a convenient way to cover up his disappearance? From what she could remember, the pilot and co-pilot's bodies were the only ones recovered. No mention was ever made about the others nor the fact that the flight recorder had never been found.

The official news release restricted comments exclusively to the political aspects of the attack, effectively avoiding any statement regarding terrorist rockets and the ultimate loss of five lives.

Even more intriguing was, although the Islamic Jihad had been accused, they had never taken credit for the act.

How many other families and loved ones lived this nightmare, never knowing what had actually happened? She, for one, often experienced night terrors so realistic they left her drenched with sweat and gasping for air. They were always the same. She was being pulled down with him in the wreckage, and when she attempted to scream for help, only bubbles rose to the surface.

Surely, the news media couldn't be that different from one country to another, especially when it came to human interest stories. She found it curious that nothing even remotely related to the personal side of the story had been printed. This event had been covered globally which made it even more surprising that the international reporters, some of the most curious people on the face of the earth, didn't come up with any human interest features.

After much deliberation, she was convinced she needed to go to Tel Aviv if for no other reason than to put ongoing doubts away once and for all. She went home and booked her flight.

Stacy checked into the Tel Aviv Hilton. She was too tired to enjoy the luxury of it all. Jet lag was quickly taking its toll. It would all have to wait until she was more refreshed and ready to explore her surroundings. She was ready for a good night's sleep.

The next morning she awoke surprisingly refreshed. She had honestly expected to feel a little groggy. She showered, dressed and went down to the lobby. Not particularly hungry she opted for a cup of coffee, sipping it as she took in her surroundings.

Where to start? Hopefully, even after five years, someone would still remember the crash. Details were few, but it was stated that the search and rescue operation had taken place from Tel Aviv's harbor. Sometime, somewhere, she recalled hearing doormen and bartenders for some unknown reason are unusually knowledgeable. She prepared to check out the validity of this theory.

Her heart pounded as the doorman held the door open and asked if he could call her a cab. She declined but cautiously told him she was interested in a plane crash that had happened about five years ago and was wondering if he remembered the event. The theory, in this case, proved right. Without any hesitation, he said, "Oh yes, ma'am, many people were interested for a while but not anymore. It wasn't a crash, you know. The plane was actually shot down by Palestinians terrorists."

When she asked him if he knew anything about it, he thought for a moment. Stacey assumed he was weighing the probable consequences of discussing such an important event with a total stranger, but she was wrong. He told her that although he didn't know anything, his cousin might. He had been at the dock when the survivors were brought ashore. She was astonished to hear there were survivors.

She commented no information pertaining to survivors had appeared in the papers. He looked a little nervous.

"True; they sometimes don't always print everything, and this rescue had something to do with a police investigation."

He hesitated and then continued. "My cousin knows more about it, but I don't know if he will tell you anything. He was ordered by the police not to talk to anyone about what he saw."

Stacey couldn't stop herself. She couldn't believe her luck. "How many survivors were there?" Her informant said he wasn't sure but thought his cousin had said two; a man and a woman."

She thanked him for his time and more than made it worth his while with a generous tip. Then she asked if he would tell her where she could find his cousin. He bowed slightly and smiled. "He works at the Sheraton Moriah."

She asked for his indulgence. She had one more question and promised it to be her last. "What else do you know?" He told her nothing more than the survivors had stayed at the Moriah after leaving the hospital. Stacey thanked him again and returned to her room.

She had a good memory but felt she needed to note down what she had been told while it was still fresh in her mind. It was a pleasant surprise to get so much information, but there was just too much to digest before moving on. It had been confirmed that the plane carried three passengers and two crew members. Logically, the survivors could not have been crew members. Upon discharge from the hospital, they would have gone home not to a hotel. So, who were they? Her mind was spinning.

She needed to adjust both to her surroundings and time zone. What she had accomplished in a short period of time, helped justify her decision to spend some time resting by the pool trying to appear as if she were a tourist in case she had aroused suspicions with her questions. After an uneventful night she felt a little more secure and headed over to the Moriah where she approached the front desk and asked for Issy Sternthal; "her" doorman's cousin's name.

The desk clerk pointed to the concierge. Tall, lean and

good looking, he smiled politely as she approached him. "How can I be of service, Miss or is it Mrs?"

"Actually, it's Ms. Whitefeather. I spoke to your cousin at the Hilton, and he suggested that you might be able to help me."

"I will do my best, ma'am." His tone was a little less friendly but still polite.

She thanked and assured him she would take as little of his time as possible and got directly to the point.

"Do you remember the plane that was shot down five years ago?" He did.

"I understand that there were survivors." He agreed. "Yes, I saw them being put on stretchers and taken away in ambulances." She stopped and looked at him. She remembered his cousin saying that this man had been sworn to secrecy. This compelled her to ask him if her questions could in any way cause him problems. He appreciated her concern but assured her they did not. It had all been so long ago.

She relaxed and proceeded. "What can you tell me about the man who survived?" Never could she have predicted his answer. "You mean Mr. Benning? Well, his head was all bandaged up and bloody when he was taken out of the boat. He was in the hospital for a week or so if I remember correctly and then he ..."

There was no mistaking what had caused him to stop so abruptly. Stacey almost fainted but managed to recover quickly. Only then did he ask her, rather cautiously, if she were his wife. She shook her head, and with that out of the way, Izzy continued.

"Well he was staying here for a few days with the lady who was rescued with him."

She wanted to know where they had gone afterward. He didn't know. A doorman at the time, he wasn't privileged to such information but what he did know was he left with the lady and two guards.

He began to look nervous and was less inclined to continue. Could she be responsible for getting him into trouble with the hotel? "No," he answered. "Not the hotel but, national security could be a possibility."

Stacey understood his dilemma, thanked him and started to leave. As a parting gesture, he remarked she could go to the rabbi who had married them if she wanted to know more and gave her the directions. He was most apologetic there was nothing more he could do for her. Her smile telegraphed her gratitude. The concierge who was well-known for his appreciation of the finer things, kept his eyes on her legs until she walked out the door.

She was on the right track; he had survived, at least for a while. Instead of going directly to the synagogue, she went to the library and scanned the local newspapers. Exasperated, by the minimal coverage of the event, she was ready to call it a day.

Packing up her things, she happened to glance at the microfiche screen next to hers. The name, Ahuva Benning, jumped out at her. She looked around saw no one and switched places. The article described a suicide bomber attack that had taken place in the Tel Aviv market. It mentioned the irony of her miraculous survival as a passenger on a plane that had been shot down at sea, only to succumb to a suicide bomber. Stacey leaned back in her chair and closed her eyes. There was no address mentioned, but it did state Thomas A. Benning was her widower. They had married in 1992, four and a half months after the terrorist attack on the plane.

Stacey had mixed emotions. She didn't know whether to be glad for herself or sad for him. The shock that he was alive would have been enough but to discover that he had married and was a widower for a second time, was more than difficult to digest.

Had he not declared his love for her and had she not willingly become his fiancée? She stared at the screen. There was no denying Ahuva's beauty, but that would never have been reason enough for him to marry her. Difficult as it was, Stacey had to admit that he must have loved Ahuva very much

In spite of everything, she couldn't suppress her joy. He was free, and she was more determined than ever to find him. She got up and asked the librarian where she could find more related information and was directed to whatever was available.

That night she tossed and turned; she just couldn't sleep. With the librarian's assistance, she had enough to keep her busy for the next few days.

Suddenly, she realized she was not alone. Her heart pounded, but for some reason, she remembered Tom had once said, "panic clouds clear thinking." She found courage in that thought and waited. She decided to pretend to be asleep, hoping the intruder would leave as inconspicuously as he or she had arrived. She did her best to keep her breathing regular and peaked through the slits of her eyes. How could anyone get in? She knew she had secured the doors.

There was no movement but she definitely smelled cologne. She carefully scanned the room and thought she saw a silhouette of someone sitting in the chair near the window and gasped.

The intruder started to speak in a quietly reassuring voice. "Please do not be alarmed, Miss Whitefeather. I'm not here to harm you."

Stacey was startled that he knew her name and demanded to know how he had gotten into her room. He told her that was irrelevant but her inquiries about Thomas Benning definitely were. He continued to speak.

"I have known Tom for a long time, and I am well aware of your earlier relationship with Thomas."

She sat up and addressed the man sitting in her chair, in her room, uninvited. There was no need for courtesy. "Is he alive and safe?" The answer was yes. Then she wanted to know who he was and why he had felt the need to sneak into her room like a thief in the night. He laughed. He told her he was just a man who believed he could help put some of her concerns to rest and he was as good as his word. She found out that Tom had returned to Canada five months previous. "There is, however, one more thing you should know. Although Thomas abhors the term, Thomas Benning was a public hero in your country, and an inconspicuous one here and that is all I am prepared to disclose National Security, you know."

It was curious. She did not fear this person even though her instinct told her he was Mossad. Who else, she reasoned, could pull off a caper like this? All she could think of was he was helping her, and she was grateful.

His voice brought her back to what he was saying. "No matter what you believe, he has always loved you, as contradictory as that may seem. He only allowed himself to fall in love with Ahuva after he was convinced he could never return to Canada. Only then did he make a life for himself here, in Israel.

His turmoil about leaving you was, and possibly still is, his worst enemy. You see, he never expected to see you again. I don't pretend to know how he feels today, but I suspect he believes he is doing the right thing by not contacting you. He is and always will be the man you knew him to be."

When her midnight visitor was finished, he walked to the door and left, but his cologne lingered.

She had traveled a long way to find out Tom was back in Canada. Thanks to the unexpected visitor she slept soundly the rest of the night and woke early the next morning to arrange her flight home.

She had only been gone about an hour when she re-entered her room. She knew immediately that the mysterious visitor had been back. Traces of his cologne permeated the air. She found it interesting that someone so intent on remaining anonymous would leave evidence of his presence. She chose to assume it was intentional; a message of some kind.

As she pondered the relevancy of it all, she walked over to the desk and picked up the list she had compiled the night before. It had been amended. Every city, except Vancouver, had been crossed off and it had been altered to read Vancouver Island.

How nice, her search had been narrowed down.

# 25

She had almost decided to move on when she saw a mailbox but not just any mailbox. It read: Thomas A. Benning. Pragmatic by nature, she was hard-pressed not to believe in fate. She had set out to find him, and here he was. The moment she had played out in her mind so many times, was a reality.

Her pulse raced. The stranger in Tel Aviv had told her Tom would never contact her, so she knew it was up to her to reach out. The heartache she had experienced ever since his disappearance had been debilitating. The relief she so desperately needed was little more than a few steps away, and she couldn't make a move. She almost raced back to the safety of her room.

There must be some truth to the saying "things happen for a reason," she mused. Initially, she had toyed with the idea of starting to look for him at one of the other beaches. What had changed her mind? Could it be as simple as the inn where she was staying was nearest to this beach? Even she couldn't answer that question. She had been on the island for three days and walked the beach with her dog every morning. This particular morning, she had changed her routine and walked around the village. Why?

The thought of having to decide what to do was close to paralyzing. She had dedicated so much time to find him and given little or no thought to how she would proceed, if and when she did. Her emotions were raw.

Was it possible he had already spotted her and chosen to ignore her? If so, how could she just walk up to him? Had she perhaps already seen him and not recognized him? The one thing that bothered her more than anything was, did she have the right to invade his privacy? Instead of the answers, she kept coming up with more questions.

She woke the dog, grabbed her wrap and went down to the beach. Quite a way into her walk, she noticed a man sitting up against a log and remembered seeing him there before. She hadn't paid much attention to him, but this time she did. From this distance, he was a rough looking character, who seemed more engrossed in his book than the boy playing at the edge of the water. As she approached, she noticed he was actually looking over his sunglasses.

The boy was jumping up and down. He had caught a fish. His father motioned for him to let it go, but he protested. There were words back and forth, but the rolling surf made it impossible to hear what they were saying. She ventured closer to eavesdrop.

The boy, his father called him Benjamin, asked if they should bury the stinking fish. It was obvious he was quoting his father who smiled and said. "No, leave it for the birds. Now, do as I say and wash your hands."

She felt like she had been hit by a thunderbolt. His voice was instantly recognizable, and she almost fainted. It was Tom. She turned around and picked up a shell. It was all she could think to do. She needed to be still.

Her dog, however, didn't. It was time to play their favorite game of toss and fetch. He had dropped his stick at her feet in anticipation, but she was distracted, and when she didn't respond, he promptly picked it up and went over to lie down next to the boy.

She watched them interact. When the dog rolled over on his back, Benjamin obligingly rubbed his belly. This was her chance and she walked over to them. "Old softy," she mumbled. It was endearing to see how easily they played together. She smiled and asked Benjamin if he liked her dog. He nodded. "Do you have a name?" she asked. He politely told her that he wasn't supposed to talk to strangers. A fact briskly confirmed by the man sitting against the log. "Benjamin, I have told you often enough not to talk to strangers. Now you come here and sit with me."

Harsh as he sounded, a smile lit up his face as the boy ran to his side. He didn't look at all like the Tom she knew. His hair was long and unkempt, and he had a beard, but there was no denying it was him.

Tom had seen her walking along the beach with her dog but that was from a distance, and now she stood right in front of him. "Hello there. I'm sorry. I didn't mean to break any rules by introducing myself to your boy. You might be interested to know he had your message down pat. In his defense, he refused to tell me his name and put me on notice that he wasn't supposed to talk to strangers."

When he got up and approached her, Benjamin ran after him. "See daddy, she isn't a stranger. So, can I go back to burying my dead fish now?" Tom didn't answer. He just looked at Stacey and accepted her apology. She remarked what a beautiful boy he was and Tom agreed willingly. "Yes I know and if his mother were here, she would agree even more vehemently."

She asked where his mother was and was told that she had died a few years earlier. "Oh, I'm so sorry," she said. "Have you lived here long?" Tom told her that they had only been in the area for a few months and volunteered they had come from Israel.

Benjamin came over when he saw his father still talking to her. He pulled on his father's pant leg. "Is this my mummy, daddy?" Tom gently reminded him that his mummy was dead. "Is she dead like the fish I caught?" He cleared his throat before answering. "Yes, like the fish." She heard the emotion in his voice and turned to Benjamin. "Why don't you go and play with the dog; he likes you." Ben happily skipped away with the dog who was only too happy to have a playmate.

Their conversation seemed to be turning into one apology after the other. "I'm sorry; I didn't mean to pry." He told her not to worry. "He asks that question about every woman we meet. It can be embarrassing, but it's a stage he's going through. It will pass."

They turned to watch his son and her dog enjoying each other's company and made small talk. Benjamin finally stood, stomped on the wet sand and proudly announced: "I finished burying my dead fish!" Tom congratulated him, told him to wash his hands and collect his things. They were going home for some lunch.

She watched them walk away. The boy was on his shoulders being bounced up and down. His squeals of delight could be heard until they reached the stairs to their back yard. Once they were out of sight, Stacey turned and went back to the inn. She wasn't proud of it but she was consumed with envy. His son should have been her son.

She slept fitfully and was up at sunrise. She puttered around her room until breakfast. It promised to be a glorious day and she wanted to be on the beach early. After the night she had just spent, she was more determined than ever to find out everything she could about him. She hadn't gone to all the trouble, to give up and walk away. She pulled her scarf a little tighter around her head and donned her sunglasses. Perhaps she could remain incognito a while longer. Her dog impatiently stood by the door.

They headed out to the beach where she unleashed him. Predictably, he immediately went to find a stick. They nonchalantly played toss and fetch as she made her way towards Tom. He was easy to spot sitting against the same log he used as a backrest every day. She called out to him and waved as she neared. "Hello, nice to see you again!" She remembered him mentioning sometimes he roamed the beach at night and said, "I looked for your ghost on the beach last night."

He sauntered over. "Well, the ghost and I were a little busy. We burned the dinner, and it took forever to get the smell out of the house." They both laughed. She found it bizarre that a parent couldn't cook and asked him why he had never learned. He said he really hadn't seen the need. He had been privileged enough to be a welcomed guest at friends' dinner tables and when that option wasn't open, a dedicated patron of restaurants for many years. "I was kind of footloose and fancy-free but employed as an architect."

Dare she probe further? Why not, she thought, that's what she was there for. "If that was then, what about now?" He scratched his beard. "I guess I'm like a piece of driftwood." This was the last thing she had expected to hear and asked him to explain. He tried but ended up being flippant. She chose to put a different slant on his comment. "I like your sense of humor, intended or not but don't forget, sometimes a piece of driftwood gets picked up and taken home by a beachcomber as a treasure." "Ha!" he quipped. "This treasure won't be that lucky. I'm one of those pieces that will be scooped up and whipped back out to sea or cremated in a fireplace."

He continued to look at the horizon, but his whole demeanor changed. "Don't you think that it is time to end this charade, Stacey?" She stood quietly before she burst out; "you knew and pretended to be a stranger, how could you?"

His defense was valid. "I didn't come looking for you, Stacey. Why did you feel it was necessary to play this game?" They were both silent; each waiting for the other to make the next move. Tom spoke first. "What I find most curious is why you came looking for me." She explained that when she had found out, he was alive; she needed to know what had gone wrong between them. He asked her how she had found out, and she told him about receiving the courier package and how one thing led to another.

She pleaded with him. "Can we at least talk; don't you think that you owe me at least that?" He agreed.

He began by saying he had returned to Canada because he was homesick. It had never been his intention to contact her because he assumed she would have married. "Well I didn't," she snapped. "Why did you leave?"

He told her about Mossad being after him. He left without telling her anything because he had no other option. Any information would have put her in danger.

"The Israelis were in a better position to keep both of us alive so, I decided to go to Israel. It was never my intention to deceive you. It was almost two weeks after the crash that Mossad had me declared dead. It was then that I knew I would never leave Israel alive." She felt weak and crouched down on the sand. It was all too much. He seemed compelled to finish his statement. "I fell in love, and the rest is history."

Eventually, she asked barely above a whisper. "And now?" "Now?" he moaned. "I am no longer who I once was. No one can come back from what I've been through and expect to live a normal life. I'm used to having a machine pistol slung over my shoulder and colt inside my jacket. Without them, I feel naked and vulnerable, yet I have to protect my son."

They sat side by side on the log, afraid to look at each other. Clearly, they could never go back and pick up where they had left off, but perhaps, they could be friends.

Stacey turned to him and made him look at her. He didn't know what to expect but was pleasantly surprised when she changed the entire atmosphere by saying. "Would you and Benjamin like to be welcomed guests at this friend's table for dinner tonight?" He accepted with pleasure but said that Ben had to be in bed by nine at the latest. She couldn't help but remark how different his life was. He had gone from free man to husband, to father to a single parent in short order.

As if on cue, Benjamin called out to his daddy that he couldn't find his dead fish. "That's okay, Ben," he called back. Not quite satisfied, he wanted to know. "Do you think he went alive again and he swam away?" This time Tom said, "maybe."

Ben picked up his shovel and kept digging the hard packed sand. Stacey remarked how determined he was but Tom corrected her. "He's stubborn just like his mother."

Stacey frowned. It wasn't easy to hear him talk about his wife and Tom sensed the mood change, yet again. He picked up his book. "Okay, I'm out of here … Benjamin … let's go!" As any normal little boy would, he wanted to know where they were going. The words "to town … a surprise!" was magic to his ears and he ran to take his daddy's hand. She watched them walk away, Benjamin chattering all the way. She wiped her tears and went back to the inn.

He had accepted her invitation, so she had something to look forward to. The three of them could have a wonderful dinner and afterward, she could walk back to his place with them. He could put Ben to bed, and they would have the rest of the evening to talk. She would apologize for her mood swing and Tom being Tom would accept it because he was not one to hold a grudge.

Later that evening and once Ben was tucked in for the night, they sat in his living room. She looked around and saw how cozy it was. She could picture herself sitting in one of the chairs near the fireplace on a stormy night.

Before Tom even had time to pour the wine, there was a knock on the door. "What the hell," he cursed going to answer it. She heard the door open and Tom's surprise. "Judah, what brings you here? Come in … dodon't just stand there, come on in."

Stacey recognized the cologne immediately. He smiled and extended his hand. "How nice to see you again, Miss Whitefeather."

"Thank you, but you have me at a disadvantage, Mr …" "Indeed, I am Judah Fink." He bowed politely. He was definitely old school but it was a rather nice change. Tom was quite taken aback. "You know each other?" "Well, not quite but we have met." Judah clarified. "It was when Stacey needed some help locating an old friend."

Tom was quick on the uptake. "Snoop, remember Judah? You called her a snoop. How are things in Tel Aviv?" Judah ignored the first part of Tom's statement and went on to say unfortunately there was no time to chat about old times. They had a problem to resolve. Tom wanted to know what or who the problem was and Judah told him it was Burman.

"Indeed, my friend. He is on the warpath. He wasn't pleased when you left Israel. I found out that he is sending a *kidon*, an assassin," he added for her benefit

Tom couldn't believe his ears and Stacey listened intently without interrupting. Judah advised them to leave immediately. Go to the Bahamas. "Why the two of us, Stacey has nothing to do with this?" Judah contradicted him.

"Well ... unfortunately she does." Tom wanted to know how much time he had and he was told none. He needed to leave right away. Judah would have Burman taken care of but it could take some time for him to arrange the *burn*.

"Shit, Judah, I don't even have anything to defend myself. Give me your gun?" Judah reached inside his jacket. It wasn't easy parting with his beloved Whalter, but he slowly handed it over. Tom released the clip and saw that it was full. He chambered a cartridge and stepped back.

Judah realizing his mistake cautioned him to be careful. Tom was pointing the gun directly at his chest.

Stacey couldn't believe what she was witnessing and interrupted for the first time. "Tom, please ... what are you doing?"

He cut her off. "Shut the hell up and stay out of this. I know this old bugger. He lies with every second word."

Judah tried to cajole him, but Tom was having no part of it. "Cut the crap, Judah. You are lying again. Burman doesn't want me. You do."

Judah insisted he had come to warn him of the impending danger, but Tom wasn't buying it. "Like hell! What the fuck do you want? It's only fair for you to know. I'll shoot your right knee cap, just to show you I mean business, if I don't like your first answer. I am willing to give you a second chance if you need it and if I like your answer, you will still be able to walk but with some difficulty. If I don't like the answer, you will be in a wheelchair. And, I will continue to torture you until I kill you."

Stacey knew Tom well enough to know he wasn't bluffing. His eyes were steadfast and cold. He uttered his words slowly so that there could be no possible misinterpretation.

"Tom, please," pleaded Stacey. "You can't do this. He's an old man, this isn't human. This isn't like you."

Without taking his eyes off Judah, he spit out. "Watch me! I told you that I'm not the same anymore. Maybe now you believe me." Tom aimed the gun at Judah's right knee.

Chaim had never seen Tom so callous and angry. He meant every word. "Okay ... Thomas ... Okay. No need to go to such extremes. I know you mean what you say. It is true; we have taken so much from you in the last years. It is time for you to get married to the woman you love. Benjamin needs a mother. You have a right to be happy again."

"So, let me get this right. This is about me getting married?"

Judah nodded.

Tom voiced his disbelief loud and clear. "Wait a minute! Wait just a goddamn minute! You want me to leave for the Bahamas with her right now? You want me to marry her and be gone forever." Tom saw Judah realize he was on to him.

Tom angrily cursed Chaim. "I have a news flash for you. Ahuva is alive." She didn't die did she, you old bastard? You had better tell me what happened or I'll peel your face with a rasp. You are worse than the devil himself?"

It gave Tom a kick to see Judah so shaken. He would never have thought it possible but Tom had succeeded where so many had failed.

Judah started slowly. His shoulders sagged, and his hands covered his face as he told the entire story. "There is no reason to withhold the truth anymore. She survived the explosion and remained conscious. She knew how badly she was injured. She still had her purse and managed to pull out her gun, pointed it at the ambulance driver and demanded a mirror. The driver didn't have much choice but to give her one. When she saw her face, she tried to get the muzzle into her mouth. The paramedic's quick reflexes saved her. He grabbed it and took it away from her."

He paused. This message was as painful for Judah to deliver as it was for Tom to hear.

"I was called to the hospital. She begged me to have her declared dead. She didn't want you to live with her out of obligation. I didn't agree with her, but I understood. So, I did what she asked me to do. She's a Jew and an Israeli. You must understand my first obligation was to her."

Tom showed no emotion whatsoever. "Who was in the coffin?"

"Some Arab woman who had no family," Judah answered flatly.

"Where is she?" Tom demanded. "Don't bother to protest that you can't tell me or, you promised her you would keep her secret or, any other asinine excuse. You know me well enough to know that I will find her with or without your help. You decide. Are you going home as a war amputee or under your own steam?" Judah sighed. "She is on the kibbutz where she grew up."

"Now, get your ass out of here with the assurance that if I meet up with any surprises, you will be arrested for treason. I guarantee it."

Judah knew when he was beaten. "You don't have to worry, my friend, you've won. Whether you believe me or not it actually feels good to get it off my chest".

The sound of little footsteps caught their attention. Benjamin had been awakened by Tom's outburst. He came down rubbing his eyes but started to smile when he saw Judah. He ran up to him and climbed into his lap. "You came, Uncle Judah, you came, you came from Iselell."

Judah's one pure love was this little guy and his eyes filled with tears at the joy of holding him.

"Yes, my boy, I came to see you, but I have to go again." Benjamin was genuinely sad. "Are you coming back?"

Before Judah could answer, Tom told Benjamin that Judah would not be coming back but that he and Tom were returning to Israel. "We're going to find your mummy." Benjamin's eyes widened at the same time as his smile. "My mummy went alive again, like the fish I caught and swam away again?" Tom was happy to say, "yes, she did."

Tom's joy was counterbalanced by Stacey's sad reality. She had lost Tom forever.

# 26

Every morning she wore her large, floppy-brimmed hat to shield her face and neck from the direct sun and one of her long-sleeved shirts to protect her arms. Her wounds were healed but she was badly scarred and her skin far more sensitive since the attack. She still preferred to wear skirts but for a different reason.

Nothing stopped her from putting in a full day in the orchard. Her sweat and fatigue at the end of each day were a testament to her diligence. It never ceased to amaze those who watched her how she managed to withstand the heat and the long hours. To her it was simple; it was expected. The offer of any concessions would have been futile. She was not only proud but fiercely stubborn and saw herself as a survivor, lucky enough to still pull her weight.

The day had been inordinately hot. She removed her hat and used her shirt sleeve to wipe the perspiration from her face and took a moment to reflect on when she first returned to the *kibbutz*. Initially, she had asked to be assigned to work in the orchard, but the decision makers felt the work would be too demanding. They suggested that she to go back to the nursery school where she had worked before her military service. They reasoned she was a natural with children and she had to admit she had loved every minute of her time with the little ones. However, so much had changed and she knew this was definitely not an option for her. The children would be a constant reminder of her son which would be too much to bear.

There were times when she second-guessed her decision to have herself declared dead. It had devastated Tom, but she held firm that it was better for him to think she was dead than to see her scarred and disabled. Four years had passed since she orchestrated the charade. Her loneliness could, at times, be overwhelming. She lived for Judah's visits and cherished the picture he had given her. It had been taken just before Tom and Benjamin left for Canada. Her baby had grown into a little boy. She had already missed so much, and her sorrow was only compounded by the knowledge that nothing could or would ever change her reality.

She put on her hat, picked up her cane and hoe and called it a day. As she made her way back, she noticed a man standing near the end of the field. It was disconcerting. Usually, someone from the kibbutz would have called out to her. She had made one stipulation when she arrived. She was there to work. Outsiders other than Judah, who could hardly be described as an outsider, were to be refused any access to her. Why was this unescorted stranger watching her? She felt vulnerable.

She had stopped wearing her gun because strapping it to her leg hurt. The pain outweighed the benefit of being armed. On more than one occasion, however, she had found herself reaching under her skirt. Old habits die hard.

Ahuva checked over her shoulder. She was startled to see him moving in her direction, and although he approached slowly, he walked with purpose. She instinctively flipped her cane around and turned to face the intruder. The heavy handle would make a good club. She surprised herself how quickly she had reacted and how prepared she was to defend herself. Had she not often prayed for God to take her?

This stranger's gait reminded her of Tom's. He didn't stop until he stood directly in front of her. She had bowed her head, so all she could see were his boots. Each silently stood their ground until she felt compelled to look up. The person standing in front of her bore an uncanny resemblance to Tom. She felt faint and leaned on her inverted cane for support.

Judah had made a solemn oath never to divulge their secret pact. How could this be happening? Her attempt to steel herself was shattered when he said her name. "Ahuva." It was him. She managed to stammer that there was no one by that name on the kibbutz. He said he didn't want to be rude, but she was wrong. There most certainly was an Ahuva and she was that person; the same person who had once said to him, "you will always be my *Tsatske*."

Tears streamed down her face, but she turned and started to walk away. Her act of rejection didn't stop him. "You are Ahuva, and you are my wife. The wife who abandoned me and our son when times got tough and if that weren't enough, the wife who chose to rescind the deal we made to die together. A deal, by the way, I couldn't honor because I had our son to care for."

Her denial was barely audible. "I … I'm not … her." His voice was precisely the opposite when he called her bluff. "Very well then if, as you claim you aren't Ahuva, it shouldn't matter to you if I finally honor my deal with her."

With her back to him, she heard him turn to walk away, and as he did, she heard a cartridge chambering in a gun, his gun. It was a sound familiar to them both. Her scream told him the ruse, cruel though it was, had been successful. He had won her back. Her sobs were interspersed with her confession that she couldn't survive to lose him again. She begged for his forgiveness for allowing her vanity and insecurity to rob them of so much time.

He tilted her face to his, kissed her eyes and then her lips. Her long-suppressed passion released, she kissed him with a vengeance that elated him. When she opened her eyes, he was smiling down at her with such love, it took her breath away. He wiped her tears and kissed each scar on her face individually. He brushed her hair from her forehead and another scar came to light above her right eyebrow. He kissed it as he had the others. "These few little scars were not worth the pain they have caused us both," was all he said. She didn't answer but continued to point out the rest of them.

She told him that she used to try to cover them with makeup, but it only made her feel, if not look like a clown. She showed him her leg brace, and he dismissed it with some inane comment about being too old for high school dances. It was the first time in a very long time, they could share such delight.

He settled her on the ground and nestled her head on his shoulder. To her surprise, he started to tell her a story. "Once upon a time, there was a little boy, and his name was Benjamin." He felt Ahuva stiffen, but he had already anticipated her apprehension and continued. "Every time Benjamin saw his daddy talk to a woman, he would ask if she was his mummy."

Tom asked her if she didn't think it was time to put Benjamin's mind at ease and answer his ever-present question. He laughed and added irreverently "before he drives me fucking nuts." She was desperately nervous but nodded yes.

Tom smiled, placed two fingers in his mouth and whistled. The pitch was shrill enough to shatter glass. He joked about being jealous that she could whistle so well so he worked at it until it paid dividends.

"Look," he grinned as they both got up. Ben's curly head peeked around from a tree near the end of the orchard. While he skipped toward them, Tom cautioned Ahuva. "Be easy, he has been told too often that his mummy is dead. Let him get used to the idea that she isn't."

Ben stood before them and looked up at Tom.

"I like Iselell, daddy. A lady back there gave me some cherries." He turned and pointed. Tom automatically asked him if he had remembered to say thank you to the lady.

The boy nodded enthusiastically and predictably asked. "Daddy, is the lady who gave me cherries my mummy?"

Tom scooped him up into his arms. "No," he answered equally enthusiastically. "This is your mummy."

Ahuva was trying her best not cry and smile all at once. Her son was indescribably beautiful and unbelievable as it seemed, he was only inches away from her. Benjamin cupped his little hands around Tom's ear and whispered something for which he was lovingly scolded. "You know it isn't polite to whisper in company. Anything you say should be said aloud or not at all. Now, say it aloud so your mummy can hear it too."

Benjamin, like all children, was totally devoid of guile. "Is this the mummy who went alive again like my dead fish and swam away?" Tom's answer opened the floodgates and questions just rolled off his son's tongue. "Is she your mummy too?" "Is he your daddy too?" Everything was going along until he asked: "can she come to Canada with us?" Tom shook his head, and Benjamin's face clouded over.

"We're staying here. We are going to buy a house so we can all live together and you will go to school in the fall." His son just about jumped out his arms with excitement, but Tom reminded him there was one very important thing he had to do first. He looked perplexed until Tom said. "I think you should give mummy a big hug. She has been waiting a long time to hold you in her arms." He put Benjamin down. Ahuva knelt and held him, tears of joy streaming down her cheeks.

Tom was enraptured watching the two loves of his life hug each other but the moment was short-lived. Benjamin began to wiggle free. As far as he was concerned, everything was settled. He had his mummy. Now, he had other things to investigate. Ahuva reluctantly released him, and he skipped away, just as easily as he had skipped towards them moments before. Tom and Ahuva looked at each other and smiled. It was clear this little person was the center of their universe.

Ahuva told Tom how much his decision to stay meant to her. He said it hadn't been a difficult one and changed the subject by concentrating one of his devilish grins on her. "Let's go and pack your things. It's time we get reacquainted." She hesitated and wondered aloud. "Doesn't it bother you that I'm not beautiful anymore?"

"It bothers me that you got hurt. Your beauty is more than skin deep, and that is why I love you unconditionally. The fact that you have difficulty believing me makes me want to do everything in my power to help you, and I believe this can only happen if you feel better about yourself. So, once we are settled here, we'll source out the best surgeons and no matter where they are, see what can be done about the scars and your leg. I think you will be pleasantly surprised."

She took his hand, and they walked back to her room. "I feel reborn, *Tsatske*."

"And, I feel that you just went undead like the fish. I guess that makes it unanimous." She stopped, and for a moment he thought he was walking too quickly but that wasn't it at all. She wanted to know the story behind the fish.

He hugged her and laughed. "That's Benjamin's to tell. You'll have to ask him."

∽∘∾